Rosy'
It's been a
getting to know you
learn about your life.
I hope to spend much more
time together in the future
a fellow writer
Barbara

DOG *Days*

Ms. Barbara C. Sattler

ISBN: 1477664963
ISBN 13: 9781477664964
LCCN: 2012911925
CreateSpace Independent Publishing Platform
North Charleston, South Carolina

To Kenney and Ben

CHAPTER
ONE

"Inmate 107656, go to Admin," the PA blares.

My cell door opens. I walk down the cellblock toward the sally port.

"You lucky fucker."

"Miss you, baby."

"Come back and visit when you're bored."

Friendly words compete with nasty looks, gestures and obscenities. I look straight ahead, don't want to see faces of those left behind . . .

I'm getting out. I'll be Kristin White, not 107656. But 'only on parole', says the little voice in my head that sounds like Mom. I struggle to shut it up, focus on tomorrow. No more sharing a cell the size of a guest bathroom. No more monotonous, barely-edible food. No more endless days lived out in seconds.

I'd longed for freedom from the moment I was arrested for a crime I didn't commit. I expect to feel ecstatic, but I don't. Sixteen months. No guard had hit me; I hadn't been raped; but the need to be on alert, the condescending attitude of the guards, and the loneliness changed you.

Still prison had benefits. You didn't have to decide when to get up, what to eat for breakfast, or what to wear. Gone was the girl who tried on half her closet before she left home.

1

The rules were clear, spelled out in a book provided for free. As long as you followed them, you knew what to expect. Now, back to real life where everyone had their own book.

In prison, I could pretend Josh waited for me. When the doors opened and he wasn't there, I'd have to leave my fantasies behind. Face the truth.

It doesn't take long to say goodbye. Early on, I learned the safest way to survive. Be invisible, don't make enemies. I succeed but as a result have few friends. The women in my pod say the right stuff, "good luck," "kick ass out there," but I'm leaving. They're not.

When I reach Administration, Correction Officer Jackson, a dour thin woman with sour breath we nicknamed Eeyore after the donkey in Winnie the Pooh, escorts me to a large, clean bathroom I'd never seen before.

With great ceremony, she takes a pair of latex gloves from her pocket and puts them on. She hands me a fabric bag, making sure our fingers don't touch, and orders me to, "take off all your DOC clothes and put them in the bag. All of them."

Next, she carefully hands me a large brown paper bag. "These are the clothes you came in. Go in there and change. I can see in the window, so don't try any funny stuff. You're still a prisoner."

Was she so out of touch she thinks I'll try to escape or steal the state's motley clothing? I never allowed myself to wonder how many bodies had worn these garments. Some of the women didn't seem to mind used stuff. Some were poor enough that clean clothes were a treat. For me, this is total humiliation. In real life, I don't borrow friends' clothes, don't go to secondhand stores. Choking back a smart remark——another thing I'd learned to do——I peel off the ugly orange jumpsuit, washed-out bra, and stained underpants. I feel a moment of sadness for the next poor soul who'll wear them.

The thought of my own clothes make me smile till I see the bag has the court outfit my mom picked——panty hose, black pumps, and a conservative navy blue dress. I hate panty hose. As I pull them on, they run. The dress is too small. I'd gained weight, but without mirrors or scales, I'd underestimated. Even the shoes are too tight. Gritting my teeth, I ask Eeyore for help with the zipper.

"I guess you've gained the 'Prison 15' and then some," she snickers. "Next time, make sure your dress has growing room."

"There won't be a next time," I reply, knowing I should keep quiet.

"I've been here almost twenty years. That's what they all say. You druggies are the worst. Even if you're clean, you won't make it three days on the outside without 'em."

All the venom I've buried comes to the surface, when I hear a familiar voice. "Thank goodness you're still here. I was afraid you'd be released before I could say goodbye. I'll take over from here, Jackson," CO Kavanagh says.

Kavanagh's the best. Unlike most guards, she treated us with kindness, even dignity. There were a few cruel ones; but the rest, even when they tried to be fair, looked down on us. Kavanagh didn't. Like a friend, she talked about our families, politics, and wasn't afraid to share her life. The other COs would blow us off if we asked a personal question. Or worse, write us up for a violation of Section 3, Rule 4, **Inmates shall not attempt to find out personal information about Staff.** Kavanagh told us about her roommates, her boyfriends, and even her problems.

Her passion was animals. If she heard someone hurt a dog, she'd get angry or cry. She understood why a person could get violent; but harm an animal, and she'd talk death penalty.

"I wouldn't be worried about saying goodbye if I were you, Kavanagh. She'll be back in a couple months anyway," Eeyore says as she walks away.

"Don't mind her. The woman's a complete sourpuss. Stuck here for twenty years despises her job and takes her misery out on everyone else. When an inmate's released, she's jealous because tomorrow she'll be back here." Kavanagh's quiet for a few moments and looks me in the eye.

"I'd like to give you some advice. Everyone thinks getting out is a piece of cake, but it's not. Once the euphoria fades, you have the same problems you had before you got here. If you have any friends left, they've moved on. And I know you're not that happy about living with your mom."

"You got that right," I answer.

"Give her a chance. A family member's better than a halfway house."

"Okay," I mumble cause I like her not cause I mean it.

"Try not to let the small stuff get you down. You have a lot of grit and smarts. Take it slow. Ask people for help when you need it. As much as I like you, I don't want to see you here again. Come on...I'll walk you to check out."

TWO

I linger over dinner, try to avoid discussion about the rules with my new jailer. Mom wakes up every day before 6:00 a.m. to exercise, works a full day, cooks a gourmet dinner and looks impeccable. Her silver hair is shiny and perfectly in place, her make-up flawless. The black tailored pants and maroon shirt she wears while cooking dinner look like she's just picked them up from the dry cleaner. Her perfect clothes showcase a flawless figure a younger woman would be proud of. She doesn't believe in serious talk while you eat.

I'd replaced my uncomfortable court clothes with a pair of loose jeans and a baggy shirt. Hope to put off the 'you need to get in shape' lecture. "Any more potatoes? They're really good."

"They're good, but full of fat and calories. You've had plenty."

"It's been so long since I've had food like this . . . come on."

"I hate to bring this up, but you've gained weight while you were . . . while you were away. It's not becoming to you and downright embarrassing for a woman in my position to have a . . . rather plump daughter."

"Mom, cut the 'while I was away' crap. Say it—-prison, prison, your daughter was in prison, your FAT out of shape daughter was in prison. Sometimes, I think you care more about my being fat than being in prison."

"Don't be ridiculous, I . . . "

"Your position. The way you carry on, you'd think you were the Surgeon General. There are more important things in life than whether you're a few pounds overweight. If it were up to you, people would need a license to go to a bakery. At least in prison, no one bugged me about my weight."

Mom glares at me, then puts her head down on her hands. She's such a drama queen. Why couldn't I be released to a halfway house? The food would be worse, but I wouldn't have to put up with all the theatrics.

After what seems like a long time, Mom speaks, "I thought you might've learned from your experience. Let's get this straight. You're released to me and to my rules. You're to go to all your appointments with your parole officer. Follow all his rules. I want to know where you are all the time. I expect you to be here when I get home from work. I don't want any of your doper friends at the house. You're to help with the cooking and cleaning at least till you get a job. I imagine I don't have to tell you I forbid you to be in contact with Josh."

She pauses and begins to speak softly. "It wouldn't hurt to come to Think Thin with me. I'll get you a counselor—-someone young. You can start working out and set up a diet plan. Getting a job isn't easy. You need to look your best. I told my colleagues you quit your job and were coming home for a break. I'd appreciate it if you'd stick to that story."

"Shit, you can't get two sentences out without a weight-loss discussion. I'm not obese. I'm a few pounds over what you and your obsessed buddies think is chic. How about being glad I'm out of prison and home? You needn't worry about what I tell anyone at your office. I'm not going there today, tomorrow or ever. I'd rather go back to prison."

THREE

Louise wished Kristin's homecoming had gone better. Prison must've been hell. Louise would've done anything legal she could to get Kristin out of jail. She was glad to have her here safe. Louise believed Kristin was grateful for her help even though she didn't act like it. Why hadn't she tried to empathize rather than nag her about being fat? Would it have been so bad to let her have more potatoes? Kristin had complained about prison food from the day she was arrested.

Worse, why mention Josh? It'd been a long time since Louise had been love-struck, but she remembered what it felt like. Before she married Kristin's father, Bob, she had several love affairs; made her share of bad decisions.

For maybe the thousandth time since he died, Louise reminisced about meeting Bob. At age thirty-one, she ended an on-again off-again five-year relationship; quit her secretarial job; and took a position as a clerk at a small, independent bookstore and coffee bar. Three months later, she met Bob. He was getting a Master's Degree in counseling at the University and worked part-time as a waiter at a café near the bookstore. Like her, he loved books and came into the store often to browse and drink coffee.

Louise didn't think Bob was her type. She was attracted to the exotic. He was average. His hair was shorter than the styles of the day, his clothes, generic jeans and a collared shirt. Every day he came in at the same time and ordered the same drink. Nothing about him was exciting. Louise knew he liked her, but she wasn't interested.

As the months passed, they spent time together, but only as friends. She dated other men, but none of the dates went anywhere. Bob took her to meet his parents, but she never took him to meet hers. He never mentioned other women. When they weren't together, he studied or hung out with friends or family.

A year passed this way until he told Louise he had a date to go to his friend, Dan's, wedding. He had asked a woman in one of his classes. To her amazement, she felt intensely jealous. As the date of the wedding approached, she worked herself into a frenzy. Pressing Bob for details, she learned there were over two hundred guests, and decided on a plan. She bought a sexy dress and decided to crash the reception.

Finally, the day arrived. She spent hours getting ready. For the first time in her life, she hired a taxi. At the hotel bar, she fortified herself with a martini (another first). In the elegant lobby, she watched chic couples, debated whether to go in. Just when she decided she didn't have enough nerve, she spotted Bob. Alone. Immediately, he came over. "What are you doing here?"

"Meeting some friends," she stammered. "Where's your date?"

"She got sick at the last minute," he replied in a soft voice.

How inconvenient for you. She was grateful not to face Bob with a date, but still upset he'd invited someone else. "That must leave you without a date."

"I don't suppose you could skip your friends and come with me?" Bob asked.

"Well, they're expecting me," she said, trying not to sound too eager to give up her non-existent gathering.

"I understand," Bob said. "It just seemed like a miracle to have you show up."

"You mean because even though your date's sick, you won't have to go alone?"

"No. I didn't have a date. Dan suggested I make one up, and maybe you'd get jealous. I told him it wouldn't work, and I was right."

"No, you weren't," she said, as she smiled up at him. Within the year, they married. Kristin was born two years later. Bob was as solid as his name, and decades later when Kristin was grown up and out of the house, he'd look at Louise and marvel at his good fortune. He was as good a father as he was a husband. Louise never regretted their marriage, which ended twenty-three years later when Bob died of colon cancer. If only she could talk to him now. He would know how to treat Kristin.

Louise looked at her watch and realized she'd been daydreaming—-a new, disturbing habit. Better make sure Kristin gets to her appointment on time. "Kristin, what time do you need to get up?"

"Seven, but I can take care of it."

If she could take care of it, she wouldn't have been in prison. "Seven's cutting it close. If you're going to eat breakfast and look your best, how about six-thirty?"

"Mom, I'm not five years old; I can take care of it. I know when to get up."

And they're fighting. She hadn't meant to provoke an argument, but again she'd said the wrong thing.

FOUR

It's hard to be angry after a long, hot shower. Mom had stocked the bathroom with exotic soaps, bottles of colorful shampoo and fragrant conditioners. For the last sixteen months, 'shower' meant a thin spray of water that switched from scalding to ice without warning. Someone was always watching. I didn't know why. Didn't always know whom. Maybe they thought I was taking too long; maybe they wanted sex; maybe I pissed them off. I never knew if they wanted to hurt me. I only knew I had to be careful. The soap was hard and thin and brown. It never lathered. I gave mine to whoever wanted it.

Feeling clean, I step out, grab a large soft towel. No need to worry about stains from another prisoner who'd used it for reasons I didn't want to think about. I hated those disgusting towels. You couldn't tell what color they started out. But when I needed one, I was glad to have anything.

Mom had left a new cotton nightshirt (my favorite sleeping gear), a new robe and slippers in the bedroom. After I was arrested, my friend, Angie, went to Josh's and my apartment to get my things. There wasn't much. I sold my work clothes when we needed money. Most of my old stuff wouldn't fit now.

Mom thought drugs had gotten me into trouble. She was wrong. I wasn't addicted to drugs. It was Josh. I still yearned for him. I forgave him for letting me face the police alone. I forgave him for not trying to get me out of prison. I forgave him for leaving town without me. He never said good by. Any rational person would never want to see him again. Would wish he suffered as I had. I thought of him day and night. Wanted him to call. My cellies wanted coke or meth. I wanted him. It was worse than drugs. I'd been clean for sixteen months, and nothing changed.

In bed, I delight in the feel of crisp sheets. Being an ex-con made me appreciate the little things: my own clothes, warm showers, a comfortable bed. Prison had done its job. I was rehabilitated. I would never use an illegal drug; never drive drunk. I'd be a law-abiding citizen. Never again would I take my freedom for granted.

My first night free. I'm tired from the stress of the day; but even in this comfortable, safe place, sleep is elusive. Until I walked out the door, I was scared they'd changed their minds, find an error in my release date or revoke my parole.

Tomorrow, I'd meet my parole officer. I wanted to be on time, look clean, and get on his good side. Please let him not be a jerk. Maybe Mom would lend me the car. She didn't know my license was suspended. Gee Kristin, your vow of being a law-abiding citizen lasted a long time. A suspended license charge isn't like a crime. That's what I tell myself. It's only a ticket, a fine. You don't go to jail. I start to drift off when I hear Mom.

"Kristin, what time do you need to get up?"

"Seven, but I can take care of it." Does she think because I was in prison I forgot how to wake up?

"Seven's cutting it close. If you're going to eat breakfast and look your best, how about six-thirty?"

There she goes again about how I look. "Mom, I'm not five years old. I know when to get up."

She wants to help but she treats me like I'm an idiot. "Maybe you could lend me the car. I need to start being independent."

"Are you crazy? You don't have a valid license. The first day out of prison you break the law. Not only break it but break it to meet your parole officer."

"Okay mom, you're right. I just want to go by myself. You can't take me everywhere."

"Your parole officer said I have to be there since I'm your legal custodian or something like that. I have to sign papers that I agree to make you follow the rules while you're on parole and live with me."

"I'm not going to a job interview—he'll be happy if I get there on time, not stoned. Seven will be plenty of time."

"Look in the closet. I bought you some new clothes. Hopefully, they'll fit."

Just like in prison, the jailer gets the last word.

Neither of us speaks on the way downtown. Mom looks good. She's wearing black wool pants with a matching gray shell and sweater. A multi-colored scarf, matching earrings and necklace tie her outfit together. She wants me to dress up. No way. She can't talk me out of my favorite jeans. I don't want to look like her. She claims a minor victory when I take off an old black t-shirt and replace it with one of the new shirts. The argument and change of clothing cause us to leave late. It's almost nine when we reach the McCain Building, which houses parole and other government offices. Parking's a nightmare downtown. She lets me off in front of the building.

The lobby's crowded. The directory lists the Parole Office in Suite 312. An elevator door opens. I join the crowd who shove into the small space. Someone pushes the button, and the elevator moves slowly as it passes the second floor without a pause and stops on three. I get off as does nearly everyone else. 312's almost directly in front of the elevator. I follow a group of people as they open the door. The room is filled with parolees, some alone and others in small groups. There are men and women, old and young, white, black, Hispanic, Asian and everything in-between. A few are dressed for work, and others look disheveled and dirty. The only thing they have in common is nobody looks happy.

At the reception desk, I remember Mom has the card with the name of my parole officer and, of course, I can't remember it. Perfect start. "I'm here to see my parole officer, but I don't know his name."

"No problem," the woman replies pleasantly. "Just fill in your name, DOC number, and time of your appointment. We'll call you when he's ready." The woman smiles at me as if my appointment is for a manicure at a fancy resort rather than an ex-con to see her parole officer. I smile back uncertainly, surprised at the woman's attitude. It isn't what I'd expected. Feeling less uptight, I walk back toward the seating area.

There are a few empty chairs, but I'm afraid to take one. Most are next to young men with lots of homemade tattoos and attitude rolling off their faces. After looking around, I walk toward the back wall, joining other standees. "What's a matter, honey, you look lost—-this your first time?" asks a thin, older woman who sits next to a young nicely dressed woman on one side and the wall on the other.

"Yeah, if it's any of your business," I retort, trying to hide my nervousness, but immediately feel bad. I'm out of prison now. Time to act like a normal person, not a paranoid ex-con.

"Don't be a bitch. I was gonna give some you info about this place, try to help save your ass," she speaks softly. Before I can reply the pleasant receptionist calls, 'Shala Miller', and my new friend gets up. "That's me. You can have my seat . . . Listen; most of the people here are bullshitters, so think before you listen to them. But you can't tell the bad from the good based on how they look."

Maybe Shala's just another bullshitter, but I'm grateful to have her chair. I'm not tired, but standing makes me too conspicuous. Should've brought a magazine or something. I'd been reading The Firm in prison. I got it from the prison library; but I was afraid if I took it home, it'd not only be the end of parole, but probably a theft charge.

As the moments pass, my mind turns to Josh. I re-live—-for the thousandth time—-how we met. I'd been down for what seemed forever before that night.

Scott was my first serious boyfriend. After three years of togetherness, he decided we needed time apart to see if he wanted to married me. Instead of being strong and giving him space, I gave him an ultimatum. If he stopped seeing me, it was forever. My strategy backfired. Scott broke up with me. After only a few months, I heard he had another girlfriend.

I spent a couple months in mourning, but soon started to party, even though my heart wasn't in it. I hooked up with a few guys, but that made me feel worse. I went to Angie's party only because she begged me. I expected nothing; but shortly after I got there, I noticed a tall, charismatic guy give me the eye. We left together.

"Kristin White." A stern-looking woman calls my name. I walk toward her. "Are you Kristin White?"

"Yeah."

"You need to take a drug test. If you're dirty, you can save yourself trouble by 'fessing up before the test."

"But I'm clean," I protest.

"You know the drill. Put your purse and jacket on this table. Before I give you the cup, I have to pat you down." I tense, remember the prison pat-downs. Hard wandering hands. No choice but to submit. Scream and you get written up. Professionally and gently she pats me down. "Here's the cup. Fill it to the line. FYI, we check it for temperature and whether it's human, as well as for drugs. I'll wait out here, but I can see you through the window." The bathroom's clean. I continue to be surprised at the professionalism of the staff. I go in, pee as fast as I can, and close the cup. I walk out, hand it to her. "Good, I'll take you to your parole officer. You're lucky; he's tough, but a sweetie."

We walk through a maze of corridors. The woman finally stops, knocks on a partially opened door and announces, "Remy, here's your next victim."

I stare as a tall, sexy black man turns toward me. "I'm Remy Cooper, your parole officer. Pleased to meet you, Kristin." Besides a terrific body, Mr. Cooper has a handsome face, a big smile and penetrating eyes. He's not even that much older than me. "Come in and have a seat." Wow, he's gorgeous. If he's half as cool as he looks, I've lucked out.

"Let's see, you got out yesterday. Living with your mom. She here?"

"Parking the car."

"Any plans for the future?"

"I guess. Get a job."

"Good . . . what type of work do you want to do?"

"I don't know—-whatever job I can get."

"We'll get back to that in a bit. I need to go over some things with you before we get your mom. Your sentence, with release credit, ends in about six months. The exact date will be on these papers. If you violate your conditions, you can spend the rest of your sentence in prison. The most important ones are that you commit no future crimes, stay clean, follow the rules at your mom's, and do something productive with your time. Both law enforcement...

"Excuse me, but I have a question. Do I have to live with her? Can't I get my own place or live with a friend?" What I want to know is if I can live with Josh, but I know I shouldn't ask that. I didn't know if Remy knows about him or not.

"Living with your mom a problem?"

"Yeah. No shit. Sorry, I mean no kidding. She treats me like I'm a kid. I was on my own for several years before I went to prison. She wants to know what I'm doing all the time. Wants to decide who I can see."

"For now, you don't have a choice. If you get a job and can afford a place, we'll talk about it. As I was saying, both law enforcement and parole have the right to search your person, your car or your home." I think of him searching my room, going through my drawers, handling my bras and underpants. Was I blushing? "You can be re-arrested and sent back to prison without a prior hearing. You can't possess drugs—-including alcohol, drug paraphernalia, guns or other weapons. You can't have any contact with parolees or felons without permission. You can't travel out of state without permission. Let's see—- there are no co-defendants in your case, so we don't have to worry about that. Any questions so far? Anything you want to ask about before your mom comes in?"

Well how about whether you're married or have a girlfriend?

"No."

"I want you to know I'm not here to harass you or get you locked up. I'll be straight with you, and I expect the same. If you have a problem, talk to me about it—-don't just blow me off. We can work on it together. Make sure you read the conditions carefully, as I didn't go over all the details." He picks up the phone. "Page Louise White and have her escorted back to my office... Thanks, you too." In just a few minutes, she appears at the door. He gets up and puts out his hand.

"Hi, Mrs. White. I'm Remy Cooper, your daughter's parole officer. Nice to meet you."

"You too, Mr. Cooper."

"I've been going over the rules with Kristin. Here's a copy of her conditions. I know we went over them on the phone when you agreed to be a third-party custodian, but feel free to read them again if you wish. You'll both need to sign them. The Court doesn't specify what the rules at home should be as long as the basic conditions are followed. It's up to you to set a reasonable curfew or decide whom Kristin can have at the house."

"I notice that Josh's name isn't on the list of prohibited people. Why not? He's the cause of most of this mess."

"I'm sorry Mrs. White; I don't know whom you're talking about. There were no co-defendants in her case, and I don't recall seeing a Josh in any of the police reports."

"Josh was her, her boyfriend," she replies venom in her tone. "They were his drugs, but he wasn't there when the police searched the house, and he never came forward. He left her to take the blame. Some boyfriend he turned out to be. I knew as soon as I met him he was no good."

"Mom, you don't know anything. You prejudged him totally without knowing him," I say not for the first time.

"Both of you relax. Mrs. White, there's no legal restriction that keeps Josh away from your daughter. You certainly have a right not to have him in your home. You can also forbid Kristin from seeing him, although in my experience, that generally makes things worse."

"You bet I'll forbid her, Mr. Cooper."

"As I started to explain earlier, Kristin, if you want help with employment, I can make you an appointment to see our job developer. What do you think?"

"I'd like to try on my own first and see how it goes."

"That's fine. If you change your mind, call and I'll set it up. I need to see you next month. How about Monday, March 13, at nine?"

"That's not a good day for me, Mr. Cooper. I have an important meeting at work," Mom answers as if what I want doesn't matter.

"Mrs. White, you don't need to come. You're welcome to call anytime you like, and you should contact me if there are any problems. But your daughter's an adult and can come alone."

"That day's fine with me, Mr. Cooper. See you then." I can't believe Mom. You don't tell these people the time's no good. Important meeting at work, no way——probably her weekly weigh in.

Two years earlier

It starts like any rotten day. I wake up slowly, groan when I hear someone knock and call my name. The clock says 11 a.m. Josh? No, it's Angie.

"Kristin, I know you're in there. Answer the door."

"Be right down." I crawl out of bed, stop in the bathroom to splash water over my face and let her in. My best friend, Angie, smart and beautiful. She's taller than me, although at five foot two, so's most of the adult world. Her auburn hair is long and wavy, and she has large brown, twinkling eyes. She laughs often about everything, including herself.

If asked to describe her in one word, it would be vibrant. She'd never be asleep mid-morning. No matter what the situation, she always comes up with ideas. Her clothes are colorful. She'd never wind up in prison. Her life's in control. She looks at me, takes in my unkempt dirty hair, slept-in t-shirt, and tired eyes.

"Just get up? I thought you were job-hunting. No one's going to hire you if you look like a homeless person on Law and Order. Do I have to come over here every morning and wake you?"

"I know. I didn't sleep last night, and I couldn't wake up."

"Where's Josh? Don't tell me he's still asleep?"

I thought about lying, but she'd know. "Josh isn't here. A couple of guys I'd never seen before came by late last night. They gave me the creeps. He didn't tell me who they were. Then he left with them. Didn't say where they were going. Didn't say good by. I haven't seen him since."

Angie looks at me but says nothing. I know she's thinks I'm a loser to stay with a guy who treats me like this. She doesn't understand. She'd been with Art since seventh grade, maybe before. He treats her like a queen. She's never been alone. "Can I make you some coffee? I don't know if we have any milk, but there's some powdered stuff."

"Yuck. I'm supposed to meet my Aunt Sara for coffee in about half an hour. Why don't you join us? You can have real cream. I'll wait while you put on some clothes."

"I'm broke. I need to use my money to do laundry."

"It's on me. Don't argue. You've bailed me out tons of times. I'll never forget when you spent hours going over years of my checking account statements. I was so happy when you found out I'd been deducting a dime per check and never had to." She gives me a big hug. "Go get dressed. Just make it quick."

Feeling better, I go back to my room. Angie always improves my mood. We met freshmen year in college and have been best friends since. We lived together until senior year, when she moved in with Art, and me with Scott.

The four of us got along great too. We had big dreams: Angie a journalist; Scott, law school; and Art and I, counselors. We graduated, and Angie and Art got married. Art got a job as a youth counselor, and Angie with the Tucson Sun.

Scott started law school. I was the only one who didn't find a 'dream job'. After several interviews that went nowhere, I took a job in the University Counseling Department as an administrative assistant. When I took the job, I hoped to interact with students. I thought I'd learn something about counseling. In reality, I was a glorified secretary; but there was nothing glorified about it.

The four of us had dinner together at least once a week and hung out on weekends. Art would tease Scott: 'When you gonna tie the knot,' 'Can I be best man?' Scott would pretend to joke he wanted to wait till we moved to a state without community property. I'd remark that marriage was passé. I'd have married Scott in a second if he'd asked. By then I didn't even love him. I just wanted the rest of the world to know someone wanted to marry me.

I hated my job. My boss, Betsy Gruper, was Administrative Assistant to the Chairman of the Counseling Department, Professorh. Betsy had a huge crush on him. "Professor Wahr, is that a new shirt?" "Professor Wahr, let me do that for you," her voice sounding fakey sweet.

"Thanks, uh, Betsy," he'd respond on a good day.

Betsy constantly harped on standards. She wanted me to dress like she did in old-fashioned suits or dress and matching jacket. She looked liked she was on her way to a funeral or a ladies luncheon circa 1950. The students wore jeans in winter and shorts and t-shirts in summer. The professors, like most Tucsonans, dressed informally. I knew I couldn't wear t-shirts or shorts, but I didn't want to dress like her. How could I establish rapport if I looked so out of touch? Not that I had much chance to bond with students. On the rare occasions when Betsy wasn't there, I'd start a conversation while they waited for their appointments. Otherwise, I kept quiet.

When not flirting with Prof, Betsy criticized me. Too much chatting with students. Didn't keep my desk neat. Handwriting too sloppy. If I married Scott, I could quit when he graduated; say bye to Betsy and her frustrated love life; find something better.

Barking, excited dogs interrupt my daydreams. I look outside but don't see anything unusual. I pull on my last pair of clean underwear; grab a worn but unstained t-shirt and my least filthy pair of jeans. More barking, loud knocks and commotion. Angie screams, "The police are outside! Come down quick!"

"OPEN THE DOOR, TUCSON POLICE DEPARTMENT." More loud knocks and again, "OPEN THE DOOR NOW, POLICE." With my heart pounding, I hurry and open the door. "WE HAVE A WARRANT TO SEARCH THESE PREMISES. Stand over here and don't move." Dazed, I watch officers with guns drawn walk through the living room, kitchen, and into the bedroom and bathroom. "Anyone else in the house, ma'am?"

"No, just the two of us." Where the hell's Josh?"

They open closets; look out the back window. Satisfied no one else is home, one of them comes over to us. "Which one of you is Kristin White?" I start to say I am, but I can't speak, so I raise my hand.

"This is a warrant to search the premises." He hands me a piece of paper. "As long as you both stand here with Officer Wright and don't interfere, we won't handcuff you. If you try to leave or interfere, we will. She's going to pat you down." I can't believe it. The female cop walks over to me and moves her hands up and down my body. She does the same thing to Angie. I glance at her. Her face is pale, her customary bravado gone.

"Who are you?" the cop asks Angie.

"Angelica Montoya."

"You live here?"

Before Angie could say a word, I find my voice, "No, she's just visiting."

"That's right. I'm a guest. Can we sit down at least?" Angie's tries to conquer her fear and figure out what to do.

"Sure, go ahead and sit over there."

As we sit down, Angie turns to me and whispers, "Remember we used to talk with Scott about his criminal law class? Don't answer any questions. He said that's how people get in trouble."

"But those were criminals. I'm not a criminal. There might be some pot in the bedroom, but just a little."

"Be quiet. Maybe you should call Scott."

"No, you can't be serious?" He's the last person I want to know about this. Why isn't Josh here?

Angie says nothing more. We sit next to each other in silence. I try to listen to the cops, but all I hear are drawers slamming and unintelligible conversation. The noise stops. One of the cops yells, "Bingo. Over here, look at this." Then, more noise.

Finally, the cop who seems in charge comes over to us, "Kristin White, you're under arrest for possession of cocaine with intent to sell and possession of marijuana. Stand up... I said stand up. We can do this the easy way or the hard way." I stand, and he handcuffs me.

"Ms. Montoya. You can go."

"Angie, I don't know anything about cocaine. It's not mine. Someone must have put it there."

"Shut up, Kristin. Don't say anything till you talk to a lawyer. Officer, shouldn't you read her, her rights?"

"Don't tell me how to do my job. I suggest you leave now. I don't want to arrest you for hindering prosecution. Officer Sainz will walk you to your car."

As Angie leaves, I feel worse, if that's possible. "Kristin, we're taking you to the police station. If you want to bring your purse, I need to look through it." I point to my purse and nod I understand.

The ten-minute ride to the station seems endless. Why is there coke in the house? Josh and I'd snorted it a few times, but always used it all. We couldn't afford a stash. How did the police know? Maybe those guys left the stuff, kidnapped Josh, set us up? Am I going to jail? Mom's gonna freak—-blame Josh. Years of 'I told you so.' Where's Josh? What must Angie think? Because of me, she's treated like a criminal. Do I need a lawyer? How do I get one? And a realization—-Josh is involved in this.

SEVEN

We arrive at the station. The cop takes me in through a back door. He leads me to a small room with a table, two chairs, and little else. The room reeks. "Sit there," he says, and unlocks my cuffs. Without explanation, he leaves me alone.

A long time passes. I'm thirsty. I'm afraid to move. Maybe they have hidden cameras and are watching me. My hands ache. I have to pee. I'm cold. The door opens, and another cop——I think he's a cop, though he's dressed in a jacket and tie——comes in and sits down. "I'm Detective Brennan. Can I get you a cup of coffee or a coke?"

"A coke would be nice. Do you have diet?" Under arrest, and I worry about diet coke. Mom would approve.

"Sure, I'll be right back." He returns with the diet coke and turns on a tape recorder. "Today's date is January 13th, 1992. This is Detective Brennan, Badge #86401. I'm at the South Stone Station interviewing Kristin White. Kristin, you have the right to remain silent. You have the right to have an attorney appointed for you before any questioning. If you can't afford an attorney, one will be appointed for you. Anything you say can and will be used against you in a court of law. Do you understand those rights?"

"Yes."

"Are you willing to answer some questions?"

"I don't know. I've never been in trouble before. Should I?"

"I can't tell you whether you should or not Kristin. I understand you told the officers the coke wasn't yours. If it wasn't yours, and you can help us find out who it belongs to, that might help you later. I can't promise you anything. Only the County Attorney's Office can make promises. But I'd tell them anything helpful you told me, and that you cooperated."

"Can I answer some questions and then change my mind?"

"Of course. So are you willing to answer some questions?"

I nod.

"Out loud please."

"Yes."

He sits quietly as if he's waiting for me to say something. After a few minutes—-or was it only seconds—-he gets up and leaves without another word.

Had I done something wrong . . .? Was he going to come back . . .? How long was he going to leave me here alone. . .? I had to pee . . . What if he didn't come back?

Finally, the door opens and he's back. "Where were we? Is your full name Kristin Elizabeth White?"

"Yes."

"You don't mind if I call you Kristin?"

"That's okay." Why's he asking now? He's been calling me that since he came in.

"Kristin, what's your date of birth?"

"June 6th, 1970."

"And you live at 134 Bean Street?"

"Yes."

"How long have you lived there?"

"About seven or eight months."

"Who do you live with?" I start to answer Josh, but before I say his name, I stop. If I say he lives there, will he get arrested too? If Josh were here, he'd never give me up. Maybe I should talk to that lawyer they mentioned.

"You said I could talk to a lawyer. I think I want to talk to one now."

"Kristin, once you ask for a lawyer, I can't talk to you anymore. The officer who brought you here will take you to the jail. It's too late tonight to see a judge.

"I can't afford a lawyer. I hardly have enough money to do my laundry. You mean I'm going to spend the night in jail?"

"As I told you, when you see the judge, the court will appoint you a lawyer if you can't afford one."

"When does that happen? Aren't I allowed to make a call? They always let you make a call in the movies." God, I'm so stupid.

"When you see the judge, he'll appoint you a lawyer. You can make all the calls you want at the jail." The detective gets up and walks around the table toward me holding out the handcuffs. "If we're done talking, I have to put these on. Are you sure whoever you're protecting would do the same for you?"

I don't know what to say. If I say yes, that would tell him something. He grabs my hands and puts on the handcuffs.

"Please, you don't need to put those on. I'll do whatever you say. Where you going?" Oh, God, what if I made a mistake? Maybe I should've talked to him. At least I could stay here. Not jail. How could Josh have done this to me? Where the hell is he? Would he have done the same for me?

CHAPTER

EIGHT

Nine p.m. Twelve hours till I see the judge. They took off the handcuffs. Instead of a cell, I'm in a large room with lots of people. There are cameras on the ceiling and guards at desks on two sides. I'm still wearing the not-very-clean clothes I put on when Angie showed up. They're sweaty, wrinkled and smell bad. No one's searched me since the pat down before they took me to jail. I've got to pee again.

The call to Mom was a nightmare. I stood in the phone line thirty minutes, wondering the whole time what to say. I've hardly said a word when the people in line yell at me to get off the "God damn-fucking phone." Everyone listens. They call out sarcastic remarks. "Mommy, I did a bad thing." "Of course the dope wasn't yours." "Stupid bitch." I can't think. How do you tell your mom you're in jail—- for dealing cocaine?

Dear Abby, Please help. I'm a 23-year-old college grad. The police searched my apartment and found lots of cocaine. They arrested me, took me to jail. How do I tell Mom? Mom's a well-dressed, middle-class woman who works as a weight consultant, is obsessed with appearances, and has unrealistically high expectations for her only child. Before my arrest, I let her down because I was fat, a walking fashion faux pas, and dumped by the perfect boyfriend. Abby, please believe me, the drugs weren't mine. I have no idea how they got in my apartment. Thank you. Incarcerated in Arizona.

It doesn't sound believable to me; why should anyone else believe it? Mom cried so hard I couldn't hear her.

"Kristin White, approach the door, attorney visitor."

Attorney? Did Mom call somebody? Maybe he'll get me out tonight. I approach the door, confirm I'm Kristin, and the door opens. I walk through several more doors, when a deputy motions me to follow him. We continue through a narrow hallway with several small conference rooms on each side. "He's in Booth 5. When you're done, wait in the hall. Don't take anything from him, not anything, including food, pencils, paper. We'll escort you back when you're done." I walk into the booth.

"Scott, what are you doing here? How'd you find out?" How humiliating. A jail visit from your ex who dumped you. Must be damn glad he did. ATTORNEY'S WIFE ARRESTED IN DRUG RAID right under CLINTON BIG LEAD IN POLLS. Not the kind of publicity to help a career.

"Did Mom phone you?"

"No, Angie. She told me what happened and asked me to come. You know I'd be here soon as I heard." Like, I believe that. "I don't do criminal, but I know enough to give you some advice."

"What's gonna happen? Can I get out of here after I see the judge? How come they didn't make me wear those orange jumpsuits? Scott, I can't believe this is happening. I'm not a criminal."

"Calm down, Kris. Being hysterical won't help anything. The jumpsuit thing's easy. You're in a holding cell. The jail doesn't want to waste clothes on you or put you in a real cell unless you're going to stay beyond tomorrow morning."

"So I'm getting out?" I look at him hopefully. Scott and I are alone for the first time since we'd broken up. In a very small room. I don't want him back, but I wonder how he feels being here. I wish I didn't look like such a mess. He still calls me Kris. It seems natural to have him here with me. I want to hug him. At the same time, he seems like a person I knew casually a long time ago.

"I don't know. That's up to the judge. He can release you ROR, on your own recognizance; to your mom; or into the custody of a court organization called Pretrial Services. Or he can put a bond on you."

"What's Pretrial Services? Is bond like bail?"

"Pretrial Services recommends whether people should be released. If the judge is worried you won't come back to court but doesn't want to keep you in jail, he can release you to their custody. If he does, you have to report to them——maybe do drug tests, things like that. Yeah, bond is bail."

"But you're out of jail?"

"Yeah."

"How much is the bond?"

"It depends. It can vary from a couple hundred dollars to a million. It's based on how serious the offense is, whether you're here legally, if you have a criminal record, if you have a place to live, a job, that kind of stuff."

" I have a place to live, you know I have no record, and I can get a job."

"You don't have to convince me. I don't decide. If you're released on bail, you can put up the cash or contact a bail bondsman. A bail bondsman puts up the bail for you, but you have to get him ten percent in cash and some kind of collateral, like a car or house title.

He sounds like he's giving a lecture in law school. I don't feel like hugging him any more.

"What happened with your job? I know you hated Betsy . . . "

"Long story. Now's not the time. What about a lawyer? You could be my lawyer, couldn't you?"

"Bad idea, Kris. I don't do criminal. I called a friend who works at the Public Defender's Office. She said if you can't afford a lawyer, the judge would appoint the PD."

Figures his friend's a she. "Even if I get out?"

"It has nothing to do with if you're in or out. It's if you can afford one."

"Maybe Mom can afford a lawyer, but she was totally pissed when I called. Thinks I'm a complete moron. She's convinced the drugs belong to my boyfriend, Josh. I'm taking a fall for him. I don't know if she has any extra money——things have been tough since dad died. Too bad the credit union doesn't have a Get Your Daughter a Lawyer Fund like they do for Christmas expenses."

"Kris, you're an adult. Your mom's not responsible for a lawyer. Is she right about the drugs? How much was there?"

"I'm not sure, but a lot. The cop said something like possession for sale. I don't know where it came from. The detective said if I helped them find out, it would help my case."

"I might not know a lot about criminal law, but I do know cops can't make promises to you, only prosecutors can. Cops lie about stuff. I remember a murder case from law school; the police told the suspect his prints were on the gun even though it wasn't true. The court said it's okay to do that."

"That doesn't seem fair. And how can I tell them whose it is if I don't know?"

"Be realistic, does anyone live with you besides this Josh? Who else has access to the house? Angie told me they found the cocaine in the bedroom. Who comes in your bedroom when you're not home?"

"Well, two guys came over last night, and Josh left with them—-maybe they left it."

"Oh, Kris, . . . don't be an idiot. No one leaves cocaine with someone else. It's worth lots of money. Seems like your mom's right. Why go to prison for this loser? What kind of man lets his girlfriend take the rap?" What kind of guy needs time out to figure out if he wants to marry you?

"Scott, stop. Don't tell me what kind of guy Josh is. You don't know him. He's always been there for me. He wasn't home when the cops came. He's going to make it right."

"I don't want to debate this. You need to listen to what I'm telling you. You're in a lot of trouble. Don't talk to the police or anyone else about your case until you see a lawyer. I gotta go. Do you want me to call anyone for you? I told Angie I'd be in touch after I saw you. She said you know that she and Art are there for you—-whatever they can do."

"Do you have to go?" Anything's better than going back there. "The jail's horrible. The people are creepy. They stare at me like it's my fault they're here. One woman asked for a cigarette. I said I didn't have any, and she called me a goddamn bitch. I'm afraid someone's going to hurt me."

"Don't exaggerate. I know it's not fun but no one can hurt you. That's what the guards are for."

"The guards don't see everything. They act like we're all criminals."

"Sorry, Kris, but I gotta go. (Probably has a girlfriend waiting.) I'll be in touch. Good luck tomorrow. Angie said she'd be there."

"Scott, wait." He walks out like he didn't hear me.

CHAPTER
NINE

Morning finally. My body hurts from the hard chair. My mouth's dry. I need a toothbrush. During the night, I drift off; but voices intrude, "I didn't do shit, he hit me first"; "Get the fuck away from me, asshole"; "I'm going kill that piece of shit." I stay as far away from everyone as I can. I don't make eye contact. I'm afraid to ask anyone what's going to happen. I try to listen to what other people say. Not that I learn much.

This place isn't what I expected. Men and women are together. Instead of bars, the room has are bathrooms, drinking fountains, chairs and tables. The phone calls go on all night. You have to call collect. "This is a collect call from the Pima County Jail. Will you accept charges?" Like mom, most do. Over and over I hear, "What do you mean, you're not going to bail me out?"

A deputy walks to the front of the room and starts to speak. Most quiet down. "Court's going to start in a few minutes. You'll see the judge on a video screen. She'll be able to see and hear you. Before you go in, you'll have a chance to talk to the Public Defender if you want to. When you hear your name, line up at the east door." He points. "What if you don't want the Public Defender?" "What if you want to plead not guilty?" "Where's my lawyer?" The deputy ignores everyone.

"Rodriguez, Sheppard, Washington, Valdez, Cox, approach the gate."
I watch the group leave. Every so often, the guard calls another group of
names. No one comes back.

When will they get to me? I get enough courage to ask a woman who
acts like she'd been here before if the order means anything. I knew it
wasn't alphabetical.

"New huh? They take the small timers first and save the bad-asses for
last. What'd you do? Stab your lover or something?"

"No, nothing like that. It's all a big mistake."

"I know. We're all innocent in here." She winks at me, and I look away,
my stomach churning.

"White, Mendoza, Kowalski, Khan." Now what? Maybe I'm better off
in here. The deputy leads us to a smaller room with a few chairs and a table.
In the front stands a young woman wearing a short, tight black skirt, black
high heels, and a silver blouse that leaves little to the imagination.

"Ms. Rainey's here to help you. Don't give her any lip," the deputy says
as he turns to smile at the sexy young woman who returns the smile.

She faces the group. "Hi, I'm Ellen Rainey from the Public Defender's
Office. In a few minutes, you'll see the judge. This hearing is called an
initial appearance. You enter a plea of not guilty, the judge will appoint
you a lawyer if you can't afford one and, most importantly, she'll set bail. If
you want a lawyer appointed, you need to fill out this form." She hands one
to each of us and points to clipboards and pens. "I have to fax them to the
judge before she sees you so hurry. Any questions?"

"I don't even know why I'm here. I didn't do anything," one of the
women blurts out, looking even more confused than I felt.

"You'll get a copy of the charges against you when you go in. Oh, and
make sure if the judge asks you something, you answer 'yes'; or better yet,
'yes, Your Honor', not 'yeah'. Act respectful, and if she asks if you'll promise to appear, say 'yes'. The judge is a real tight ass, ask CO Sullivan," and
this time they exchange laughs and heavy eye contact.

"Are you going to be my lawyer if I get a PD?" I force myself to ask.

"No, it'll be someone else." Thank goodness for that. She looks more
interested in flirting.

Eventually, she calls me over. "Last night you told Pretrial you have no
previous arrests, have lived in Tucson all your life, and can live with your
mom. No job, though. Is that right?"

"Yeah, but the no job is temporary. I had a good job, and I can get another one."

"We don't have much time, so just answer my questions. You want to get out, don't you?" she asks, as if I'm wasting her time.

"Of course, I want to get out."

"You're not working now?"

"No, but I worked at the University for two years, and then at a restaurant. It's just . . ."

"But not now?" she interrupts me.

"No."

"Send in White," calls a voice from the next room. The lawyer follows me into another room that has a video screen in front. There are two rows of chairs in front of the screen. A few people watch the proceedings. Mostly deputies. The lawyer shows me where to stand. On the video, I see a dark-haired woman wearing a black robe. She must be the judge. There's a young blonde woman seated on one side of her and an older bald man on the other. Later I realize the woman is a clerk and the man is the prosecutor.

"State of Arizona vs. White. We're on the record. The Public Defender's Office, Ms. Rainey, specially appearing for the defendant. Robert Barron for the State." The lawyer hands me a piece of paper. "Ms. Rainey is handing you a copy of the charges against you. Do you waive reading?"

The lawyer looks at me but responds, "Yes, Judge, we waive reading." I have no idea what they mean. 'Wave reading'?

"How do you plead?" No one speaks. "Ms. White, how do you plead: guilty or not guilty?"

"Say not guilty," the lawyer whispers. "I told you that." Why did the lawyer seem angry with me? Wasn't she supposed to be on my side?

"Not guilty. I didn't even know the drugs . . ." I begin to explain.

"Now's not the time to discuss your case, Ms. White," the Judge interrupts. "I've looked over your financial form, and I'm going to appoint the public defender to represent you. You're assessed $250, payable at $25 a month, starting ten days after you're released."

"Ms. Rainey, as to bail."

"Well, Your Honor, Ms. White has no prior arrests or convictions; has lived in Tucson all her life; and can live with her Mom."

"Mr. Barron?"

"Your Honor, at least eighty pounds of cocaine were found in Ms. White's residence. She was the only one present when the police served the warrant. The apartment is leased in her name only. There was also marijuana and narcotics paraphernalia. If convicted, she faces five to fifteen years in prison. According to pretrial, she hasn't lived with her mother for several years. She's also unemployed."

"Thank you, counsel. I am going to set bail at $50,000. Your next court date is a preliminary hearing on the fifteenth. Should you make bond, you're ordered to appear, or a warrant will issue for your arrest. Call in Khan."

"Hurry." When I don't move, the Rainey woman pushes me out of the courtroom. A deputy thrusts a paper in front of me. "You need to sign this, promising to appear."

"Am I getting out?"

"Didn't you listen to the judge? You're not getting out unless you come up with fifty grand." I look over to ask the Public Defender what to do, but she's already gone back in the courtroom. "Sign the paper. I don't have all day. You don't want me to tell the warden you're a trouble-maker, do you?"

TEN

Please God I'll do anything. I promise. Give up sex. Pot. Go to church every Sunday. Please, do something. Help me. Don't let them do this to me. I didn't do anything wrong. I'm innocent. Mommy, help me, oh, God . . .

"White, come in." I stand in place trembling. Crying. My feet feel like concrete. "Move it, honey, we don't have all day." I walk into the room, try not to drop the jumpsuit, the underwear, and at the same time cover as much of myself as I can with the skimpy towel they gave me. The unfamiliar clogs are too big, but I'm grateful for the warm socks. The room is icy cold.

"Put your clothes on the chair and stand in front of me." I allow myself to look at the woman who issues the orders. She towers over me. Mom would call her fat, but to me she looks tough and physically strong. Not a woman to fuck with. Her black hair is cut short like a man's, yet she wears make-up, earrings, a delicate gold necklace. And latex gloves.

"First time, huh?"

I nod yes, unable to trust my voice.

"It isn't my favorite job either. Just do what I say, try to breathe, and it'll be over in a second. Try to pretend it's a doctor's visit."

Doctor's visit, what the hell's wrong with her? I almost chuckle.

"Ready? You can try to keep the towel on but it's gonna drop, so you might as well put it on the chair. You won't get another one for a week. It's not like I haven't seen a naked woman before."

I do as she says. The last thing I want to do is piss this woman off.

"Okay." She looks my body over quickly. "Now turn around." Later I would find out being nearly flat chested is an advantage. The big-breasted women are told to raise their breasts while the guard checks for contraband. How can you hide anything there anyway?

"Good. Now bend down and spread your cheeks." Was she going to touch me with those gloved hands or worse? I make another silent prayer. My legs are visibly trembling. Off in the distance, I hear two men talking; but this room is totally silent. Cold and silent. The guard says nothing more. I wait another moment for rescue but know it isn't coming.

I do as she asks.

ELEVEN

Josh wakes up, spaced out, groggy. His head hurts. His mouth tastes like crap. Sunshine streams through the windows. A typical morning. But he's not in his bed. Not in his house. For a minute he doesn't know where he is. Then he remembers. Kristin's gonna be pissed. Really pissed.

He hadn't planned to crash here. Whatever he smoked last night was amazing. JT said hash, but it was fucking stronger than any hash he'd smoked before. He touched his hand to his pocket, checking for the cash. When Kristin saw the money, she'd understand. One thousand fucking USA dollars. For one night's work. If you can call being stoned work.

He walks out of the bedroom. "Carlos, JT . . . Carlos, JT, where the fuck are you?" No answer. Room's empty. Where are those fuckheads? He checks the fridge. Empty too, except for half a six-pack and an empty carton of OJ. The place doesn't look like anyone lives here. They said it was a party house. Way too clean. Last night, he hadn't noticed a thing. As soon as they walked in, they got high. Never even turned on the lights.

He stops at McDonald's as much to put off Kristin's bitching as to get something to eat. Maybe they can go out for a decent dinner. Money'd been short lately. The last time they'd gone out for a good dinner was her birthday. Josh had forgotten to get her anything, and she was angry. Didn't care that he was broke.

"You have enough money to buy dope!" Kristin nagged.

"Like you don't smoke it with me. You sound like a little brat. Why don't you go spend your birthday with your mommy? She'll make you a cake and get you a present. I'm out of here," he said opening the door.

She cried, begged him to stay. Apologized for complaining, but he'd left. Spent the night with a friend. And the next night. Didn't call her. Imagined she was frantic. That'll show her. Two nights later, he'd calmed down and went back. Used almost the last of his secret stash to take her to dinner.

As soon as he walks in, he knows something's wrong. Drawers open. Papers scattered. Neither he nor Kristin would get a prize for housekeeping, but some weird shit has gone on here. "Kristin, Kristin, where are you?"

He wonders if someone burglarized the place. Then he sees an official-looking paper. 'Search Warrant Return Pursuant to the laws of the State of Arizona, That on the 13th day of January, 1994, I executed this Search Warrant, issued by Judge Adam.' Fuck. He scans the words—-drugs, ledgers, pipes, narcotics paraphernalia. Holy shit, the coke. Why would the cops come here? Had JT and Carlos set this up? Is that why they weren't there this morning? Did the cops think he's a drug dealer? Where's Kristin? Fuck, Fuck, Fuck.

Calm down. Think. Where would Kristin go? He dials Angie and Art. No answer. He wishes he'd paid attention when she talked about her friends. What about Leslie? He and his cuz hadn't spent much time together since he'd moved in with Kristin. She disapproves of his lifestyle even though she doesn't know the half of it. 'You know Josh God doesn't approve of a man and women living together if they're not married.' Know-it-all bitch. Just 'cause she's a fat pig who can't get a man. Shit, she won't know anything. Kristin wouldn't be desperate enough to call her. Kristin's mom? She hates him, but Kristin might be there. If the cops scared her, it was a safe place. He dials.

Shit her friggin Mom. "Hi, Mrs. White. It's Josh, can I speak to Kristin?" Dry-mouthed, he speaks hurriedly as if she'd react nicer if he talks fast.

"How dare you phone here? Kristin's in jail. It's all your fault. I told her you were no good. You're the one should be in jail."

"In jail? The cops arrested her . . .?"

"Of course, they arrested her. What do they usually do when they find illegal drugs? I imagine you didn't write your name on them."

"What do we have to do to get her out?"

"We don't have to do anything. Her bail is $50,000, but I don't want your help or your drug money. If you're any sort of a man, you'll go to the police station and tell the police who the drugs belong to."

He doesn't know what to say. Who's she to give him a bunch of shit? It isn't like he did the deal only for him; it was for both of them. "Why are you blaming me? Why do you assume the drugs were mine? Maybe they were hers. Maybe the cops planted them."

"Don't act like more of an ass than you are. The police don't go around planting drugs in people's house. I can't believe instead of helping her, you're blaming her. If I had any doubts about what kind of man you are, I know now. At least in jail, she's away from you."

No point talking to her. The old witch doesn't understand anything. Turning myself in wouldn't save Kristin. If someone's after me to pay for the stuff and Kristin gets out, they'd come after her. He stays quiet.

"As far as I'm concerned, don't ever call here again, and stay away from my daughter." She slams the phone down.

Shit Kristin in jail. How fucking stupid can I be? A thousand bucks to hold the stash. 'Look man it's only for twenty-four hours.' Carlos and JT fucking played me. All that missing coke. What the fuck should I do? I can't pay. They'll kill me.

CHAPTER
TWELVE

"Kristin, your lawyer's here, wake up."

"Huh?"

"Get your ass up. Your mouthpiece ain't gonna like it if he has to wait."

"Okay, I'm up." I fell asleep often in the overheated dayroom during the endless TV watching. Soaps. Sitcoms. Never thought I'd miss news. By now, I know some rules, like what to do when you have a visitor. I walk down the corridor through several doors that leads to visitation. I stand in what's called a sally port, but it's just a small space with doors on both sides. One set leads into the jail and the other to visitation. Guards in the control unit open and close the doors electronically. I wonder if my lawyer will be like the other one. Will she care about me? Can I trust her?

"Booth three," booms the guard. The doors unlock, and I walk over to the small room, open the door. The woman seated in the chair stands. "Hi, I'm Becky Bernini, your lawyer. Good to meet you. Have a seat." She point to the only other chair in the tiny space.

This is my lawyer? She isn't wearing a party outfit like the other one. She's dressed professionally in a dark blue suit that almost reaches her knees. Her hair is dark brown and curly. She looks so young. If I saw her on the streets, I'd think she were a freshman or sophomore in college. "You're really a lawyer?"

"I sure as hell am. You can't get into these luxurious accommodations without showing ID. If I weren't a lawyer, I'd have better things to do than hang around here. I'll show you my ID if you like, but we should talk about your situation. I don't have all day. I have other clients to see, and I assume you have a few questions."

Is she pissed at me already?

"Let's start over. I'm your attorney, Becky Bernini. Everything you tell me is confidential. I'll be honest with you—-the best way to help yourself is to be honest with me. Now, you're supposed to say, 'Nice meeting you, Ms. Bernini. I know you're really busy. Thanks for coming down to see me.'"

I stare at her blankly for a moment. Then she smiles at me. "Thanks for coming," I stammer. "When can I get out?"

"I talked to your Mom. She's very concerned about you . . . "

"If she's so concerned, how come she hasn't bailed me out? Why are you talking to her?"

"She called the office, and we spoke about getting you out."

"She's going to bail me out?"

"She's worried you have a drug problem but agreed to bail you out if you go to a halfway house."

"What's that?"

"A place you live and get drug treatment. You can't leave except for court and approved doctor's visits. After awhile, the rules loosen up."

"Sounds like here."

"Much better than here. No bars, better food, freedom within the house. It could help your case. It'll show the judge and prosecutors that you want to be drug-free, lead a productive life."

She must think I'm a total loser. "You don't understand. I'm innocent. I'm not an addict. I don't need drug treatment. I lead a productive life now. I don't want to go there."

"I'm not going to force you. I want you to make your own decisions but after you have enough information. I've already filed a motion to see if we can get you out ROR, which means you're released if you promise to come back to court. If it works, you can live anywhere you like. If that doesn't work, I'll try to get the bail reduced or get you released to Pretrial

Services. If neither of those alternatives works, we'll talk more about the halfway house."

"So it's possible I can just get out?"

"It's possible but no guarantees. I know you want out but we need to talk about your case."

"I'm innocent. I didn't know it was there."

"That's a lot of coke they found."

"But it wasn't mine. I didn't know anything about it."

"Did you have roommates? Was it theirs?"

"I live with my boyfriend, but it wasn't his."

"Before we go into more detail, I should explain the law to. You're charged with possession of over the threshold amount of cocaine with intent to sell, which means if you're convicted, you're facing five to fifteen years in prison. The most likely sentence is ten years."

"Ten years . . . Ten years is for people who are big-time criminals like burglars or robbers. I've never been arrested before. The coke wasn't mine. They can't do this to me. Oh, my God!" Tears spill down my face.

"Calm down, Kristin." Prepared for meltdowns, she hands me a tissue. "That's worst-case. They're lots of other possibilities. I haven't seen the evidence against you. I should get most of it in a week or so. I need to determine if the search was legal, things like that. We need to talk more about where the coke might've come from. No one else was arrested with you. How come they didn't arrest your boyfriend? What's his name?"

"Who told you about my boyfriend? Must've been my mom. You can't believe what she says about him."

"You told me about your boyfriend. Don't worry about what your mom said. It's not important. What you say is what's important."

"Are you going to tell her what I say?"

"No, I told you, everything you tell me is confidential. I'll get information from other people, but I won't tell them anything you say."

"Josh Harrison." I can't focus on what she's saying. Prison—-ten years. I'd been here for less than forty-eight hours, and I'm already losing it. Should I tell her about Josh and those guys? What if she tells the police? "If I tell you something that will get someone else in trouble, will you tell the police?"

"Of course not. Confidential means I can't tell anyone what you tell me even if you tell me you killed someone. If I told, I'd lose my law license.

The only contact I have with police is to interview the ones involved in your case to find out what they'd say at trial. It's done on tape, and you get a copy. I don't tell them anything you say. If you don't talk to me, I can't help you. I'm here for you. I don't work for your mom, the police, the prosecutors; just you."

I try to grasp what she said. Scott and I'd watched a TV show about a young lawyer who represented a guy accused of rape. The guy denied the rape to police but confessed to his lawyer not only that he committed the rape, but also killed three other women. Shortly after he confesses to his lawyer, another guy's charged with killing the three women. The lawyer wants to save the innocent man but couldn't figure out how without violating her client's confidentiality. Finally, she told the innocent guy's lawyer what her client told her. She gets in trouble and can't be a lawyer anymore.

I have to trust someone. "Okay, Ms. Bernini, what do you want to know?"

"First, tell me a little about you and Josh, and then, will talk about how the coke got in the house."

"Well, Josh and I met at a party about a year ago. It was love at first sight. He'd just moved from San Diego and didn't know anyone in Tucson but his cousin, Leslie. She brought him to the party. She acted bitchy towards me for no apparent reason. Josh put her in her place. We've been together since and started living together about eight months ago.

"Did you both work? How did you pay rent?"

"It wasn't an expensive apartment. When I first met Josh, I had a job as an administrative assistant in the counseling department at the U. I hated it. It turned out I was only a secretary and my boss was a witch. Josh convinced me to quit. I was unemployed for a while. Then I started waitressing at Vintage Pizzeria. Josh was a bartender at the Downtown Hotel."

"So you both had jobs before you were arrested. I thought you told Pretrial you weren't employed?"

"I quit that job too. I hated working days when Josh worked nights."

"Okay, tell me about the cocaine."

"Well, I'm not sure. Josh and I smoked weed, but hardly ever did coke. We couldn't afford it. I've never seen more than a gram or two. The night before all this happened, Josh worked at the bar. He usually got home around one-thirty but he got back late that night. I tried to wait up, but I fell asleep.

"When I woke up, Josh was home, and two guys I didn't know were there. I heard them, but I couldn't make out what they were saying. After awhile, the other two went outside. I thought they'd left, but they were waiting for Josh. He told me he was going out, and he'd explain later. He never said who the guys were or why they were at our house. He mentioned something about a lot of easy money. We were totally broke. I didn't like the whole thing. I asked Josh if he was doing something risky.

"He smiled and said, 'No way.' He told me he loved me and left. I haven't seen him since. I'm worried about him."

"You're worried about him? You need to worry about yourself. He's not sitting in jail—- you are. You think he got the coke from those guys?"

"I guess. But I know Josh, and he wouldn't sell coke. We've had chances to deal before, and we never did. Didn't even consider it. We're not criminals. My mom probably went on a rant about what a jerk Josh is, but she never gave him a chance. She adored my ex-boyfriend, Scott, and thinks no one's as good as him. She acts like I dumped Scott, but he dumped me.

"Josh is a good guy. He's sexy and funny. More than anyone I've ever met, he makes me laugh. He has this—-I guess you'd call it a collection—-of moron stories about idiotic things people do. Like these California kids who brought home three abandoned puppies they found on a hike in the mountains. The puppies turned out to be bear cubs!"

Shit, I'm facing fifteen years and telling puppy stories.

"OK, I get it. When you were arrested, did the cops question you?"

"Yeah, some detective did, but I don't remember his name."

"Do you remember if he read you your rights?"

"Yeah, he did."

"Did you tell him anything about the coke?"

"I told him it wasn't mine. He asked me whose it was. I didn't know what to say. He asked me who I lived with. I was afraid I'd get Josh in trouble, so I stopped talking. I remember he said I didn't have to talk, so I didn't."

"Good. Have you talked to anyone else?"

"My ex-boyfriend, the one who dumped me, came to see me the night I got arrested. My friend, Angie, called him. He's a lawyer, Scott Downing, maybe you know him?" She shook her head no. "He doesn't do criminal law. He said he talked to a friend at your office—he didn't tell me her name. He told me a little about bail, when I'd see the judge, and told me not to talk to the police, that's all. My mom hasn't even come to see me."

"Your mom can't because you don't get family visits till you're here four days. Did the cops show you a warrant?

"Yeah, but I don't remember what it said."

"No problem, I'll get a copy later. Was anyone else in the house?

"My friend, Angie."

"I need to talk to her. Will that be a problem?"

"No, she's my best friend. She'll help anyway she can."

"What's her last name?"

"Montoya; she's a reporter for the Tucson Sun."

"Good, I'll call her. After I leave, I want you to write down every detail of what happened from the time Josh got home that night till the police showed up, everything that happened when the police were there, and what happened at the police station. Don't leave anything out even if you don't think it's important. And don't talk to anyone about your case, not anyone. Not your roommates or anyone at the jail, not your mom, not your friends if you get out, no one but me. Don't show your notes to anyone either. Don't leave them out if you're not in the cell. Be careful, there's always inmates who'll snitch anyone off. Lie and tell the prosecutor you confessed."

"I get it."

"You'll be in court in a few days to see if I can get you out. Hang tough. I'll try to get your bail reduced, but give some thought to a halfway house if it doesn't work. Judges are more likely to release someone to a place like that. I'll see you in court, and then we'll get together again. Do you have any questions?"

"Am I really going to go to court, or will it be on that video thing? What if the police come and question me? Are you sure I'll be in court soon?"

"The police won't question you. Once you have a lawyer, it's illegal for them to talk to you without my permission. You're going to court, not the video thing. The hearing will be in a couple days. Here's my card. It has my number and my paralegal's, Coleen. The office takes collect calls between eight and five. If I'm not there, ask for Coleen. She'll know your court date by tomorrow afternoon."

Ms. Bernini walks out, leaving me alone. Ten years. Mommy, help me. I can't breathe.

THIRTEEN

Louise sleeps soundly and rises early. She doesn't need an alarm clock but sets it just in case. She's believes in being prepared and is always on time. When her clients at Think Thin complain about insomnia, Louise lectures then on the value of exercise and healthy eating. Stress is an excuse. That's what she thought until her daughter's arrest.

Since the call from the jail, she can't sleep more than an hour at a time. The alarm clock rings; she hits the snooze button. Ten minutes later it rings, she hits it again. And again and again . . . then she realizes it's the phone.

"Hello, Mrs. White. This is Becky Bernini, your daughter's attorney."

How'd Kristin get an attorney? She can't afford one. "I'm confused. She can't afford an attorney. Who's paying your fee?" Josh wouldn't . . .? He has no money either.

"I'm appointed by the court. I work at the Public Defender's office."

Why's she calling me? "Kristin's okay isn't she?"

"Yes, she's fine. Her bail hearing's tomorrow morning at nine. It'd be helpful to have you in court."

"I'll be there. Will I have to say anything; I'd be too nervous to talk?"

"Just yes or no. If the Judge gives you custody of Kristin, she'll ask if you're willing to let her live there. She'll ask if you'll make sure she gets to court, and if you'll contact the court if she fails to follow her release condition."

"I can do that. You think she'll be released?"

"I hope, but I'm not hopeful. It's more likely her bond will be reduced. I discussed living in a halfway house with her; she's opposed, at least now. Are you willing to bail her out? If you use your home or a relative's as collateral, all you need is ten percent cash."

"Do I lose the money?"

"Unfortunately, yes, that's the bail bondsmen's fee."

"How much is the bail going to be?"

"I can't tell you for sure. With this amount of cocaine, it'll stay high. It was originally set at $50,000 so that should be the maximum."

"I have more than $50,000 equity in my house. Will that work?"

"Yes for collateral. I need to tell you that if Kristin were to be released and not come to court, you'd lose the collateral, too." Bernini always felt weird when she told a family member that.

Louise grimaces. "I don't even know who she is any more. She has a college degree, had a decent job and was going with this terrific fellow who was in law school. Had a great career in front of him. Then she meets this Josh and no job. No money. Now she's in jail. I'm afraid if she was released Josh could get her to run away with him."

"You know her better than I do. I'm going to do my best to get her out but it's your choice how much you want to help."

"You probably think I'm a horrible person, but I need to think about it. Kristin's made lots of bad decisions lately, not that I thought it would come to this. I need to decide what's best for her in the long run."

"It's tough. If she's using or under Josh's influence, it's possible she'll screw up. On the other hand, if she's innocent, it's outrageous for her to be in jail."

"Is the hearing in the same place where I saw her on that video screen?"

"Same building, different courtroom."

Watching Kristin on camera had been painful. This time she'd be in person, maybe in one of those unflattering orange things. Oh God, my little girl in handcuffs. She lays back and puts the covers up to her neck. If only Bob were here.

It isn't the money. She's not rich, nowhere close; but somehow she'd come up with the cash. Use her house as security like the lawyer said. Take a loan. What bothers her is what happens next. Can she make Kristin follow her rules? They hadn't gotten along since Kristin and Scott broke up. Their relationship Ralph Wahr after she started seeing Josh. That damn Josh was the cause of all of this.

Doreen, Louise's coworker at Think Thin, had a daughter Amy who had been a meth addict. A high school cheerleader and homecoming queen, she dropped out of college, got arrested then sentenced to jail. Louise spent hours listening to Doreen cry. "Amy's lost interest in her looks, lost so much weight." Later, "Amy's dropped out of school." Later still, "Louise, she tried to kill herself. She took an overdose . . . She's in jail again."

Doreen's daughter got sober only after she lived in a halfway house for almost a year. At home now, drug testing three times a week helps her stay straight. She told her mom there were more drugs in jail than on the street. She's doing well now. Gone back to school, gained weight.

Louise knows little about drug addiction besides what Doreen told her and what she'd seen on TV. She wouldn't know whether Kristin was using. She's never even seen marijuana. What help could she be?

Is this the time to practice tough love or take a chance on Kristin? Can she forbid Kristin to stay away from Josh and enforce it? She'd try to see Josh any chance she could, and lie. For the hundredth time, she wonders what kind of man treats a woman like Josh did. Maybe it's a good thing Bob isn't around. God knows what he'd do.

Bob, I miss you. If only you were here to give me advice. Our daughter's in jail. I'm too embarrassed to talk to anyone except maybe Doreen. I never told anyone about her daughter, but I looked down on her. Figured she wasn't a good mother.

She's even considered talking to Josh. Maybe she can force him to stay away from Kristin? She stares at her favorite picture of Bob taken after Kristin's high school graduation. She hopes to get a sign, something. But the picture stays silent.

Louise thinks about it all day. What has she got to lose? If he hangs up or yells at her, so what. If he refuses to stay away from Kristin, she's learned something. As soon as she gets home from work, she dials the familiar apartment number, afraid if she waits, she'll lose her nerve.

The phone rings and rings. Josh finally answers. "Hello?"

"Hello, Josh, this is Mrs. White, Kristin's mom." Out of habit, she almost asks how he is.

Before he says a word, Louise senses she's made Josh nervous. Thinks he might hang up. To her surprise, he apologizes. "I'm so sorry Kris is in jail. I'm sorry I wasn't there when she got arrested. I'm sorry . . . She lets him talk; gives her time to get her courage up.

"Josh, there's only one thing you can do for Kristin now. I'll bail her out and let her stay here if she doesn't see you. I want your word you'll stay away from her."

She expects him to rant, rave, call her names; but he does none of those things. He's quiet for a few moments and then, "I've decided to leave town. I know you don't like me and probably won't believe me, but I love Kristin. I'd never hurt her on purpose." Funny thing, Bob, when Josh agrees, I'm almost angry? Doesn't he care enough about Kristin to fight me? Why is he so gutless?

Louise calls the lawyer back. Kristin can stay with her.

FOURTEEN

"Good news, Kristin," Ms. Bernini says, as she walks to the prisoners' section where I sit in my preowned orange jumpsuit, handcuffed, chained to another inmate. "Your mom agreed you could come home instead of the halfway house. It's up to the judge. That's the tough part."

"Whatever you said must've worked."

"It wasn't me. I don't know what made her change her mind. You'll have to ask her. She'll be here, but the deputies won't let her talk to you. It's against the rules."

"Big surprise. Do I have to say anything?"

"Usually not, but the Judge can ask you questions The important thing is that you tell her you'll come back to court and follow whatever conditions are set, like drug testing. I'll be right next to you if you need help."

"What if she asks about the coke?"

"This is a bail hearing. Nothing else will be discussed. There are other hearings besides yours going on in here, and I have hearings in other court-rooms, so don't worry if I walk in and out. They can't start without me."

"Is this the same judge as before?"

"No, but she's assigned to your case from now on."

"Good—-that other judge was so mean."

"This one's polite but tough. She's not my favorite, but there's nothing I can do to change it. At least she listens . . . "

Before she can finish, one of the deputies interrupts, "Be quiet, the judge is coming in. Don't talk unless the judge asks you a question. Act respectful if you can," he said, looking at us like we're pond scum. Too bad he has such a shitty attitude; he's buff, with a sweet baby face. One of the women tries to flirt with him, but he ignores her.

"All rise, Honorable Judge Thomas presiding," says a young woman with a quiet voice. The courtroom is silent as the judge walks in and sits down.

A case is called, and the courtroom's noisy again. I listen to other hearings, but it's hard to pay attention. All I care about's getting out. The judge like Bernini looks young. She's pretty, with shoulder-length reddish-brown hair. "She doesn't look mean," I whisper to the woman I'm chained to. I've never seen her before, but she looks friendly.

"Are you fucking nuts?" whispers a male prisoner in the next row, his arms covered with what looks like homemade tattoos. "She's a first-class bitch. Gave my cousin twenty years for screwing this slut. The bitch said it was rape, the fuckin liar."

"When I say be quiet, that means you," the deputy glares at my new friend, who rolls his eyes and gives me a conspiratorial smile.

Time passes. My friend who talked about his cousin stands next to his lawyer as his case is called. (I'm not surprised when he asks the judge for a new one.) "My lawyer never comes to see me, Your Honor. He ain't doin' nuthin' on my case." The judge says something about not being entitled to the Cadillac of representation. Tells him to try to work with his lawyer. His lawyer looks more disappointed than the prisoner.

"Bitch," he mouths silently when the judge starts another case.

More time passes. The judge takes a break. A female deputy takes me and another woman to a small filthy bathroom. The wastebasket's overflowing with what looks like used toilet paper and bloody tampons. The floor's wet and sticky. "This is your only chance to use the can before you get back to the jail." She uncuffs us, but we're still chained together. Am I supposed to pee attached to someone while both watch? The other woman looks at me, sensing my hesitation. "Don't be a prima donna. We don't have much time, and I gotta go." She takes a loud, stinky shit. I hold my breath and pee, grateful I don't need to do more. We go back to the courtroom. I'm relieved to see Ms. Bernini's back.

"State v. White, Case #103089. Set for bail hearing. Lawyers announce your appearance, please."

"Leo Bryce for the State."

"Becky Bernini for the defendant."

"I've read defense's motion, State's response, and the Pretrial Service report which recommends a bail reduction. Ms. Bernini, do you have anything to add to your motion?"

"Your Honor, the bail in this matter is clearly excessive. My client has no prior convictions and has never been arrested. She's lived in Tucson her entire life. Ms. White graduated from the University of Arizona and has been employed most of the time since she graduated, although now she's between jobs. Her mom, Mrs. Louise White, is present in the courtroom and is willing to have Kristin live with her. 'Mrs. White, would you stand up, please.' Mrs. White is a widow. She's been employed for three years at Think Thin and has lived in Tucson for forty years. No one else lives in the home. 'You can sit down now, Mrs. White.'"

"Thank you, counsel; let me hear from the State."

"Your Honor. The defendant is charged with a mandatory prison offense, minimum five years if convicted. Pursuant to a search warrant of her residence, the police found over eighty pounds of cocaine. Street value would be at least half a million dollars. No one else was arrested at the residence, and no one else's name is on the lease other than the defendant. State also believes the defendant is a flight risk. For all those reasons, we strongly object to bail being reduced."

"What's does he mean 'a flight risk'?" I whispered.

"Ms. Bernini, do you wish to respond?"

"Your Honor, calling Ms. White a flight risk is outrageous. My client was born in Tucson and went to school here, as well as graduated from the U of A. She has never lived anywhere else and has no significant ties outside of this community." She turns and glares at the prosecutor.

"As you are well aware, I haven't been provided with all the discovery material, so I'm unable to respond to some of the particulars. To the best of my knowledge, no large sums of money, scales, packing material, ledgers or other indicia of drug trafficking were found in the home. There was evidence of at least one male resident living in the home, as men's clothes and toiletries were in the bedroom where the drugs were found. Most importantly, Ms. White is presumed to be innocent."

"Thank you, counsel. I agree with the County Attorney's Office. The amount of drugs is, without doubt, indicative of dealing; and the defendant is facing mandatory prison time. Motion denied. Ms. White, I need to advise you that if you post bail, you're released to third-party custody of Pretrial Services. That means you're to contact them three times a week, live with your mother, not change residences without the court's permission, and drug test twice a week. You're also to attend all court hearings or a warrant will issue for your arrest, or a trial could be held in your absence. Do you understand?"

"Yes, Your Honor." I lie. I look at Ms. Bernini. "What happened? First she says I have to stay here, and then she says I have to live with my mom and take drug tests. I don't get it. Am I released?"

"I'm sorry, Kristin, the Judge wouldn't budge. Your mom has to post $50,000 or ten percent plus collateral."

"You mean nothing's changed?"

"That's right."

"I have to stay here till my trial?

"After I get the police reports, if I can find something in your favor, I can file another motion. I know you're upset, but we can't talk now."

"When are you coming to see me?"

"Tonight or tomorrow at the latest," she says as she walks toward the spectator section where Mom's sitting. Mom looks upset but waves. I'm afraid to.

The deputy hands me a paper to sign. I sign without reading it. What's the point? I sit back down and watch Bernini try to calm Mom as tears stream down her face.

FIFTEEN

The days are much the same. Up too early. Straighten the cell. Tasteless breakfast. Watch TV. Tasteless lunch. More TV. Tasteless dinner. More TV. Lights out. Occasionally, a letter, a class, or a visit.

Sometimes talking to the other women breaks the monotony; sometimes it makes things worse. Tania has long since gone. She went to court one morning, and I never saw her again. Rumor had it she'd pled guilty and been released, but I don't know what to believe.

Since then, a series of "roommates." Cecelia's a nut job. She babbles on and on about 'the ones coming to get her.' She never sleeps, so neither can I. After the second unbearable night, the guards take her away. One of the few deputies who treated me okay said she was in the mental health ward.

Brandy's gorgeous and feisty until she starts coming down. "Nick's loaded. He's gonna hire a lawyer to get me out of here. I'm not having no public defender." She repeats it over and over. As time passes, she becomes edgy and screams constantly that she needs to go to medical. One morning, she refuses to get out of her bunk and, when I come back from breakfast, she's gone. No one told me where.

My new roommate, Ina, is quiet. She wants to hang out only with black women and makes that clear. I try to talk to her. "If you and me gonna get along, you stay on your side and leave me alone, bitch," is the friendliest she gets.

We both sign up for any class offered. I don't care if it's Building Self Esteem, Substance Abuse or Bible Studies. Anything to change the routine. Neither of us makes the list. Finally, we both get selected for Principles of Nutrition. She sits with a couple of black women, and they glare at me every time I look their way. I think about asking for a change of cells, but I'm too scared.

Mom's allowed to come twice a week, but only makes me sad. She stops blaming Josh out loud, but I know what's in her mind. She doesn't ask me what it's like being in jail or how my case is going; she acts like I'm in college, and we're having a weekend visit. "I ran into that woman, Beth Sanders, I think is her name, at the grocery. You went to college with her; she came to Thanksgiving dinner once. She's pregnant, expecting in June. She asked about you. I told her you were working out of town. She said to say hi." I couldn't care less.

Angie writes almost daily letters, visits often, and sometimes makes me laugh. "Maybe the paper can do a story on the jail, and I can go under-cover—-stay with you for a couple weeks. We could be cellies and have a slumber party every night." If I want to talk about Josh, she listens but doesn't bring him up if I don't. Neither she nor Art have seen or heard from him.

At first, every time I get a visit, I'm sure it's him. Finally, he writes to me.

Kristin,

I'm sorry about everything. I never meant for you to get in trouble. Do what you need to do to save yourself. I told the office you had moved out and paid what was due. You need to find another place when you get out. Angie has your stuff. I'm leaving town. I hope you don't hate me.

Josh

I don't know what to think. He didn't say he loves me. Didn't sign it "Love." I wish I hated him. I read the letter over and over, but it doesn't change; it just gets greasy and harder to read. If only I were out of here. Maybe we could run away together.

I can't stop thinking about him. I read the letter so many times I've memorized it. Why's he leaving? Is he in trouble because of the missing drugs? Why had he been so stupid? We needed money, but nothing was different about that. I could've gotten a job.

I must have fallen asleep, when I hear my name on the loudspeaker. "Kristin White, attorney visit. Report to visitation."

Usually, I'm glad to see anyone, especially Ms. Bernini, but not today. What can she say that matters? I'd tell her I'm sick and to go away, but she won't believe it. Maybe you get in trouble if you refuse an attorney visit? I'd ask Ina, but the one time I asked her something, she said, "I ain't no information booth," and gave me the evil eye. I go to visitation.

"Hi, Kristin."

"Hi," I mumble and sit down. As usual, Bernini looks energetic and put-together. I wonder what she thinks about me. I look particularly gross today. Usually, I stop to comb my hair; and, if I know she's coming, I put on some makeup and brush my teeth. I haven't done that today or even taken a shower. I feel sweaty and ugly. Did she notice anything beyond the orange jumpsuit? I wish I had enough nerve to ask her if I stink.

"I finally got all the police reports. Not a whole lot's new. I did find out why the cops showed up at your place. They got a tip from a confidential informant that someone in the house was dealing. The good news is no one's claiming you made any incriminating statements."

"What do you mean 'confidential informant' what's that?"

"A scumbag who works for the cops snitching off people. Usually, they have drug charges. Get a better deal by giving names of people who supply them drugs or more often who they sold to. Sometimes they set people up to do deals with undercover cops. Sometimes they make the whole story up."

"Is that legal?"

"It's legal, but the cops have to get a judge to sign a search warrant before they can act on a tip from one. The judge isn't supposed to sign it unless the CI has given reliable information before, and gives enough detail so you know it's not made up. Usually, there's some other corroboration. I hate them; they would say anything to save themselves. Turn in their girl-friend or mother. And some judges sign almost anything."

"Who was it?"

"We might never know. That's why it's called 'confidential.' The judge won't order the prosecutor to tell us without what they call a compelling legal reason, which we don't have. You should be able to figure it out, if you think about it."

I close my eyes. "Those guys who came to the house, Carlos and JT?"

"Maybe."

She pushes a pile of papers towards me. "It's hard to get a search thrown out under these circumstances. I've made copies of everything for you to read. You have any questions?"

I know I should ask questions, but I can't focus. "Please, can't you get me out? I can't stay here. I have stuff I need to do on the outside. File another motion or something. I'll go to that halfway house. Just get me out."

"Did something happen, Kristin? You don't seem okay."

"No, nothing." Of course I'm not okay, stuck in here. Josh's leaving town. But why should I tell her? She's my lawyer, not my therapist. She'll tell me to turn him in.

"Kristin, I wish I could get you out, but nothing's changed since the last motion. I've talked to the county attorney, and they won't budge on prison time. The cops are pissed off because they think you know more than you're saying. They don't think you're a drug dealer. In a fair world, that would matter; but life's not always fair."

Ms. Bernini's voice seems like it's coming from far away. Suddenly, our eyes meet; and I can't stop myself from tearing up. She looks at me and hands me a Kleenex. "What's the matter, Kristin? You can talk to me. It doesn't have to be about your case."

What did I have to lose? She can't make me turn him in. I'm sure it wouldn't surprise her my boyfriend dumped me. "I got a letter from Josh today. He's leaving town. I thought he'd visit me or at least be there when I got out. He just said he was leaving—-didn't even say he loved me."

"I'm sorry. You must feel like shit. I've been dumped, more than once, and it's one of the worst feelings ever, till you meet someone else or realize you're lucky to be rid of the asshole."

"Someone dumped you? You're smart, pretty; you have a good job. What kind of jerk would do that?"

"That's sweet of you to say, Kristin, but I'm no different from you. I've had my heart broken more than once. Happens to everyone sometime."

I stop crying. "So Ms. Bernini, when are you going to start lecturing me to turn Josh in, and my best interest and all that?"

"I'm your lawyer, not your conscience. And cut the Ms. Bernini. It's time you started calling me Bernini—-everyone else does. I think you understand the position you're in. If you cooperate with the cops, we can deal. I don't know how good a deal, but at least a lesser sentence—-maybe probation. You'd have to turn in Josh and tell all you know, plus agree to testify against him and those other two guys—-if they catch them. Even if they got Josh, from what you say, he's only a minor player; and he might not be willing to talk. That's a lot of ifs. I won't decide for you. Whatever you decide, I'll do my best for you."

"I can't do it Ms., uh, Bernini. Even knowing he's leaving. In the letter, he told me to save myself, but I can't. I love him. He wouldn't turn me in."

SIXTEEN

Never thought I'd look forward to washing dishes, but I am as close Josh uses some to happy as I'd been since my arrest. The pans are large, the water scalding, and the soap harsh; but working in the kitchen's a perk. It makes time pass. If you work hard, you might get a piece of fruit, an extra dessert, or the cook would give you a plate of food she was cooking for staff. The kitchen crew doesn't hesitate to yell at you if you mess up, but their attitude's different from the CO's. If you work hard, they accept you. They joke around a lot. After a few days, I feel part of the group. The work's hard enough that I sleep at night.

Ina laughs bitterly when I fill out the work application. "I'm sure you'll get whatever you want, you white girls always do." I put down law library as my first choice, data entry as my second, and wherever needed third. When I'm selected to wash dishes, I overhear her tell her friends, "That white bitch ain't gonna last a day. She never done no real work before." I'll last. Anything's better than being ostracized by Ina and her buddies or having nothing to do besides being alone hour after hour with my thoughts.

Why isn't Ina gone? My other roommates had only been around a few days. At night, whenever I heard footsteps, I hope the guards are coming to take her away. When I return from a visit or work, I fantasize she's gone. Instead, there she is, "Didn't your mama teach you not to work for free?"

When I'm not busy, I spend endless time going over the 'what ifs'.' What if the cops hadn't been tipped off; what if Josh hadn't met Carlos and JT; what if I'd never met Josh? When I'm done with the what if's, I obsess over 'did you hear.' Did you hear Kristin White got arrested? Did you hear she's a drug addict—-maybe even a dealer? Did you hear Kristin's boyfriend set her up and then dumped her?

When my thoughts quiet down, Mom's take over. My God, Kristin, you were raised in a decent home, taught values. No one in our family has been in jail before. What am I supposed to say to my friends? They tell me their daughter's an honor student or has a great job or got married. My daughter's got a job washing dishes at the jail. Sounds bad, but really, it's considered a plum—-like student-of-the-week or employee-of-the-month. And, worst of all, thank goodness your dad isn't alive to see you now.

I couldn't care less what Mom told her stupid friends, but I love Dad. He wouldn't care what his friends thought. What their kids did. He'd be there for me and know this was all a horrible mistake.

But my thoughts always return to Josh. I relive the day we met and all the good days before our life began to fall apart. How excited Josh was when I got home from work. We'd tell each other about our day, cook simple dinners, and spend the rest of the night in bed. My mind would skip the bad times. I'd imagine the police realizing they made a big mistake and releasing me. Josh picks me up, we're together; but this time, we work hard, make good choices.

On Tuesday, when I make my weekly phone call to Bernini, her secretary says she'll see me Friday. Friday finally arrives. It's already past three. She's not here. I shower, but if she's not here soon, it won't matter. The last few days, the cellblock's hotter than usual. Sweat's rolling off my face and under my arms. Everyone's miserable and on edge. Ina tries to charm one of the new arrivals into buying her a coke from the commissary. When she refuses, Ina reverts to her usual routine. "You better watch your back. I got friends. We can carve you up anytime," and pushes her. A CO sees. They toss our cell. When Ina mouths off, two CO's drag her to solitary. Maybe she'll never come back.

I tell Mom about the heat and, in her clueless fashion, she asked why I don't complain. "Deputy, tell the warden it's too warm in my cell and to turn down the air conditioning. The sweat's ruining my jumpsuit." Right.

Where's Bernini? She's never this late. I try to watch TV, but I hate talk shows—-favorites with the women. Today, the host's interviewing women who take pride in being obese. They make me sick. I shouldn't be so judg-mental. The jail diet makes even the skeletal druggies gain weight. The food's tasteless and starchy, but everyone looks forward to meals and piles on seconds of potatoes, tortillas, rice and beans while they complain about the quality. Eating's something to do. No one's on a hunger strike here. The stupid show seems to last forever. The clock strikes five, and just when I give up, "Kristin White—-attorney visit."

Bernini chats for a few minutes. I'd gotten more comfortable with her and tell her about the heat in the cellblock. She laughs sympathetically at Mom's response. I'm lucky she's my attorney. Inmates complain constantly that their lawyers never come to see them. Mine comes every week. Private lawyers get the most respect. A common belief is money can buy justice—-I'm not sure. Most of the women believe public defenders are incompetent, stupid and uncaring. Some think they aren't real lawyers. Still, Bernini has a good reputation around the jail.

After a few minutes, she gets down to it. "I finally got the CA to listen to me. He agreed to stipulate to a two-year sentence and drop the allegation of over two pounds of coke. The time you've been in here counts, so you'd be eligible for parole in about fifteen months. Because of your background, I'm sure you'd make parole. As I've explained if you go to trial and lose, you're facing five to fifteen years. There's nothing the judge can do to change that if you lose. You have to decide by next Wednesday, or they'll pull the plea."

"That's less than a week—it's not fair."

"You're right, it's not fair; but that's how the CA's office operates."

"Why'd he change his mind? You said he wasn't willing to give me a deal."

"I don't know. Maybe he knows I'm not bluffing about going to trial. I fight hard, and I've won more than my share of cases. Maybe because they've tried everything to find something questionable in your background, but they can't. I've sent them character letters from your mom, friends, rela-tives, employers and your coworkers; but usually they ignore them. It's pos-sible the prosecutor knew Scott. His letter was persuasive and he's known you intimately for a long time. It's most likely he's overworked, has a lot of cases set for trial, and has to plead some. The important thing isn't why; it's whether you're interested in the plea."

"I'm interested. Five years is like forever. It's almost a fourth of my life. I can't imagine fifteen years in here. I'd rather die. I'd be an old lady when

I got out—-almost forty. Do you think I'll get a better deal if I hold out? I'd heard about this guy who was facing twenty years for a bunch of armed robberies, and the day of trial, he got probation."

Bernini looks at me and shakes her head. "Haven't you learned not to believe everything you hear in here? It's true once in a while someone gets a great deal the day of trial. Maybe the State can't find their main witness or a witness gets arrested. Usually it happens because the prosecutor has two trials set on the same day, so they have to plead one. Your case isn't complicated; if he has two cases, he could probably get one of his colleagues to try yours. It's a gamble where all the cards are stacked against you. If you don't get a deal, you're screwed."

"What chance do I have at trial?"

"I can't give you a number. To convict you, the state has to prove you knowingly possessed the coke. If the jury believes you, they should acquit you. Juries are usually more reliable than Judges in this kind of situation, but they don't always do the right thing.

"I'm scared about testifying. I wouldn't know what to say. Couldn't you write me a script or something?"

"I can't tell you what to say. That's called suborning perjury, and its illegal and unethical. We can practice your testimony, and we will many times. I'll get another lawyer from the office to come here with me and cross-examination you. All you have to do is tell the jury what you told me."

I get up and start to pace, try to warm up. The air-conditioning always worked great in the attorney's room. "I can't implicate Josh. If I testify, will they ask me about him?"

"They definitely will. You don't have to testify. No one, not the judge or the prosecutor, can make you. But if you don't, all the jury's going to hear is eighty pounds of cocaine were found in your house, and you were the only one there."

"What should I do?"

"I can't decide that for you. I'm not the one that has to do the time. Why don't you talk it over with your mom? Or Scott?"

"It was a total humiliation to ask Scott to write me a letter. I'm not going to ask his opinion. When he was here, I could tell how glad he was not to be involved with me. My mom's no help. She doesn't know anything about law. All she cares about is if her friends find out I'm in jail. Angie's the only one I trust."

"I think you're too hard on your mom. She wants to help; she just doesn't know how. If you think your friend's advice is helpful, talk to her. She's on your visitation list, isn't she?"

"Yeah."

She hands me some papers that look like they've been stapled together, but the staples are removed. I guess the jail folks worry about suicide by staples. "This is a copy of the plea agreement. I'll go over the main points; you can read it later. I want to make sure you understand everything before you decide. You'll plead guilty to Possession of Cocaine with Intent to Sell. The state would agree your sentence would be two years. There's a mandatory $2,000 fine, plus an additional fee called a surcharge, which amount to another $1,620.

"How am I supposed to pay a fine while I'm in prison? That's more than $3,500."

"Don't worry about the fine. You don't have to pay till you're released. Your parole officer will help you set up a payment plan. Twenty dollars a month is enough. You won't get assessed the surcharges. This Judge is known for not imposing them. She thinks it's unfair to burden people with that much debt if they're going to prison."

"Can I get out earlier if I get Mom to pay it all now?"

"No, it wouldn't make any difference."

"Where will I go to prison?"

"First, they send you to a reception center in Phoenix and give you a battery of tests to figure out where to put you. You'll be in minimum security, but there are several of them around the state. We can request Tucson since your family's here. No guarantees. Go ahead. Look it over."

I try to read it, but all I see's a blur. I'm going to prison. Seeing it in writing—-even blurred writing—makes it more real. No matter what I do, I'm not going home.

"I'll come back Tuesday, and you can let me know what you decide. If you have questions, call me. I'm out of town this weekend, but I'm going to have Coleen, my paralegal, come out and meet with you."

"Am I gonna get beat up or raped?"

"In minimum, it's not likely. Most of the women will be in for crimes like fraud, DUI or possession—not violent stuff. It's not that different from here. The best advice I have is to lay low. Don't piss anyone off, guards or inmates. You'll be okay."

"Are you sure?"

"No."

SEVENTEEN

Bernini's coming today. Do I take the two years or go to trial and gamble on five, ten or more? I wake up fantasizing about donuts.

You can buy overpriced stuff from the commissary——toiletries, socks, and food——most of it high in fat and calories. Every morning, a trustee passes out a list of stuff available that day. Before lunch, another trustee picks up your order. A third brings it before dinner. (Prison full employment.) I read the choices over and over; visualize small, powdered sugar donuts that melt in your mouth; soft chocolate chip cookies a bit under baked; and oatmeal crème pies, like the ones I bought as a kid. It takes a long time to choose.

By the time the trustee comes with my order, I'm salivating. The food's never as good as I imagine. I don't care. I try to ration, but as soon as I eat one thing, I keep on until I finish everything. I used to exercise some control, but since I came here, I can't turn down anything that makes me feel good. Lucky for me the jail only lets you get three desserts a day.

Why bother trying to be thin? Josh's gone. It doesn't seem likely I'll meet an eligible man. The next several years are women only. Unlike Mom and her friends, my cellies aren't obsessed with calories. At least Mom doesn't criticize my weight gain. Jail silences even her.

The more crap I eat, the friendlier Ina gets. She came back to the cell three days after the incident. She never told me what happened, but she's subdued. Like me, Ina's a sweetaholic. Unlike me, she has no money. I know she's using me. Feeding her's worth it. To stop her hostility. Have someone to talk to.

She's charged with lotsa counts of theft and misuse of credit cards. When we talk about our boyfriends, we realize our situations are alike. We became closer. Unlike, Josh, Ina's guy, Dwayne, isn't gone. They'd both been arrested when the cops stopped him for speeding and searched his car. "Stopped for being black in a white town," Ina said. "We were screwed. Dwayne was on parole and carrying."

"Carrying what?" I ask.

"A piece."

"A 'piece'?"

She looks at me and shakes her head. "Where the hell you been livin' your life? A gun."

"Where's Dwayne now?"

"Prison. Doin' the rest of his sentence for burglary. And they charged him with havin' a gun on parole and the same thefts and credit card shit they got me for."

I talk to Mom about the plea. She offers to get a loan to hire a private lawyer. She's so goddamn clueless. "It'd be a waste of money."

"How could you know that?" she asks.

"Bernini's the best. You've talked to her. Everyone thinks I'm lucky."

"You trust these people's opinions? They're criminals. You'd take their advice instead of mine?" Mom looks at me like I'm a total moron.

"Oh, so you think I'm a criminal too?" And on and on it goes. I think both of us feel more comfortable arguing about whether I need a different lawyer than my probable future. Ten minutes before the visit's over, she gets quiet, looks me in the eye.

"I feel like a horrible mother. I want to help you, but I don't know how. I don't want you to go to prison for something you didn't do, but I can't do anything to stop it. I wish I could go in your place." She starts to cry.

I don't know what to say. I know Mom cares, but we're not the kind of family who hugs and says, 'I love you' every time we meet or talk on the phone. Mom and I were inseparable when I was young. We both loved animals. Dad was allergic; we never had pets except fish. To compensate,

Mom took me to zoos, pet shops, and to visit friends with dogs. When I'm old enough, we go horseback riding.

I volunteer at the Humane Society during high school and college because of her. Being with dogs made me feel good and gave Mom and me something to talk about.

Dad died the summer after my sophomore year of college. I convinced Mom she needed a dog. I help her rescue a small white one we name Sparkie. He's part poodle and maybe part dachshund. I've never had a stable enough lifestyle to get my own dog, but after I move out, I visit Sparkie often and consider him part mine. Then I meet Scott.

From the time Scott and I start to date, he and Mom get along fantastically. Scott often invites her to join us at dinner or a movie. I think she's more devastated than me when we break up. She blames me. Said if I hadn't given him an ultimatum, if I'd had more patience, we'd still be together. Should have talked to her before I did it. You'd never guess he's the one who left me.

Ironically, after Scott and I split, Mom and I spend more time together. We eat dinner and watch movies. Take Sparkie on walks. Then I meet Josh. Mom hates him from the first. Not only isn't he going to be a lawyer, he looks "fast"—-whatever that means. I figure she'll hate anyone I date. She's upset we spend less time together. No one can measure up to Scott. We start to argue and never stop. It'd been a long time since she said loving words to me.

Her sobs release my fear. "Mom, I don't know what to do. Prison sounds like death. Jail's horrible, but not scary anymore. I follow the rules, the guards leave me alone, and none of the women have tried to hurt me.

"I hear the women talk about prison, mean guards, violent women. There's this one girl, really pretty, looks about eighteen. She's been in prison before. Told me the guards leered at her all the time. Watched her shower and in the bathroom. Another woman, big and tough, looks like she could hold her own with anyone, got raped by two women in her pod. Said the guards knew but didn't care. I'm not tough; I don't know how to defend myself." The words I'd held back tumble out.

"They talk about gangs. I thought that was only guys, but the women say even if you're female, you have to join—-you have no choice. You can't stay to yourself. If you're not with them, you're against them. They'll get you. You need someone to watch your back.

"I'm so lonely. I don't know whom to trust. Every time I find someone I like, they get transferred. They change my roommates all the time." I stop to catch my breath.

"I'm sorry, honey. You got used to being in here; the same thing will happen there. People exaggerate," she replies, desperation in her tone, as I become her scared little girl again.

Before either of us could say more, the guard walks over, lets me know time's up. "Bye, Mom, talk to you soon, see you in court," I put the phone down eyes dry. I no longer cry so easily.

My visit with Angie's calmer. She'd talked to Scott, who said I should take the plea. My chance of winning at trial isn't good with that much coke. Who'd believe I didn't know? Scott, the jerk, still can't understand why I won't testify against Josh. Angie and I write lists of pros and cons. She promises to write, visit, and send food.

Even though Bernini warned me not to talk about the case, I do. Besides Josh, there's not much else on my mind. Ina talks about her case to anyone who'll listen. "I got no chance going to trial. I ain't gonna be acquitted by no white jury, and all I'll get here is white folks. Arizona ain't Harlem."

She keeps bugging me. Finally I show her the plea. She asks lots of questions. She's smarter than I thought. I feel bad for underestimating her and hope it's because of how she treated me—-not cause she's black. She agrees with everyone else. "Take it. Only way you're gonna win is if you get some gangbanger with the hots for you on your jury." Then she chuckles. "With that amount of blow, you'll need more than one."

"Bernini said if the jury believed me, I'd win."

"On Law and Order maybe." She gets quiet. "You been decent to me. Two years you can handle. You be in minimum. Your time here counts, and there's a bunch of early out bullshit. Honkie girls like you get time off. You get five or ten; you come out different, bitter and used up. They'll send you go to a yard with tough, nasty bitches like me. Don't take the chance."

A few days before I have to decide, I'm in the dayroom killing time. For once, the TV is off. A couple of women talk about trials. Tell horror stories. A friend of one of their cousins is offered a plea of six months, goes to trial, and gets ten years. An attorney's disbarred after her uncle's trial, but he can't get his case reversed. Trials are a crapshoot. You can't trust juries. One woman who's waiting to be transported to prison says her lawyer was high during her trial. I tell them about my case. They all agree, "Take the plea."

The night before Bernini's wants my answer, I hardly sleep. Every time I drop off, I wake up sweaty, scared. I dream I'm asleep in a tiny cell, when two large men with small eyes and cruel mouths unlock the door and scream at me to give them the stuff. I protest I don't have any stuff. They search my room, break my things and read my letters. They get angrier and angrier as they find nothing. One grabs me, calls me girlie, pats me down over my clothes. Then he lifts up my nightgown. I explain only women guards are allowed to touch me, but they laugh. One holds me down, and the other begins pulling my legs apart, when thankfully my screams wake me. Ina too. I expect she'll be mad cause I woke her, but she comes over to my bed, hugs me and tells me it'll be okay.

Early in the morning, I get up and look at the list Angie and I made. I see the words 'tell the truth' written under testify. Bernini said to win I need to tell the whole story and snitch off Josh. If not, I'm dead meat.

I can't. It doesn't matter what Josh did. Or didn't do. I have to take the plea. I lie back on my bed and sleep till breakfast. I dream of donuts.

CHAPTER
EIGHTEEN

From the moment he wakes up hung over in a strange place, no Carlos or JT, a thousand bucks in his wallet, his life begins a downward spiral. He knows immediately something's wrong when the apartment's empty except for remains of a meal. But he never expects his own apartment ransacked, a search warrant on the table. Never expects the coke to be seized. Never expects Kristin to be arrested. Kristin's mom's blaming him for all of it— that's the only thing that's no surprise.

He's afraid to go back to their place. Someone or someones are after him. Since he can't deliver the drugs, he owes money, more money than he can imagine earning in his entire fucking life. And if he can't pay, they will hurt him, maybe kill him.

Time to split. The car's packed. He said his few goodbyes. Can't face Angie and Art. He thought about visiting Kristin. Why bother? She probably hates him. He could try the "I love your routine"; but if he loved her, he'd help her. Josh doesn't know law, but thinks he could turn himself in, snitch off Carlos and JT in exchange for getting her out. If he tries and it doesn't work, it'd show he cared. People talked about loving someone so much they'd sacrifice their own lives. If that was love, he didn't love Kristin.

What if Kristin talked? She wouldn't rat him out, but if she had- the cops might want to talk to him or worse. If he went to see her, he could get arrested. The longer he stays in town, the more danger he's in. God, he's an asshole.

His dad's voice swirls around his head. "A real man would take responsibility." Throughout childhood, his dad bombarded him with pronouncements about real men. Real men don't cry. Real men work hard and don't complain. Real men protect their women. Real men don't have ponytails. He believed his dad's values had roots in the Middle Ages, didn't apply to him, but he kept hearing his voice. His dad's long dead. They rarely talked when he was alive, so why did he hear him now?

Over the years he'd had a passion for what he called moron stories: An idiot on probation with a suspended license calls 911 because he needs a cigarette; a crook leaves his prison ID cards at the scene of the crime; a drunk woman hits a man with her car—-the man's embedded in her windshield and, instead of getting help, she drives home and leaves him in her garage to die. (They made a movie of that one.) Now, he's the moron.

Not since the bully in second grade has he hid. His dad told him real men don't hide. Real men take on the bully. Josh stole money from his dad, mom and aunt. Paid the bully off with Snickers, Chuckles and rock candy. Only dumb luck saved him this time. Driving by his place in a borrowed truck, he sees two big, menacing men at his door. Thinks they have a gun.

He considers using the citizen tip line to snitch out Carlos and JT; but he doesn't even know their last names. Carlos, a Hispanic guy, mid twenties with darkish skin, average height and build, brown eyes, tattoos on both arms that he couldn't describe. And JT, a white guy, also mid twenties, tall, skinny, with stringy brown hair and a beard, no visible tattoos. He can show the cops their apartment, but nothing's there to back up his story.

"How did you meet them?" Well, officer, I bought pot from a dude named Heavy; and he introduced me to Carlos. Carlos offered me a thousand dollars to store some blow overnight. Heavy? Don't know his last name either; but the dude's real old—-maybe forty, Polynesian, short, fat and hangs out at the biker bar downtown.

He mulls his choices again. Turn himself in. Stay here and hide. Face Carlos, JT, and their people, tell them what happened. Leave town. If he's not going to turn himself in, leaving's the only choice. He hates that

Kristin's mom think she'd talked him into abandoning Kristin. His dad's right. He's a coward—-a stupid coward.

Josh used some of the money to settle the rent on their apartment. Luckily, the office is on the other side of the complex. Even with the borrowed truck, he's a nervous wreck. At least Kristin can get her stuff back. Her credit won't be ruined. Great. She's doing time for me, in exchange; I take care of her credit.

He has enough cash to leave. But where? Back to San Diego to live with Mom or some old friends, or someplace new? Why not make a new start? He'd always wanted to go to New Mexico. A couple girls he knew from high school might give him a place to stay. Linda was a dog, but Jody . . .

CHAPTER
NINETEEN

I wait my turn to plead guilty. Court's boring. Not scary anymore. When Bernini leaves the courtroom, I barely notice. At breakfast, I skip coffee (no loss) so I don't need to use the bathroom. When the inmate I'm chained to panics because her lawyer's not here, I calmly say, "Don't worry. They can't start without her." Mom and Angie are here, but I know enough not to wave.

Bernini and I have gone over the plea agreement almost word by word so I'm ready for the judge's questions. "Can I read and speak English?" Duh. "How far have I gone in school?" Does it matter? "Has the lawyer gone over the plea with me?" About fifty times. "Have I had any drugs, alcohol or prescription medication in the last twenty-four hours?" I wish. "Had anyone forced me to plead guilty?" Josh. "Had anyone threatened me?" Josh again.

Some of the questions Judge Thomas asks are really dumb, but I think the reason is to make sure I know what I'm doing. Make sure I don't make a mistake. Later, Ina tells me she asks those questions so I don't have grounds to appeal.

After what seems forever, the judge gets to it, "What did you do that makes you think you're guilty of cocaine possession with intent to sell?" We'd rehearsed the answer I was supposed to say, but I can't get the words out. If I say I didn't do anything or Josh did it not me, what would happen? Bernini takes one look at me and asks the Judge, "Can I give the 'factual basis.'" Without waiting for a response, Bernini says, "In Pima County, Ms. White knowingly possessed less than two pounds of cocaine for the purpose of sale."

"Do you agree that's what happened, Ms. White?" Before I can answer, Bernini asks the Judge for a moment, and whispers if I say yes, it's all over. I still can change my mind . . .With no hesitation, I say, "Yes, Your Honor."

I won't be sentenced for a month. Bernini says the delay's normal because probation has to write a report about me for Judge Thomas, which seems ridiculous, since I'm not going to be on probation and everyone has agreed I will serve two years. I don't ask her to explain. Little of what goes on in court makes sense.

Ina had court today, too; but even though we leave the jail together, we come back on different vans. I get back first. When she returns, I'm on my bunk waiting for the trustee to bring the food. "How'd it go?" I ask.

"Shitty. My asshole lawyer told me he had some motion to get my case dumped. He said I had a good chance. In court, he didn't seem to know shit. The fuckin' prosecutor was much smarter. Hot too. I wish I had Bernini. Mine's a burned-out old fart. The judge probably gave me a shitty one on purpose. He didn't even ask that worthless judge to get me a medical visit."

I don't know what to say. I change the subject. "I ordered us donuts, Little Debbie cakes, and Red Vines. Should be here soon."

"I don't know what I'd do without you, girl, maybe be fifteen pounds skinnier. Dwayne use to bitch that I was just a bag of bones, not that I'm going to let him look at my ass any time soon. I've told you all about Dwayne, but you ain't told me nothing 'bout your guy."

"He's probably not 'my guy' anymore. You saw the letter."

"Maybe. How long you together?"

"About a year."

"How'd you meet?"

"Why do you want to know that?"

"Just tell me. Take my mind off how much my stomach hurts." Ina got off my bed and lay down on her bunk. She looks pale and sweaty.

"Maybe we should get the guards?"

"No, just talk. Maybe you'll put me to sleep. You never tell me the good stuff."

I don't know whether to laugh. "Okay. My friends, Angie and Art—-Angie's the one who visits all the time; I told you about her—-had a party. Almost didn't go. I was still hung up on my ex. I didn't feel like partying but both of them kept on me. This woman, Leslie, who worked with Art, brought her cousin, Josh, who just moved here from California. Didn't know anyone. He kept looking at me."

"Go on," she groaned.

"Later that night, I can't remember exactly... His cousin Leslie was gossiping about some celebrity's love life. I didn't know who the person was. I made a mistake and asked her. She made a sarcastic remark like, 'What cave do you spend your time in?'

"I couldn't think of anything to say, so I just stood there looking stupid; and Josh said, 'You know, Leslie, some people have more important things to do with their lives than know trivia about every passing pop star.'"

"She sounds like a real bitch."

"Yeah. Josh said they got along off and on, but she's been on his case about me since we got together. She didn't like me—-thought I wasn't good enough for him. Said I was ugly. Ugly. I might not be gorgeous but compared to her. Leslie outweighs me by forty pounds, has short, greasy hair, zitty face. Yuck. Ironic the way it turned out."

"So Josh got his mojo working?"

"His what?"

"Jesus, girl, you do live in a cave. Is he a good fuck?" Ina grinned, then groaned again.

"Ina."

"What do you mean 'Ina'? It's not like we're in high school. We're in jail—-probably both heading to prison. You act like you're a virgin."

"Well, I'm not; but that doesn't mean I have to tell you all my personal stuff."

"Nothing personal about it. Once they take off their clothes, they're pretty much the same. Some just take longer than others."

"You're horrid." I look over at Ina. She has her eyes closed, so I keep quiet. l must have drifted off. A sound outside the cell wakes me.

"Hey, get your lazy asses up. I got your goodies. You two sure like the sweet stuff. Here you go: donuts, cakes, Red Vines. See ya tomorrow, I'm sure."

"Ina, food, get up."

"I can't. My stomach's killing me. I gotta get to medical."

I don't know what to do. We didn't go to the dayroom so next time we get out isn't till supper. Still a couple hours away. "Hey, you with the cart," I yell at the trustee.

She turns around. "My cellie's really sick. Can you tell the CO on your way out? Hurry," I call as Ina continues to moan. Ina'd complained about not feeling well for several days. She'd filled out slips to go to medical, but nothing had happened.

A few minutes later, CO Miller comes over. Shit, she won't help.

"What's going on here?"

"Something's wrong with me. My stomach's killing me. I need to see a doctor," Ina moans.

"You know the procedure. Why didn't you request medical?"

"I have at least three times, but nothing's happened."

"She has, I've seen the forms."

"No one asked you, White."

"I can't take you now—-I'm on yard duty. You'll have to wait till dinner." She walks away.

"Fuckin' cunt," Ina whispers.

"Please, get someone else if you can't." I yell but Miller doesn't even turn around.

Ina's crying. A first. I touch her head. It's hot. I sit on her bed, say things to calm her down. Time passes slowly. Finally, the guard calls our pod to dinner. "Can you make it to the cafeteria? Once you get there, someone will help you."

"No, I'm too dizzy. You go; you don't want to get in trouble." It's against the rules to skip a meal. They don't care if you eat, but you have to show. I hadn't gotten a write-up since I got here. Bernini says it's best not to get in trouble. Your judge and the prosecutors find out if you do. I think about Scott and Josh, how they weren't there for me. I decide to stay.

After a while, Ina stops moaning, falls back to sleep. I grab the rest of the desserts and eat them. I'd saved her some, but she won't be eating them. I'm almost finished when I hear footsteps. Two guards walk toward us. "Stay on your beds, hands to the front," orders the taller one. "What's going on here?"

"She's really sick. She's been trying to get to medical all week." One guard walks in the cell and over to her bunk. The second one follows.

"Hey, you, get up. We're taking you to medical." Ina opens her eyes and looks confused. She stands up slowly, holds her abdomen. One woman on each side of her, they drag her out the door. One of the guards gives her a paper and then turns to me. "White, this one's for you."

I look at the paper. It's entitled Notice of Violation and Disposition. "Inmate White, 107656, has committed a Class 5 violation; failure to follow procedure. Pursuant to Rule 27(a), Code of Jail Conduct, it is ordered that inmate will forfeit three days of commissary, starting the day after the infraction. Inmate is advised that, due to the minor nature of the sanction, there is no right to appeal."

TWENTY

The last month's the worst yet. I never saw Ina again. For all I know she could be seriously ill or dead. The guards say they don't know anything. I say they won't tell. My cellies come and go never staying more than a few days. I haven't the energy to befriend anyone. Yesterday in the yard, Mama Carla, one of the inmates I knew only by reputation, tried to pass me a note.

Passing notes, which the frequent fliers call a 'kite,' is illegal. A Class 2 Violation. I don't want to get in any more trouble. Mama Carla's trouble. Big trouble. She looks about thirty or so, tall, plump with long black hair and nasty eyes. Head of female Brown Pride. "Listen, bitch, open your fucking hand, or we'll both be busted. And you don't want to get me busted. Now," she whispers. I look at her and open my hand. Better to get a write up than my face busted. It's from Ina:

Hi Krissten, Went to hospital for apendicks. Doing ok. See you soon. Ina.

I feel messed with by everyone. After three days with no commissary, I get moved to another pod. All strangers. I lose my job. Don't get picked for classes. Bernini won't admit it, but she's upset with me for the write up. I'm proud of it.

Today's my last day in court. The place is packed. Standing room only. I look out at the spectators and see Mom, Angie and Art. I told Angie not to bother. They smile. Mom brought me 'court clothes,' but I can't wear them because this is a sentencing, not a trial. They'd probably be too small.

A young girl, who's not in custody yet, is pleading guilty to resisting arrest. Dressed in jeans and a t-shirt that look like they'd fit a large doll, she's nervous and unsure how to answer the judge. Her lawyer asked to go out of order; he has a trial in another court. It doesn't seem to me there is any order. When the judge asks how far she went in school, the girl frowns, "What do you mean?" Her lawyer whispers to her, and she answers, "Dropped out of ninth grade." Between the judge repeating the questions and conferences with her lawyer, the hearing takes forever.

Finally, the Judge asks what she did that makes her guilty of resisting arrest. The courtroom gives a sigh of relief. This time, she doesn't ask him to repeat the question. She looks at her lawyer, then at Judge Thomas. "I didn't do anything. They were trying to arrest my brother, and I was trying to help him . . . and she breaks into loud sobs. The lawyer asks to continue the hearing. She leaves still free. The judge moves on.

At last, Bernini says we're next. The bailiff calls my case, and the lawyers say their names. This time, the prosecutor's a David Lusk. "Your Honor, the State requests that you sentence the defendant to two years under the plea agreement. This case involves eighty pounds of cocaine, with a street value of $500,000. Ms. White was given numerous chances to cooperate, but failed to do so. She's shown no sign of remorse."

How could he say that? I told the probation person who write the report that I was sorry. Didn't he believe me?

I'm furious and miss most of Bernini's speech. When I calm down, she's finishing. "I ask you, Judge, when is the last time you sentenced someone with no previous convictions—-felony or misdemeanor—-who's never been arrested before?"

Then it's my turn. I stand up, my legs trembling. Bernini and I'd talked about what I should say. Keep it short, take responsibility, and sit down. "Your Honor, I just want to tell you that I'm sorry for everything that happened. I take responsibility for the drugs that were found in my house. I've learned my lesson and I promise you that I'll never break the law again." I sit down relieved I'm done.

"It is the order of the Court that, pursuant to the plea bargain, I sentence you to two years in the Department of Corrections, with credit for the one hundred and twenty-two days you served in jail; and a fine of $2000, to be paid in installments beginning thirty days after you're released. Your Parole Officer can explain how to make payment arrangements.

"The Court finds in mitigation the defendant's lack of prior record and in aggravation the amount of drugs.

"Ms. White, you come from a stable household and have a college education. There's no reason for you to resort to drug dealing to make a living. I better not see you again.

"You have no right to direct appeal, but you have ninety days to file a Petition for Post-Conviction Relief. Do you have any questions?"

Questions? What's going to happy to me? I'm going to be locked up for two years. Someone else will decide everything for me. What prison am I going to? Will I be okay? Do I have to join a gang? Will I see Mom or Angie again? Is my life ruined? Where's Josh?

"No, Your Honor. No questions."

TWENTY-ONE

THE PRESENT

I feel guilty for choosing Starbucks. There are three independent coffee shops close by, and I believe you should support local business. Another belief I don't follow up. But at Starbucks, you get coffee the way you want it every time. No worries it'll be too weak or too cold like the crap in prison. The customers look prosperous, like they have places to go, only stopping for a break from their busy lives.

I'm early—even taking the damn bus. Angie's meeting me at ten-thirty. It's barely ten. I feel like I've put in a day's work. Job-hunting's a bitch. Every morning, I scour the want ads. Stop at the post office. Send off resumes. Save the hard part for last, businesses you have to apply in person.

Resume writing's painless. A section on education, on employment history and a few references. Unlike job applications, no one expects you to list prior arrests or convictions. I'm thankful for rules that prohibit employers from asking about marital status and kids. Maybe they think the two-year gap means I was a stay-at-home mom not a stay-in-prison daughter.

Job interviews suck. They start okay. I look put-together due to Mom, unless the wait for the bus is more than ten minutes, and I'm all sweaty. I have a degree, job experience. Then they ask, "Have you ever been arrested?"

Some say upfront they won't hire a felon. The rest try to act like it's just another question, not a deal-breaker. But all of a sudden, the job's been filled or the smile disappears, and I'm told "We'll call you if something comes up." After a few rejections, I'm ready to call it quits. And these jobs don't require a degree. Pay shit. I'm not stupid enough to apply for anything to do with counseling.

Halfway through my soy latte, I see Angie. Unlike me, she isn't wedded to one drink. Last week, a macchiato; today, "Coffee mocha with whipped crème, lots of it. How goes the hunt?"

"Same old, same old. No one's willing to take a chance on an ex-con. I could write a song: 150 Ways to Tell a Job Seeker to Fuck-Off, like the Paul Simon one. I'll never get a job. My PO told me he could help, but I hate to ask."

"Why? You said he's a hunk. That'd be a legit way to spend time with him."

"Yeah, but I don't want him to think of me as a typical parolee who can't do anything. I want to show him I can do it on my own."

"I'm going to make your day. You know my Aunt Sara, the dog trainer? Her assistant's having a tough pregnancy, and the doctor wants her to stop working. Sara's looking for a temporary replacement. She couldn't care less if you have a record. Thinks she's psychic about people: If she gets good vibes from you, nothing else matters, as long as you like animals—-which I know you do."

"Sounds too good to be true. I think I met her once at your house. Does she kind of look like you, same wavy hair but dresses kind of funky?"

"Yeah, that's her. No question she's a tad different, but she's smart and compassionate. If she likes you, there's nothing she won't do for you."

"Like you. How do I contact her?"

"She'll see you at ten tomorrow."

"Angie, you're terrific." I give her a big hug. For the first time in a while, I feel like life might improve. "Any tips? What should I wear?"

"You'll work with dogs, so I don't think you need to dress up. She's won't care what you wear. There are a couple things you need to know about her. She's passionate about rescuing dogs. Hates dog fighting, any kind of dog abuse or neglect. She doesn't eat meat. As long as I can remember, she's told people she can see into the minds of people and animals. In spite, or maybe because of that, I adore her. Just remember, it all depends on your vibes, so make sure they're good tomorrow. Here's her card."

I decide to enjoy the rest of the day. In one sense, every day since prison is the best; but in another, it's not. I appreciate my privacy and mom's food, but the stress of no job, no money, and life with Mom is always there. Mom gives me money for lunches and stuff like toothpaste, but I want to go out and buy clothes I like or the new Eric Clapton CD. Mom bought me clothes to look for work, and outfits she thinks I should wear at home but they're not me. I should be grateful.

I go to the mall, look around. All I can afford is a couple of cookies from Mrs. Fields. I haven't had desert since I got out. Mom's food's great but always low fat. And no treats. As I eat the cookie, I think about Ina.

I'm home before Mom. Decide to cook dinner without her having to ask. The salad's finished, chicken and vegetables cooking when she walks in. "Hi, Kristin. How was your day?"

"Great. I have a job interview tomorrow at ten with Angie's aunt, who's a dog trainer. She knows about my record and doesn't care. I think I have a good chance."

I wait for a smart comment, "You graduated from college, and you're going teach dogs to sit"; but she just smiles and says, "Good luck."

TWENTY-TWO

I knock hesitantly on the front door of The Dignified Dog. No answer. I'd left the house at eight thirty and rode two buses to get here early. It's a few minutes before ten. Stay calm—-maybe the place isn't open yet. Or maybe she's running late. I pace back and forth in front of the small businesses that make up the strip mall. A few minutes later, I knock harder, but again no answer. I check the card with the address and time. Right place. Right time. Should I call Angie? What good could she do?

I walk back and forth again and again; now I'm concerned. Sweaty. Maybe the job's too good to be true. But Angie'd never mislead me. I'm about to leave, when I see a phone booth. My hand shakes as I dial.

"The Dignified Dog, Sara speaking." Thank goodness, except now I'm late.

"Mrs. Sanchez, it's Kristin White, Angie's friend. I'm here for the interview. I know I'm late. I'm sorry. I was out here knocking . . .

"My fault. One of the dogs in day-care threw up. We were all back there making sure Dudley was okay. You're here now. I'll come open the door. See you in a moment."

The door opens. I'd know this woman was related to Angie if I ran into her on the street. Same long, brown wavy hair; similar facial features, and a smile that warmed your day.

Unlike Angie, who dresses casually, Sara's wearing a long, crinkly purple skirt, lacy white blouse, and lots of costume jewelry. Beside her is a large, older black Labrador retriever; and a smaller, younger, pudgy brown dog of mixed parentage. Sara puts out her hand, "Hi Kristin. I'm Sara, the black one's Samantha, and the brown one's Theodore. Welcome."

I follow her to a small room that looks like the office. Sara motions for me to sit down on the chair in front of her desk. Both dogs sit down in front of me and give me their paws. As I shake 'paws' and pet them, my nervousness abates.

"Angie probably told you my assistant has medical issues. I need a fill-in. It's full-time, but I can't promise it'll be permanent. I expect Gail back between six months and a year." She fills me in on salary and benefits, which are better than I expect.

"My assistant has a variety of duties, from supervising day care, making sure the dogs have water, answering the phone, paperwork. I need help teaching obedience class; and on busy days, someone to see to Samantha and Theodore. I board clients' dogs. They need baths, feeding, and interaction."

"I love dogs," I blurt out "Terrific. I do a weekly radio show and write columns, so sometimes I need you to do research. You need to work independently and get along well with the clients—-which is the easy part—-and their 'people,' which is a lot harder. Do you live with any animals?"

"Yes. No. I mean I don't have one of my own. I never had the right place to keep one. I live with my Mom now, and she has a dog—Sparkie, mostly poodle not too big. She got him at the Humane Society about three years ago."

"I'm glad your mom rescued her dog. Animal rescue's my passion. There are thousands of dogs in shelters in every state. It'd be great if they were all no-kill, but many of them keep the animals for a certain period of time and, if no one adopts them, they kill them." She looks at me with sad eyes, "And of course, there's the dreadful treatment of greyhounds."

Over the next half hour or so she asks questions about my education and job experience. She never asks about my drug conviction or prison. She never asks me to fill out paperwork. Mostly, we talk about my views on animal issues. I feel comfortable with her, but I don't want to get my hopes up.

After she's finished, she looks at the dogs. "Either of you want to ask Kristin anything?" Each barks a couple times. She asks Samantha for clarification, and

Samantha barks again. The first question is from Theodore. "Theodore wants to know your position on between-meal snacks."

Does this woman seriously believe she talks to dogs? "Between-meal snacks?" I repeat, try to think. Sparkie gets treats, but who knows what this strange woman would think was the right answer. In kiddie day-care, new moms have all these rules about what their kids can eat. No between meal snacks. No meat. No food with dye. Maybe I should play to the dog. "I'm all for treats," I answer. Theodore runs over to me and again puts his paw out to shake. Seems like I got that one right.

"Samantha's more intellectual than Theodore," Sara says. "Teddy thinks mostly about his stomach. She wants to know if you believe pit bulls are dangerous and should be treated differently."

I almost laugh out loud. After college, I never read much, but the prison administration pushed it. Gave you perks for each book you read. Reading for Donuts. Mom and Angie sent books, but never enough. Like everything else in prison, too many rules. To get an intact hardback book, the publisher had to send it. Hardbacks from anyone else had to have covers removed. Never could figure out if they were worried about suicide or contraband. Books about explicit sex, prison escapes, and true crime were prohibited.

The prison library was a mess. The books were old, pages torn out or full of repulsive stains. Too many Bibles. A few guards brought us their old books and magazines. The public was encouraged to donate. Mostly they sent stuff charities would refuse.

CO Kavanagh brought animal magazines. Several articles were about the treatment of pit bulls. Before I read them, I thought pit bulls were violent and dangerous. This question was a no-brainer. "Pit bulls should be treated like all other dogs. It's outrageous to label a dog because of its breed. A dog should be considered dangerous only if it exhibits aggression, whatever its type." Samantha looks at me when I answer but, unlike Theodore, doesn't show approval or disapproval. Still, I think I'd gotten that one right.

Sara asks if I have questions. I hate to bring it up. "I'm not sure if you know, but I've been convicted of cocaine possession for sale and I'm on parole. Do you want to ask me anything about that?" I want everything in the open. If I'm going to lose the job because of my past, I want to lose it now.

"Angie told me. I know everything I need to know about you from our conversation. I have the ability to look into the hearts and minds of humans and animals," she says the same way you'd say you had a degree.

The interview's over. She asks me to wait while she talks with Samantha and Theodore. Both stop for a quick pet and sniff before they follow Sara out of the room. I can't wait to tell Josh about the interview, and then I realize that's impossible. He'd have found Sara hysterical, but liked her. Or maybe not.

If I don't get the job, it'd be the first time I'd be rejected by a dog or dogs.

A few minutes later, Sara, Samantha, and Theodore come back into the room. "Congratulations, the job's yours if you want it."

TWENTY-THREE

"Mom I need my license. It takes two buses and more than an hour to get there from here."

"Are you sure it's legal to get one. You're still on parole."

"I looked at the paperwork Mr. Cooper gave me. It says eighteen months after conviction you can get it back. There's a fifty-dollar fee. I promise I'll pay you back. My old car just sits in the garage."

"Lucky for you I've kept it useable. You need insurance, too."

"I'll pay you back for that too. I can do it. My salary covers my expenses and fines and I have a lot left. I could pay you some rent."

" I don't want you to pay rent. I'll make you a deal. I'll pay the fifty dollars and the first two months of insurance as long as you're working. You have to agree that if you quit or get fired or mess up on parole, you'll stop driving."

Oh, God, there she goes again. Always doubting me. I'm surprised it isn't a condition that I join Think Thin. "Sure Mom, that's fair, I'll do it. How about we go this afternoon?"

"Can't—-I've other plans. I could do it early tomorrow. I don't have to be in till ten."

I'm up early, ready to go. We get there shortly after it opens, but I'm number one hundred two. It's so crowded we can't sit together. Mom's brought a book but I didn't. I grab a driver's manual, but I know the stuff. Took 'Safe Driving' in prison. The teacher was a retired cop. Had great war stories and taught us the rules.

"Hey Kristin, is that you?"

"It's me," and for a moment I can't figure out who it is-. "Rita?" I try to keep a smile on my face while I wish she'd disappear.

"Yeah, it's me. Haven't seen you in ages. Always wondered what happened to you. One day you're at the desk next to me, and the next thing you're gone. Nobody would say a thing about why you left." How could they since they never knew?

I check to look for Mom. Luckily, she's engrossed in her book and far enough away not to hear.

"It was no big deal. My mom was in a car accident. I had to quit and help take care of her. What are you doing now?"

"I'm still at the counseling department, but things are much better. Gruper's gone——moved out of state."

"I never thought she'd leave as long as Wahr was there. He didn't leave, did he?"

"No, he got remarried, and she couldn't take it. Walked around with tears in her eyes. Sniffling. Poor thing. Wahr never got it. She finally quit and they give me her job. You?"

"I'm working out of state. A small college you never heard of . . . in . . .

"Number eighty-seven, Report to Window Eleven."

"That's me, Kristin. Thank God. I've been here for hours. Nice to see you."

"You too," I lie, and sneak another look at Mom. She's still reading. Another lie cause of Josh. I have no choice. Couldn't tell her I left cause Josh forbid me to go back. And I listened. The thousands of times I've thought about Josh, I've never thought about that day. Josh and I never mentioned it. It almost seems like it never happened. Like I saw it in a movie.

Was it three years ago? Rita and I were both admin assistants at the counseling center. Dean Wahr announced Professor Jacobs was leaving the U. He'd gotten a better position at some university in California. Betty arranged the potluck, probably so she could spend more time with Wahr. I liked Professor Jacobs. Unlike most of the others, he remembered my name and talked with me about subjects other than the Wildcats or the weather. Usually, I skipped events like this; but since it was for Jacobs, I decided to go.

After dinner, some of the staff decided to go for a drink at "The Inn of Court," a bar owned by a couple lawyers and frequented by downtown lawyers and wannabe law students. It was known as a good place to meet the 'right' people.

I didn't want to go. I knew Josh was waiting for me. Rita kept pushing—-even taunted me. "Come on, don't be such a wuss. Can't your boyfriend handle it if you have a drink with friends? Aren't you allowed to go out without him?" I went.

Almost immediately some guys Rita knew sit down with us. Buy a pitcher. She whispers they're law students. I rarely drink, and after a few, I'm high. The guys are funny. I haven't laughed so much in a long time. The cutest one flirts with me. I'm not used to this. Josh and I stay to ourselves. Somehow, it's eleven o'clock. I grab my purse and leave.

The drive home takes forever. I have to pee. Should have used the bar bathroom, but I want to get home. I drive slowly; worried I'll get pulled over for a DUI. I deserve it.

I drive into the parking lot. Walk to the door. Josh's gonna be mad. The door's locked. The apartment dark and silent. Maybe he's asleep. Quietly, I open the door. I take off my shoes and begin to tiptoe toward the bathroom.

"Where the hell you been? You know what fucking time it is?" Josh screams at me from somewhere in the house.

"It's late, I know. I guess I should have called. I've got to go to the bathroom."

Josh appears and blocks the bathroom door. "You're not going anywhere till you tell me where you were."

I can tell he's drunk. "I'll tell you anything you want to know, just let me pee."

"I said no. Where the fucks were you?"

Scared. I'd never seen Josh this bad. "I went to the potluck—-I told you about it. It's a going-away thing for one of the professors I work for."

"I'm not a goddamn idiot. That started at five. You weren't there all this time. Don't lie to me."

"Please, Josh, let me in. I can't hold it."

"Too bad. Go outside."

Maybe I should. I know a spot near the dumpster that's hidden from view. Or I can drive to the McDonalds. I need my purse and shoes. "Okay, I'll go outside."

"Don't you dare leave, you stupid bitch. Where the fuck were you? Screwing one of those big shot professors."

"No, of course not. It was no big deal, Josh. After dinner, the girls went to the Inn of Court by the university. I had some beers—-that's all." I feel sober now, but my bladder's bursting. Urine trickles down my leg and tears down my face.

"Josh, please. Why are you doing this? I didn't do anything?"

"So drinking and flirting with guys is nothing. Glad to know that. You won't mind when I do the same."

"It wasn't like that," I say, knowing that it was like that. "Some guys who knew Rita just came by the table. I don't even know their names."

"So you're a slut as well as a fucking liar."

"Stop, Josh, please. I didn't do anything. I just talked to these friends of Rita's. Please stop."

Josh moves away from the bathroom door. His face has a look of rage. As he walks toward me, I think he's going to hit me, but I can't move. He pushes me hard out of his way, grabs his keys and leaves.

. . . .

"Mom, what do you want?"

"They've called your number twice. What's wrong with you?"

CHAPTER
TWENTY-FOUR

At the end of the first week, I haven't decided if Sara has psychic powers; but I know she works hard and expects the same from everyone.

No days are the same. I start in doggy day-care, which is housed in two large rooms separated by a small doorway. The larger room is for dogs over twenty-five pounds and holds up to six dogs at a time. The small room holds eight. Both are furnished with soft couches, boxes of doggy toys, and water bowls. Sara has even taped a series of dog cartoons at their eye level. "A scotch and toilet water bartender." Each room has a doggy door leading to a small fenced yard. My main responsibilities are to make sure the dogs are secure, happy, and have water.

Most dogs drink out of the communal bowls, but others—-like Bubbles—-a spoiled brown Pekingese, brings her own bowl- her name engraved in pink. Bubbles drinks only imported water from France that her person, Meredith, provides. No other dog's allowed to drink out of her "sweetie's" bowl. Meredith's a tall, big-boned woman with a baby face and short blonde curly hair. She has her name engraved in gold on her purse. Sara told me Bubbles prefers the communal bowls, or, if she can, the employees' toilet.

When day-care's crowded, I have to make sure no dogs are mistreated by the others; and every dog who wants a toy gets one. Like kids, dogs fight over a few toys and ignore the others.

Snack times twice a day, except for Otis, an aloof Weimaraner, who eats only organic food his people buy from a holistic pet store. Otis isn't allowed to eat between meals. I haven't met his people yet, and I'm not sure I want to. Someone has to take him outside during snack time so he won't feel left out or grab treats from more submissive dogs. I want to give Otis treats, but I won't till I find out more about Sara. My mom's voice tells me to follow the rules if I want to keep my job, but my voice says you don't lose your job or get arrested for being kind to a dog.

When I was a teenager, I earned money babysitting. One couple didn't want me to feed their two-year-old any dessert. I felt sorry for the kid, but obeyed the parents till one day when she wouldn't stop crying. I called my mom, asked her to bring over some cookies and gave the kid one. She shut up immediately and wanted more. I didn't want to get in trouble, so I called the cookie a "banana." I found out later she kept asking her mom for a banana and would cry when her mom gave her one.

On slow days, Sara's dogs, Samantha and Theodore, are allowed to play with the clients; but if day-care's full, they hang out with Sara, one of the other employees, or me. I already love both of them.

Wednesday afternoon, Sara asks me to take Samantha for her weekly ride. We're to pick up supplies at Choice Feed Store on Alvernon. "Samantha looks forward to visiting the store, but I can't take her. Channel Four's going to interview me about the danger of leaving dogs in the car during warm weather. Every year, thoughtless people kill their pets this way. Often, it's people who care about their animals but are just plain ignorant—-not evil."

She continues to talk, but my mind wanders to stories Josh told me about dumb pet owners. I remember the woman who parks in valet parking and asks the attendant to take care of her dog. When he refuses, "It's not my job, lady," they get in a fight and she's arrested. Some of the stories Josh heard from his friend, Zach, who worked at Pet Palace. "How do you bathe fish?" "How come my dogs don't know which beds are theirs even though their names are on them?"

Sara hands me her car keys, a list of supplies, and walks off, leaving me to figure out what kind of car she has, where it is, and how to pay. I assume she's covered this while I was daydreaming. Good thing I have my license.

Thank God for Samantha. I put on her leash, and she leads me to Sara's car. I open the front door, but she stays put. I stand there clueless till she paws the back one. I open it, and she gets in. I'm about to get in the front when she barks softly and paws at a leather contraption. I realize it's a harness. Once I get it fastened, she sits quietly. At the store, the employees fuss over her; and, as Dignified Dog has an account, all I have to do is sign.

When I get to work the next day, Sara tells me Samantha liked our trip and hopes I'd take her out again. As I leave her office, she adds, "I know it's hard not to give Otis snacks; but I try to follow my client's wishes, if at all possible." How could she know that?

Two other people are employed at the Dog. Taylor is tall and handsome, although I later learn he's almost sixty. He has thick hair, but the brown is interrupted by streaks of gray around the temple. His brown eyes are intense, but he has a ready smile and laughs a lot. Every time I feel unsure of what to do, Taylor magically appears. He seems psychic. The dogs love him and treat him like alpha dog. If they're squabbling, all he needs to do is walk into the room, call the dogs' names, and they calm down.

I don't know how long I'd have remained ignorant of his status if Angie hadn't told me. He'd been Sara's significant other for almost ten years. Before moving to Tucson, he'd owned a small ranch near Sahuarita with his now ex-wife. When they divorced, she kept the ranch, and he moved to Tucson.

The other employee is nineteen year old Sam, who goes to community college. Sam has red hair, and he's long and lanky. He seems not used to his body size, often tripping over non-existent items. So far, he'd hardly said a word to me. I can't decide if he's shy or a jerk. Like everyone else around here, he works hard and is crazy about all the dogs.

My favorite job so far is assisting at obedience class. Sara offers group classes, but before a dog can join, he has to have six private lessons. The first group I watched was a shock. I expected classes to be segregated by size or breed or something.

Instead, the dogs are different as possible. Mutts and purebreds; young and old; big and small. Each a different breed. Gerti's taken the class twice before. Sissy has ribbons in her hair. Apple's a rescued greyhound, and Casey's a recently adopted Shepherd mix who seems insecure. Dusty, an eight-month-old golden retriever, bounces clumsily around the room and steals my heart. They all seem to get along.

Their people are as diverse as the dogs—-married couples; a few college-aged kids; an older woman who brings her two preteen daughters; and Dusty's owner, a man named Kelly about my age. He's almost as cute as his dog.

I love to watch Sara work with the dogs. No matter how stubborn they behave with their people, as soon as she takes the dog, it behaves impeccably. For now, my job during class is "go-fer"—-get treats, leads, and other supplies; hold dogs while their people go to the restroom. I fetch. Sara says as I learn more, I'll do more.

CHAPTER
TWENTY-FIVE

Since I have a job, Mom and I get along better. She enjoys hearing about the dogs, laughs when I describe the oddities of their people. After a week with Sara, I stop using the word "owner." Sara hates that word. She doesn't believe that people can own dogs any more than people can own people.

"Are you busy after work tomorrow?" Mom asks.

"I'm not sure," I answer, concerned what she has in mind.

"Tomorrow night's graduation. Three women met their weight-loss goals. We show 'before' pictures, and the women talk about their struggles, if they want. Past graduates and women in the program show up. Afterwards, we have vegetables and low-fat dip. It's inspiring."

"Why would I want to do that? Maybe if you served ice cream sundaes."

"Don't be ridiculous."

"You want me to feel bad because I'm overweight. You think if I listen to these women's stories, I'll be inspired."

"You're wrong, Kristin. I thought you might want to see something that's important to me. Think Thin is more than just a place I work. I believe in what we do. Everything in the world's not about you. And, if you became motivated, what's wrong with that?"

"Gee, Mom, I can see me in aerobics class talking to the other women. 'I never used to be overweight until I had the twins'; 'After Jack and I got together, we went out constantly for happy hour and dinner and, before I knew it, I'd gained 25 pounds'; 'I've been thin all my life until the freshman fifteen; how about you, Kristin?'"

"For me, it was the prison twenty-five. Like college, before you know it, you put on the pounds. It's hard to date, and there's not much else to do, so you eat. At least if I say I'm not a drug addict, they'll believe me. I'm too fat."

"Just because someone asks you a personal question, you don't have to tell them your whole life story. All you need to say is you stopped working out and gained weight. I'm not trying to give you a hard time; but if you want to meet someone, you need to shape up."

I say nothing. Do I want to meet someone? Sure. But who'd want to date a fat ex-con? I have friends who'd struggled to confess to new guys they had herpes or an abortion, but we'd never thought about how to tell a guy we'd been in prison, or on parole. And if someone looked twice at me? I still want Josh.

"I'd like to meet someone; but I'll do it my way. Let's take Sparkie for a walk and watch a movie?" I try to be conciliatory. "I stopped at Blockbuster, picked up Sleepless in Seattle."

"Okay. Sounds good."

. . . .

The following day, I'm in daycare, when Taylor approaches. "Sara wants you to sit in on her two o'clock consult. Sam can cover day-care. If you haven't seen her do one, you're in for a treat. She's amazing."

"Thanks, Taylor. Wouldn't miss it." I'd heard of Sara's ability to diagnose dogs' problems and want to see her in action.

A few minutes before two, I walk into Sara's office. "I'll greet the new client," she says. "Her name's Bunnie. Her person's name's Jane." She returns with a lively brown and white husky mix with beautiful blue eyes, accompanied by a pretty woman around forty with two kids. Sara introduces them to me. Spends a few moments petting and talking to Bunnie who stares at Sara with adoration.

"Tell me about Bunnie. How long you've had her, what's she like, who lives with her?"

"We've had her about five years. There's my husband, my children, and me ten and twelve," she points to the kids, who've been introduced as Tasha and Jared. "She's totally lovable and was house-trained when we got her. No problems at all until a month or so ago."

"What happened a month ago?" Sara asks.

"It's hard to explain. She seems sad. When my husband came home from work, she'd run over to him and act excited to see him the way dogs do. Same with when the kids came home from school. Now, if she's outside and someone comes home, sometimes she doesn't even come in. If she's in the house she'll stay in her bed and ignore us. If she were a person, I'd say she was depressed."

"Is her behavior the same with all of you?"

"Except maybe me but I feed her."

"Is she eating and pooping like always?"

"Yes, she still gets excited about eating, and no problems pooping."

"Any changes in your lives, your routine?" Sara continues.

"Not really. Everything's the same," Jane replies.

Sara turns her gaze from the family to Bunnie. "You sad, Bunnie?" she asks. Bunnie tilts her head and stares at Sara.

"Are you sure there's no change in Bunnie's environment or routine . . . even something small?"

"Mom, she changed when you got the new couches in the den," says Jared. "The ugly ones you won't let Bunnie sit on. You don't even want us on them most of the time."

"They're not ugly. You're right that's when she changed. You saw what she did to the old ones."

"Jane," Sara interrupts. "How often did Bunnie sit on those old couches?"

"Whenever someone was in the den, and that's where the TV is, so someone's usually in there."

I notice Bunnie alerts at the word "couches." Sara again speaks to Bunnie. "Bunnie, you feel excluded from your family?" This time, Bunnie, who'd been silent till then, gives a soft bark. Sara turns to Jane.

"You got your answer. It's one thing to keep dogs off furniture from the beginning. But when you suddenly change the setup, they get confused or, as you said, sad. She feels less part of the family . . . thinks she did something wrong, that you're punishing her by keeping her off the couches. Even though it's different furniture, she used to be able to sit there."

"My husband's kind of a clean freak, and Bunnie makes a mess shedding and drooling," says Jane defensively. "He used to get irritated every time he'd sit down and see how terrible the furniture looked. The last straw was when we had his family over to watch a basketball game, and his mom's white pants got full of hair and dirt."

"Grandma doesn't like dogs. She's always blaming Bunnie for something."

"I'm not saying you're wrong about what you're trying to do. I'm just saying it's tough on Bunnie. Don't worry, I have some suggestions."

Before Sara can continue, the girl looks at her mom and moans, "I have to go to the bathroom."

Sara shows Jane and her kids where to go, and turns to me. "I assumed we'd have a chance to talk earlier, but I got tied up talking with Samantha. Before you go to obedience class today, I wanted to let you know Dusty's person, Kelly, likes you."

"But how do you know, and what do you mean?"

"I think I was clear. I don't mean to interfere in your personal life. I wanted to tell you so if you like him, you can help him out. He's shy. If you're not interested, you can make sure he knows that too. That's all I have to say," she says, as Bunnie's family returns, "other than I think he's a decent guy."

I try to listen to the rest of the consult. Sara says something about getting furniture covers or a special pillow for Bunnie and putting it in the same room as the couches. She tells them they should go out of their way to treat Bunnie special. At the end of the consult she spend some time alone with Bunnie. Tells her she didn't do anything wrong and everyone still loves her. Bunnie looks like she understands.

I want to learn, but my thoughts keep going back to what Sara said. A man, a man Sara thinks is decent, is interested in me. I can barely remember what he looks like; but I remember his golden retriever puppy. My hair's a mess. My pants are full of dried slobber. Calm down I tell myself. You don't even know him.

TWENTY-SIX

Starbucks again. Angie and I meet Saturday mornings. She's tells me about a story she's working on. "Ten men have been charged in Tucson Federal Court with being Irish terrorists. Sending explosives to the IRA in Belfast. The case was transferred from New York District Court. The defense attorneys believe it was moved because there's a smaller Irish community here. Less support for the accused. I didn't even know they could transfer cases. I've got lots to learn."

"Aren't you in Lifestyles?"

" I though I told you. I got transferred to crime beat. This is my first big story. I want to make sure everything's right."

I try to listen patiently—-God knows, she's listened to me. It's hard to keep quiet. I'm brimming over with my news. I'm also hungry, and her cranberry muffin doesn't help. Today's the third day of my new diet. I order my usual soy latte but minus the scone.

Finally she winds down. "So, what's up? Did you see your parole officer this week?"

"Yeah, it went well. Seemed pleased I have a job and I'm clean, but he won't let me move out. Says I don't have enough money saved, and it's too soon."

"I know you want to be independent. It must be tough, but it has to be a hell of a lot better than prison. Your mom's a great cook."

"She is. But she's into making these healthy meals, all lean protein and veggies. I want biscuits, desserts, those au gratin potatoes she used to make. Art loves 'em. She's harps on me constantly about my weight."

"Speaking of weight, I notice you didn't order a scone. Is that significant?"

"I guess. I started another new diet a few days ago, but it's so tough. I think about food all the time, and everywhere you look, temptation." My eyes are drawn to the other tables where people eat scones, muffins, coffee-cake and drinks topped with whipped cream and sprinkles. "I don't want Mom to know. She's too crazed. The combination of her being proud of me and nagging me to join Think Thin will sabotage the whole thing."

"Your secret's safe with me. Are you still hot for your PO . . . what's his name?"

"Remy Cooper, not anymore. He's gorgeous, but I've met someone I have a chance with. Cooper sees me as just another parolee. He'd never date me."

"Kristin, I can't believe you haven't told me. Where'd you meet him? What's he like? Tell all." Angie crams a third of the muffin in her mouth. I'd eat tiny pieces, savor each bite, make it last.

"It's barely started. Between work, community service and life, I'm busy. I wanted to tell you in person. You're the only one I'm telling. I'm afraid it won't last, or maybe I should say I'm afraid it won't start."

"You still haven't answered my question. Who is he? Where'd you meet him?"

"His name's Kelly Mordelli. I met him at work. He's got a golden retriever puppy, Dusty, who takes Sara's obedience class. I thought she might've told you——she's the one who told me he was interested."

"She never said a word, and wouldn't. She doesn't gossip, particularly about employees. I had dinner with her the other night. She never mentioned your name."

"Glad to hear it. She's terrific, but I'd feel creepy if she talked behind my back even good stuff. Anyway, Kelly's thirty, sexy, dark wavy hair, dark eyes, reminds me of Al Pacino. Works at Superior Court in the IT department. I'm not sure about Kelly, but the dog's crazy about me. Anyway, yesterday, Kelly and I went for a walk in the park after class and for coffee. Tonight's our first real date——dinner and a movie."

"Wow, can't believe you didn't call me. What do you mean Sara told you he was interested? Before you explain, I need more coffee." Angie walks towards the counter. It didn't take her long, thank goodness.

I keep on as if she hadn't left. "I was sitting in on a consult. The family left the room to use the bathroom. She blurts out Kelly's interested in me. She called him Dusty's person. Her psychic vibe, I guess. The only other thing she said was he's decent."

"Aunt Sara's a trip. I wish I knew if there was any truth in any of it. My mom thinks it's a bunch of shit. They're not close," She laughs. "I don't know what to think. She's told me stuff about people she couldn't know, and later I find out it's true. Warned me off a friend who turned out to be bad news. I've heard similar stories from other people. Helped my sister find a lost ring. She's always been my favorite aunt. Whether or not she's psychic, she's a good judge of character."

"I'm glad she's okay with me."

"How can you keep Kelly a secret if you're going on a date tonight? Won't your mom find out when he picks you up?"

"No, she's going out. I told her I was going to dinner and a movie with people from work. I don't wanna tell her until there's something to tell. She'll make a big deal out of it like she does with weight. Have me married off next week, or else she'll disapprove. You know how much she hates Josh."

"I know she never gave him a fair chance, but it's hard to like him after what he did." I don't reply and, for a few rare moments our table's silent. Then Angie asks, "Any reason you're worried you and Kelly won't go anywhere?"

"Maybe you're psychic. Kelly doesn't know about me. I'd have to tell any guy at some point but, with most guys, I could wait and see how things go. I'm worried Kelly could look at my court records. Maybe he checks out everyone he dates. I don't want him to find out before I tell him. On the other hand, I'm afraid if I tell him, either I'll scare him away, or he'll think I'm getting serious too fast. You don't usually tell secrets on your first date."

"I never thought about that. Art knows all my secrets. You're right, though; it's better if he hears it from you, but I wouldn't think he checks out his dates. Wouldn't that be illegal?"

"I don't know. Convictions must be public record because employers get them. I hope it's unethical, but privacy and ethics don't seem to mean as much as they used to," I sigh. "What's wrong with me? My first date in over two years. I should be worried about what I'm going to wear, not the big picture."

"Wear something sexy, flirt all night, and blurt it out at dinner, 'By the way, I was in prison for something I didn't do, and I'm still on parole; but I really don't want to talk about it.' How 'bout that? It'll make you seem mysterious." Angie grins at me and runs her fingers through her hair.

"Sounds great, but I couldn't pull it off. I don't feel very sexy with these extra pounds." I'm not a flirt. You know that. You really think I should tell him tonight?"

"Hard to say. Why don't you see how the evening goes and play it by ear? Any guy who's worth it would like you. You look fine. You're not fat. Your mom's made you paranoid. She thinks if you don't look anorexic, you're fat."

"Thanks, Angie. I wish people could see me through your eyes. Got to go, though. I'm doing as much community service as I can to impress Cooper."

"Where do you do it?"

"Cooper gave me a list of places like the Food Bank, Humane Society, Parks and Rec. I'm doing it at The Muscular Dystrophy Foundation 'cause it's near my house and they treat me decent."

"I tried the Salvation Army first, but the supervisor watched me every second like I was gonna steal something. Could she seriously think I'd want the clothes they collect? I had to sort them, and some of the clothes were gross like the stuff they gave us at jail. At MD, they let me type and file and treat me like I'm a normal person.

TWENTY-SEVEN

Kelly's exactly on time. Even though Mom isn't home, I hurry outside when he knocks. He gestures to his car, a small blue one—-Honda, I think. Cars aren't my thing. He holds the door open for me. We've hardly said a word. Kelly dressed up. He's wearing a blue polo shirt and a pair of khaki Dockers. He turns, smiles at me and says, "You look really good."

"Thank you," I say, trying to hold back all the 'buts.' I don't look bad for a fat girl. This old outfit? Is that what you say to all your dates? I'd tried on half the clothes I own before I settle on a pair of old black pants and a short-sleeved black tunic. The combination makes me look thinner. I add silver jewelry and debate on a scarf when he arrives. I go without it. Unlike Mom, I never can figure out what to do with them.

"You like Mexican food? If you do, we can go to Maria's. I've eaten there for years. The food's great, and there's tons of it. I always overeat."

"Sure, that would be fine." Terrific- food by the bucket. I'd eaten there before and know they have salads, so I can stay on my diet if I want. Josh and I never ate there, so no memories.

Dinner goes well. I order a salad, but almost don't because I'm afraid Kelly will think I'm on a diet. I don't want him to, but I'm not sure why. If I order a big plate of food, he might think I'm a pig. I don't want that either. He probably doesn't even notice what I eat. We talk about our jobs and dogs. I relax even enjoy myself. Kelly suggests Jurassic Park, a film I want to see. Good signs—suggests, not decides and similar taste.

After the movie, we go for coffee. I'm pleased he's a Starbuck's fan and prefers a coffee house to a bar. Kelly asks me questions about growing up, and what I like to do. I could mention my prison days, but I can answer his questions truthfully without going there. Already I knew it'd be hard to tell him. I like the way he asks questions about me instead of talking about himself. The insane magnetism I'd had (have) for Josh is missing, but I sense Kelly and I are alike in fundamental ways, and that our relationship has a chance. I don't want it to end now.

On the way back to the house, Kelly's quiet. Was I worried for nothing because he'll never ask me out again?

"I had, um, a great time tonight. Unfortunately, I'm going to a conference in Houston on Tuesday and won't be back till late Friday. I'm going to miss class—-I already told Sara. Um, what I mean is, can we get together again next Saturday?"

"I'd like that. We'll miss you and Dusty. What do you do with him when you go away?"

"My roommate, Justin. He loves Dusty. Has no problem taking care of him when I leave."

"That's great. I'm sure you'd hate to put him in a kennel." A casual remark, but an answer that would haunt me.

"I left him at a kennel once. When I got him back, he didn't seem okay. I took him to our vet. She said he had an infection, possibly because of neglect at the kennel. I went back there to complain, but the place was out of business. I read in the paper the owner was a meth dealer. He's in prison now."

"Oh, that's horrible," I say, feeling sick inside.

"I'm sure you know addicts are responsible for a huge percentage of crime in this country," he says as he walks me to the door. "If it were up to me, they'd all be locked up."

I smile at him like he said something smart or at least something I agree with. What's worse? Being gutless, a hypocrite, or desperate for a man's approval? I'm all three.

It's after one. Shit I planned on being home before Mom. She and her friends usually gab half the night. Hoping against hope she's in bed or at least in pajamas and won't come to the door, I say good night to Kelly. I jump out before he has a chance to kiss me. I want him to, but if he doesn't try . . .

Mom doesn't come to the door, but she's looking out the window. Sees Kelly drive away. Can I bluff my way out of this?

"Something you want to tell me?" Mom asks, her facial expression unreadable.

"Not really. Did you have a good time?" I ask her.

"At first, until I went to see Jurassic Park, and guess who's sitting a couple rows in front of me with her date?"

"I guess you're mad I didn't tell you I had a date."

"I guess I am. It's not just that you didn't tell me—-you lied to me. Why? Something about this guy I wouldn't like? Did you meet him at the parole office?"

"Don't be ridiculous, Mom. I met him at work. He brings his dog to obedience class. He has a good job at the courts working on computers. Sara likes him."

"So your boss knew before your mom?"

"Stop overreacting; she doesn't know we went on a date."

"If he's such a great guy, why'd you lie about where you were going, and make sure I wouldn't be here when he picked you up? Are you ashamed of me?"

"Of course not. It's hard to explain. This was our first date and I didn't know if he would like me or not. I didn't want you to keep nagging me—- make a big deal, like you do about my weight."

Instead of answering, Louise takes a deep breath and tries to understand Kristin's side. She doesn't want to start a fight she'll regret later. Kristin's an adult. There's nothing wrong with her going out as long as it's not Josh. But she didn't need to lie. Let it go, at least for tonight. "I'd appreciate if you'd be honest in the future. I'll try not to pry into your business so much. He seems like a nice young man, from what I saw. If you like him, I hope it works out. See you in the morning."

That's it? No third degree? No remarks about my bad judgment, Josh, or how I'd better start to diet or it won't work? What's got into her?

TWENTY-EIGHT

Samantha and I give our shopping list to the clerk. While we wait, I take her outside for a romp in the grassy area behind the store. Out of nowhere, a little girl runs full speed toward Samantha yelling, "Big Doggy," followed by a woman (I assume is Mom) trying to stop her. Before I can scream, "The dog's okay," the kid grabs Samantha and hugs her. To her delight, Samantha sits and gives her several slobbery kisses. "Mommy, doggie kiss. Sticky face."

"Emily, get away from there. You can't touch strange dogs. They'll bite you, and you'll have to get rabies shots." At the word "shots," the girl lets go of Samantha and frowns.

"She won't hurt your daughter," I say almost angrily. Samantha puts out her paw for a shake, but the girl doesn't take it.

"That's not the point. I'm trying to teach her something." Yeah, to be scared of dogs.

I smile at the little girl. "My dog likes you." As we walk back to the store, I feel the mom glare at me.

My order's ready. A different clerk follows me out with the stuff. I'd noticed him last time due to the combination of his large biceps and strange accent. Maybe Australian. "New haircut?" he asks, as he looks me over not so subtly.

"No."

"Something's different. A good different."

"Nothing's different." I've lost five pounds. Not even Mom noticed. Right now, I crave a chocolate chip cookie or several.

"You gonna be picking up the order every week?"

"I think so."

"Great. My name's Nick. Sure you didn't get a haircut?"

"No haircut," I answer, wish I could say something clever.

I put Samantha in the car, buckle her up and get in. He's still looking at me. I smile but say nothing as I drive away.

"Samantha, he was flirting with me." She looks up and gives me a big grin. (If you don't think dogs can grin, you don't know as much about dogs as you thought.) "We deserve a treat. How about McDonald's? I'll get a drink, and I'll get you a cheeseburger." Normally, a treat for me would be a Big Mac, large fries and a coke. Suddenly, my diet seems easier.

As I drive back to work, I worry Sara will be angry. She wouldn't eat at McDonalds. Maybe she wouldn't want me to feed Samantha there. The hardest part of working for someone like her is feeling she knows everything you do. And if she doesn't, would Samantha tell?

Soon as we get back, I 'fess up. "I hope you don't mind, but I stopped at McDonald's——bought Samantha a cheeseburger. I should've asked before I fed her, but I thought she deserved a treat."

"You worry too much, Kristin. It's delightful you and Samantha get along. I've been meaning to tell you I'm very pleased with your work. Why don't you take the rest of the afternoon off? You've earned it and probably have a lot to do."

"Are you sure?" I ask. "I don't need to leave early."

"Of course I'm sure, go."

What did she mean "a lot to do"? It's like she knows I'm cooking dinner for Kelly for the first time. No time to wonder. I want the meal to be perfect. His roommate, Justin's, going to be there too. From everything Kelly's said, his mom's a great cook. She doesn't do Mexican, so I make tacos. Everyone likes tacos. They're easy to make, but I need to stop at the store. Like most men, all they have in the kitchen are drinks, cereal, and snacks.

I'd cooked tacos hundreds of times, but worry I'll screw them up. It's been a long time since I cooked for anyone. Like all my experiences with Kelly, everything works out. The food's good. The three of us get along.

Dusty's in retriever heaven, running from one to another, as each of us surreptitiously feed him taco meat.

Shortly after dinner—-as if by prior plan—-Justin takes off. Kelly and I do the dishes, and afterwards he puts on some music. "Eric Clapton okay?"

"Terrific," similar tastes again. We make small talk until he blurts out, "Kristin, would you like to go to a wedding with me? My cousin, Al, is getting married in LA, May 31. I don't want to go, but my family's pushing it. If you go, it'd be fun. There's a rehearsal dinner Friday night. If you could take Friday off, we could fly over with my family. If that wouldn't work, we could miss the dinner and go Saturday. We can stay at the hotel the wedding's at—-I can't remember the name of it."

"I'd love to go. A day off shouldn't be a problem. You'll have to meet my mom, though. It's absurd for someone my age to need permission to go on a trip, but since I live with her, she'll raise a fuss if she doesn't know you."

"No problem, I'd like to meet her. You're so mysterious about everything, I wasn't sure I'd get the chance." If only Mom was my biggest secret.

I can't wait to tell Angie but I settle for mom. "Kelly invited me to his cousin's wedding in LA. I know you'll want to meet him before you're okay with me going, so I'm inviting him for dinner next weekend."

"I'd be delighted to meet him, but have you talked to your parole officer?"

"Why should I talk to him about inviting Kelly for dinner?"

"Don't be ridiculous. Not dinner, the wedding. You have to get his permission to go out of state. It's one of your parole conditions."

"Oh, God, what am I going to do? This is gonna ruin everything."

"Calm down. What's the problem? You've got a job, you're clean, I won't object. I doubt Mr. Cooper will. Just make an appointment with him."

"You don't understand. Kelly has to get airline tickets in the next few days. They're nonrefundable, and I probably won't see Mr. Cooper before he has to buy them. He's out of town for two weeks."

"Call the parole office tomorrow and find out if you can see someone else. I'm sure Mr. Cooper has a supervisor or a coworker who can give you permission."

Maybe she's right but I obsess all night. Should I tell Kelly the truth, or let him buy the tickets and hope it works out? I picture Kelly explaining to his family he can't buy tickets till his girlfriend checks with her parole officer. If mom wasn't involved, I'd just go. How would Mr. Cooper find out? I hate Josh, at least tonight.

TWENTY-NINE

"State Parole. Please listen carefully as our menu has changed. Press 1 for directions and hours. Press 2 for drug-test results. Press 3 to check your appointment time or schedule an appointment. Press 4 for the operator. If you know your party's extension, you may press 1 plus the number at any time."

"Shit, I guess 3."

"Scheduling, may I help you?"

"I'd like to make an appointment with PO Remy Cooper as soon as possible."

"Mr. Cooper's on vacation until a week from Monday."

"Can I see someone else? He must have a supervisor or something . . . it's urgent."

"I don't have the authority to schedule you with his supervisor. If you like, I'll transfer you."

"Yeah . . . okay." Oh my God. They hung up on me. Oh, shit, what was that number again?

"State Parole. Please listen carefully because our menu has changed. Press 1 for directions and hours. Press 2 for drug-test results. Press 3 to check your appointment time or schedule an appointment. Press 4 for the operator. If you . . .

"I'll try 4."

"Operator, may I help you?"

"I was trying to schedule an appointment with my PO, and they hung up on me."

"I'll transfer you to scheduling."

"Wait. Please. My PO is out of town, and I was trying to reach his supervisor. The scheduling person said he didn't have the authority to transfer me, so he was transferring me to someone else."

"Whom were they transferring you to?"

"I don't know—-I got disconnected."

"Well, which PO did you want to see?"

"Mr. Cooper."

"We have two Mr. Coopers . . . which one?"

"Remy Cooper." I don't believe this. Idiots. I'm gonna be late for work.

"Okay. I'll transfer you."

"Supervisor McKane's office. Can I help you?"

"Yes, thank you. I need an appointment to see Mr. McKane. Right a way. My PO's out of town. I need approval to go on a trip."

"You can't wait till Mr. Cooper gets back?"

"If I wait, it'll be too late."

"He has Wednesday at three o'clock open, but there's no guarantee he'll approve your trip. What's your name?"

"Kristin White. I'll take it. Thanks."

"Be on time, Kristin. He's busy that day, and gets irritated when people are late."

Wednesday three o'clock. Shit. I won't be able to take Samantha to pick up supplies. No Nick. I'll have to ask for time off to see the guy and Friday for the wedding. Better ask one at a time.

Soon as I get to work, I tell Sara I have an appointment to see my PO Wednesday afternoon. Ask if I can take part of the afternoon off. She looks at me strangely, but says, "No problem, but I know Samantha will miss going out with you."

I'm working daycare. No new clients today, and the dogs are doing fine—-only the usual spilled water and fights over toys. Twice, I catch Bubbles in the employees' bathroom drinking toilet water. Midmorning, the phone rings. "Hello, can I speak to someone about a dog issue?" a woman says, sounding breathless and worried.

I look at the employee board. Sara's in a consult, Taylor's doing a dog class, and Sam isn't working this morning. "I'm the only one available. I can take your number and have someone call you back."

"You work there, don't you?" Without waiting for an answer, she begins speaking rapidly. "This morning, I was out walking my Ginger, she's an AKC registered Poodle, on a leash, of course, and a coyote comes out of nowhere and bites her on her rear end. We have lots of coyotes in the neighborhood, but nothing like this ever happened before. What should I do?"

"Do you know a vet to call?"

"I don't need a vet. The physical injury is minor; it's her emotional state I'm worried about. She's terrified. I am too. I don't know anything about coyotes. What if it had rabies?"

"I'm sorry, I don't know much either. I've heard of them attacking dogs before, but I don't know how you tell if they're rabid. You should check with your vet about the bite and ask about rabies. I assume Ginger's had her rabies shot. Sara, the owner here, can help you with the rest. She knows how to handle terrified dogs. I can have her call you when she's free, which shouldn't be too long."

"She's had her rabies shot, but I'll call the vet. I guess I can wait, but I'm so worried. I hate the thought of Ginger being scared. She's usually such a happy dog."

"Stay close to her. Pet her and talk to her." I try to help in some way. "Give me your name and phone number, and I promise she'll get back to you soon."

On my way back to daycare, I eye a candy dish full of M and M's. I'm nervous about seeing a different person at the Parole Office. Worried about whether I'll get the travel permit. My snacking is way down, but today every candy dish glows like a bright neon sign that reads, "Kristin, come here . . . umm, umm, good." I walk away.

Kelly's the high point of my days, but it's hard to talk about the wedding, pretend to be enthusiastic when I know I may not get to go or worse we could break up. Part of me wants to see him as much as I can, but part wants me to stay away from him until I find out about my travel permit.

As if the thoughts of Kelly conjure him up, the intercom buzzes. "Kristin, call, line two."

Should I pick up? I know it's him——he usually calls around this time. "This is Kristin."

"Hi, it's me. Have you asked your boss for Friday off yet? My parents are ecstatic I'm going, and they credit you. Can't wait to meet you. They want you to come for dinner Friday night."

"Dinner Friday night, uh, sure, that'd be good. I didn't ask Sara because I have another problem. I have to take Wednesday afternoon off because I have an appointment, and I couldn't ask her for two days at once. I haven't worked here long. I'll ask soon, I promise."

"What appointment?" he asks.

I don't know what to say. No way could I tell the truth. I have no choice other than to lie, but the lie comes too easily. "I have a doctor's appointment."

"You okay, Kristin? You're not sick or anything?"

"No, nothing like that, just routine."

"Good. I gotta go. One of the judges is having trouble with her computer. They expect you to drop everything and help them."

"Wait. I forgot. Mom wants me to invite you for dinner Sunday night."

"Terrific. I'll see you Friday; pick you up say six o'clock? Give you enough time to get ready?"

"Perfect. See you then."

I hang up feel like shit. What if Kelly mentions my doctor's appointment in front of Mom? What if Mom mentions my PO in front of Kelly? Why is everything so fucking complicated?

The next few days pass quickly. It seems like every coyote in Tucson attacks someone's dog. Sara's swamped with new clients and their frightened people. My job's to research coyotes.

"I can't communicate with coyotes. My abilities don't extend to wild animals."

I'm surprised to find out coyotes can live almost anywhere. Relieved to know they're timid, rarely attacking humans. You can frighten them off with a loud noise or a rock. They only get aggressive to protect their territory or their cubs, or if they have rabies. Strangely, if they're protecting their territory, they attack bigger dogs rather than smaller ones because a bigger dog's a bigger threat. Lucky for the dog, the attack is often a bite on the butt, not an attempt to kill.

. . . .

Finally, time to see the guy at Parole. By now, I know the routine. Check in at the front desk and scan the room for a seat. I find one next to a well-dressed woman about my age. I barely notice the gangbangers.

I'd forgotten to bring a book, so I grab a magazine. Article after article about dieting. Is Mom stalking me? I try to read, but all I think about is a man I don't know, who doesn't know me, can ruin my life. My stomach's in knots. Ten long minutes later, my name's called, and I'm directed to McKane's office.

"I'm Unit Supervisor Jack McKane, Mr. Cooper's boss. I'm told you urgently need an appointment. What couldn't wait?" He motions me to sit. His desk's bare except for three pens in a row and a couple of folders neatly stacked. His perfectly ironed shirt and creased pants add to my impression that he's an anal by-the-book guy. It doesn't bode well.

"I need a travel permit, and I can't wait till Mr. Cooper gets back."

"Where and when do you want to go?"

"My boyfriend's cousin's getting married in LA on May 31. I want to go on the 30 and come back June 1. I'd be traveling with my boyfriend and his family. I'm on release to my mom, and she's fine with it."

"Today's May 7th. You're supposed to request a permit thirty days in advance." Oh, my God, he's not gonna let me go.

"I couldn't. He asked me to go over the weekend. I called immediately. Look at my file. My drug tests are all clean. I've never missed an appointment. I'm employed, and the job's going well. You could call my boss and check."

"I'm sorry, Ms. White. I looked at your file. You seem to be doing well; but rules are rules. You were given a copy the first time you met Mr. Cooper. You signed them."

"But that's so unfair. It's not like I'm going to a concert. It's a family wedding." Can he hear the desperation in my voice?

"It's not about where you're going. I can't change the rules for you, or I'd have to do it for everyone."

The jerk's enjoying this. Reminds me of the guards who loved to write you up for nothing. Same smirky expression on his face.

I don't cry or yell profanities. Won't give the asshole the satisfaction. Why did Mr. Cooper have to be on vacation? He'd let me go. This idiot's ruining my life over a technicality.

What if I lied to Mom and told her he said okay? Hmmm. But I'd have to lie to Sara too. Never work. Way too risky.

I should go back to work, but I can't pretend everything's fine. I drive to Starbuck's—-diet be damned. I'll start with a latte, add whip cream and vanilla syrup. A maple scone. Maybe two.

CHAPTER

THIRTY

For the first time someone's late to pick up their dog. Any other day it wouldn't matter, but Kelly's picking me up at six. What kind of idiot's late to pick up their dog? How could she have no consideration for anyone but herself? Daycare closes at five. Can't the bitch tell time? Baxter, a neurotic mini-dachshund, picks up on my mood and paces around the room.

Finally, I see her Lexus SUV pull in. Lori leaves the car running and walks briskly into the room. Before I can say a word, she begins to apologize. "Sorry for holding you up. It's inexcusable. I'd be angry if someone did this to me. I have no good excuse. There was an emergency at work, so I left a few minutes late, and got stuck at Grant and Campbell in a traffic jam. There was a bad accident . . . terrible corner."

She grabs Baxter, who'd stopped pacing and was jumping up and down wagging his tail. As she walks toward the door, she opens her wallet and hands me a twenty-dollar bill. "Tell Sara to add the late fee to my bill. This is for you."

"I can't take this," I say, as I try to hand the bill back.

"I insist. You don't want to upset a customer," she adds, as she closes the door and gets back into her car.

I close up, get into my car, and see that it's only five-fifteen. I feel stupid for getting upset, confused about the money. I'll worry later. I have to get

129

home—-fast—-and change before Kelly gets there. Which is worse: Mom being alone with Kelly, or my being late to the first dinner with his family?

I shower quickly, put on make-up, and fix my hair. I'd asked Kelly if I needed to dress up, he laughed, "Of course not, it's a family dinner."

Shit, shit, shit. Kelly's here. I put on a pair of long shorts, but the shirt I like to wear is dirty. I've gained back the five pounds. I try a sundress Mom bought, but I look like the Goodyear Blimp. Thank God for black pants. I grab a pair and add a long black V-neck knit shirt. It'll have to do. Earrings, a bracelet, ready.

"Hi, Kelly. I see you and Mom have introduced yourselves. Sorry I wasn't ready, but a lady was late picking up her dog."

"No problem. It's not like we're on a tight schedule. We should probably leave, though. I promised Mom I'd pick up some wine."

"We'll have all evening to talk on Sunday, huh, Mom?" I smile at her; glad she hasn't trashed my clothes. "I won't be late."

"Bye, Mrs. White. Nice meeting you. I look forward to Sunday. I hear you're a great cook."

"Have a good time," Mom says. We're off . . .

On the way to the Wine Barn, Kelly tells me about the new computer system they're using at the courthouse. I'm interested, but it's hard to follow. Kelly's still explaining as we walk through the store. He knows what he's looking for, as he confidently navigates the rows and rows of red wine and grabs two bottles. We go to the shortest cashier line and wait. Kelly finally finishes. Usually, he gets me to talk, but I love his passion for his work.

"Kris, how are you? What's up?" Startled, I look toward the voice. Scott's in front of us. Oh, my God! What if he says something about prison?

"Hi, Scott," I say in as unfriendly a tone as I can. I hope he thinks I'm sour grapes about our relationship and leaves me alone.

To my surprise and dismay, Kelly sticks his hand out toward Scott, "Hi, you're Scott Downing? I'm one of the courts IT guys. I met you at the meeting about the new court computer system."

"Sorry, I didn't recognize you," Scott answers. Of course you don't recognize him. He's only an IT guy, and you're a lawyer."

"No problem. There were lots of people there."

"What kind of wine is that?" Scott asks. What a jerk! Who cares?

"Oh, just some Chianti my mom likes. We're having company for dinner," he said, as he smiles proudly at me. I can't mess this up; he's so great. He's proud of having me over for dinner.

"Chianti . . . I guess it could be a good dinner wine if you're eating spaghetti. I got an 1990 Chateau Margaux . . . won several prizes for best red that year. Of course, it's pricey."

"I don't know much about wine myself. I'll have to get Kristin to teach me."

"Afraid that's not my thing either," I say.

"You two an item? Congratulations, Kelly; she's a great gal." Right asshole. I'm such a 'great gal' you dumped me.

"Nice seeing you, Scott. Kelly and I have to get going."

I'm fuming. When had Scott gotten to be such a wine snob? Great gal my ass. Now I'll have to tell Kelly about us. At least he didn't mention prison. Kelly and I hadn't talked much about our past relationships beyond telling the other we'd never been married, didn't have children or STD's. I assumed Kelly had been in relationships before, and I was sure he assumed the same for me; but having him meet someone from my past is different.

"Scott's become a major jerk. I hate that wine snob attitude."

"Well, I'm no wine aficionado myself. I gather, you had a relationship, or he wished you had?"

Scott as my rejected lover sounds attractive. It would be easier to explain. I'd told too many lies to Kelly, so I tell him the truth—-at least most of it. "Scott and I had a relationship when I was in college and he was in law school, but it was over more than three years ago."

"What happened?"

"We decided to go our separate ways. Different values. What's for dinner?"

"Kristin, you're so secretive. Is there some reason you don't want me to know what happened between you two?"

"No, it's not like that. It's just that the past is the past. Go ahead ask me anything about Scott . . . I'll tell you."

Kelly says nothing. Our first argument. I'm not sure what to say, but he's right. I want to hide my past. "Look, Kelly, we can talk after dinner. I wouldn't feel comfortable going in there with us fighting. Please, let it go till later," I say, tears roll down my face.

Kelly stops the car and puts his arm around me. "It's okay, Kristin. I care about you; but I get the feeling sometimes that our relationship isn't that big a deal to you—-that there's something or someone more important."

"No, Kelly, no. I care about you. There's no one else. I haven't been involved with anyone for almost two years. You mean a lot to me." (How stupid does that sound.)

"Good. No reason for tears then. Let's go in. Mom's dying to meet you. I haven't brought anyone home for a long time."

Dinner goes great. Kelly's parents and sisters and brothers are warm and friendly. It's easy to feel part of this large, noisy group. Kelly's mom cooked a feast: antipasto, lasagna, meatballs, ravioli, bread and gnocchi. For dessert, she made a luscious lemon cake, brownies and cappuccino. Living in this family, I'd weigh a ton.

Kelly's mom's attractive, with shiny brown hair, plump; but, unlike Mom, seemingly unconcerned. She's dressed casually in a knee-length denim skirt and flowered blouse. His dad's tall, with distinguished gray hair and a small potbelly. He wore shorts and a Diamondbacks t-shirt.

Dinner conversation ranges from politics to sports to movies. Clinton's the family choice for President; they follow the Arizona Wildcats, like everyone else in town; and the latest movie they'd all seen was Sleepless in Seattle. Everyone talked over each other. I mostly listen, until Mrs. Mordelli talks about the wedding. "We're so delighted you've agreed to go to Al's wedding. The whole family will be there, and we hated having Kelly miss it."

"Glad I could be useful," I say, feeling like a fraud and liar again.

"No one ever thought Al would tie the knot. He switched girlfriends more often than I change underwear," Mr. Mordelli says laughing.

"He's not kidding about that underwear," one of the siblings says looking at me.

They all laugh, and the wedding isn't brought up again. Every few minutes, someone asks me a question, but nothing too personal.

By the time we leave, it's almost ten. I'd eaten too much. I should've felt good about fitting in, but all I can focus on is how much I'm going to lose if I mess this up.

I expect Kelly to grill me about Scott, but he doesn't. I think about letting it go, but I know Kelly wants to know. The only hard part's telling how it ended. "Toward the end of Scott's second year of law school, everything in my life seemed stagnant. I hated my job. My friends, Art and Angie, would tease us about getting married, and Scott would joke his way out of it. I don't think I was in love with him, but I wanted life to change. I gave him an ultimatum about getting married, and he said 'no'. That was the end of it."

Kelly looks at me quizzically for a moment, and smiles. "Guy's a moron, if you ask me."

"That's your reaction?"

"What did you expect? Relationships don't always work. People move at different speeds sometimes. Thanks for telling me. I know it wasn't easy."

One family dinner down, one to go.

Any other time, I'd be a wreck about bringing a boyfriend over to meet my inquisitive, judgmental mother. I can hear her blurt out, "When she got out of prison . . ."

But all I think about is when I have to tell Kelly I can't go—-and worse—-what I'll say when he asks why. I should have lied to Mom, worried about the consequences later. We could have skipped the rehearsal dinner, gone Saturday and then I wouldn't have had to tell Sara. I could have told Kelly someone else had the day off or something. Never would have worked.

Sunday evening, Kelly arrives on time dressed in a short-sleeved striped collared shirt and slacks. He treats Mom like she's special, acts interested in Think Thin, and eats multiple helpings of her oven-fried chicken, scalloped potatoes and biscuits. Mom is charmed.

She's on her best behavior in return. Doesn't blurt out a word about prison or ex-boyfriends. Doesn't even comment when I eat two helpings of potatoes and two biscuits. (Any more family meals, and I'll be back to prison size.) Sparkie and Kelly get along great too, but that's not surprising, as Kelly feeds him under the table.

I'm glad Kelly has to leave early. I don't want to be alone with him.

THIRTY-ONE

I wake up Monday with a sense of dread. Mom misreads my mood. She's excited and asks a million questions about Kelly, "What does his father do? Does his mother work? How many brothers and sisters does he have? What's their house like?" First time she's shown enthusiasm for a boyfriend of mine since Scott. I get swept up in her fantasy, share details. I mention Scott, how he acted at the Wine Barn. She doesn't defend him even agrees when I criticize him. I hear her think, "Maybe's there's hope for my daughter after all."

My fantasyland conversation with Mom takes too much time. I'm late for the monthly staff meeting. I arrive, mouth an apology and sit down.

The meeting begins with a discussion of client numbers and problems with specific dogs or their people. Sam's concerned Max never socializes with other dogs, spends all day in the same chair. Usually, I'm quiet; but I bring up Lori and the twenty dollar tip. "Since this is the first time, we'll let it go," Sara replies. "She's a longtime customer. As for the tip, people have gotten them before, but rarely so large."

"Why don't we put the tips together and split them each month?" I suggest.

"Lovely idea, Kristin. The split would be you and Sam. That okay with you, Sam?" Sara asks.

"Of course. Who'd complain about that? Thanks, Kristin," Sam says, acknowledging me for the first time.

We discuss Max. Sara, for once, seems impatient. Business out of the way, she explains, "I talked to an old friend this weekend whose spouse is disabled. She got a service dog, named Kazu, whom they both adore. Next week, they're coming to Tucson for a conference, and we're all going to meet him. I'm going to learn more about service dogs and see if it's something we could get involved with."

As Sara continues to talk about the pros and cons of her service dog idea, my mind drifts to my problems. I focus back in at the word 'prisoner.' Prisoners had trained Kazu, like many service dogs. Wish Arizona DOC had that option. Dog training might have led to a decent job and been fun. We suffered outside weeding the vegetable garden or made license plates. Not much future in either. At least I wasn't in Phoenix where they lived in tents without air conditioning.

Finally, the meeting ends. As we walk out, Sara stops me. "What a lovely gesture to share your tip money. I'm proud of you."

I wish I were proud of me. It's hard to be proud when your life's partly a lie. I have two days' breathing room till Kelly returns; but I know when he does, he expects me to tell him I'm in.

I'm meeting Angie for dinner. Maybe she can help figure out what to do. Tuesday night Mom's talked me into going to see a motivational speaker Think Thin might hire. I got tired of saying no. It'll make the time pass.

Work calms me. Dogs are less stressful than people. They're forgiving, humble and loyal. They don't gossip, spread rumors, or take credit for your ideas.

. . . .

Angie's not much for vegetables, but suggests "Corn 'N Cabbage," a salad restaurant, to make it easier for me. The Irish terrorist trial has started, and Angie spends her days in Federal Court. "The prosecution isn't very impressive, but a few of the defense lawyers are the best I've ever seen. Today, a detective from Scotland Yard was on the stand. He looked and sounded like the Feds had gone to central casting to request a British spy type. He testified about two men not on trial who were under surveillance for months. I can't figure out what they have to do with the case. They spent most of their time ordering pizza and drinking at Irish pubs. One had two girlfriends. Each though she was his only one."

"Not like TV?"

"I wish. Everything takes much longer. Lots of breaks. There are seven defense lawyers and two prosecutors. Each lawyer gets to question each witness. When the lawyers object, which they do a lot, they all go up to the bench and talk to Judge Nunez. No one else can hear. I want to know what they say. Sometimes it's just boring. At least one of the defendants is great looking."

"I've never been on a jury. With my record, I'll never get the chance."

"I was on one in state court when you were in prison. I followed that case, no problem, but it was less complex. House break-in. The whole trial took two days not three months like this one's supposed to. Can't you get on a jury if you get your rights restored?"

"I think I have to be off parole first."

"What'd Kelly say when you told him?"

"I didn't."

"What are you waiting for, the night before you leave?"

"No. It's so sad. I finally meet a guy who seems to care about me and isn't a jerk and I'm going to lose him. He's compassionate, responsible, loves dogs. His family's cool, his parents like me, and Mom even approves. I think she's planning the wedding."

"If he's that great, he'll understand."

"That's what Mom says, but you're both wrong. He hates secrecy, believes all drug addicts are criminals. He'll think I should've told him everything when we first met."

"Speculate all you want, but you won't know till you tell him. How 'bout the good news and the bad news? The good news is I can prove I'm clean, but the bad news is. . ."

"Jeez, Angie. It's a good thing you didn't go into comedy." I change the subject. "Your Aunt Sara's totally excited about meeting a service dog that belongs to a friend of hers. She wants to learn how to train them."

"I love it. It's perfect for her." By the time we leave, I feel better, even though nothing's changed.

. . . .

Tuesday passes uneventfully. Sara's concerned Theodore and Samantha have been neglected lately. She asks me to take them for a ride to Mt. Lemmon. It's an hour's drive to the almost ten thousand foot summit where the temperature's cooler than Tucson. The trip takes more than half a day. I don't know who enjoys it more—-the dogs or me. Even a call from Kelly doesn't destroy my mood.

Mom has dinner on the table when I get home. Tonight is salmon with some sort of glaze, salad and green beans. We leave the cleanup for later, as the speaker's scheduled at seven. I protest half-heartedly about going, but Mom reminds me I've promised; and if I stay home, I'll eat. Who knows? Maybe I'll learn something.

We'd barely sit down when a hugely obese woman dressed in a long-sleeved, ankle length tent-like dress walks, waddles, to the microphone. "Hi, I'm Candy. I'm going to talk to you about not looking like me. I'd like to blame it on my parents for naming me after a product made of chocolate, nuts and sugar, but that would be too easy."

"I can't believe this. I heard she was an inspiration," Mom mutters. "I can't let someone her size be a role model."

"I don't believe in diets, only in life changes," she continues. "Anyone can live on cabbage soup or miracle cookies for a while, but when you stop, you'll gain it all back and more. I know . . . I've tried them all. And it's not good for your heart to lose and gain, lose and gain." Several in the audience clap.

The woman gives simple advice on portion size and not too much self-deprivation. "Give yourself a treat often." Mom can't get past her size, typical of her. Who better to relate to fat folks than fat folks? After thirty minutes, there's a short intermission. Three svelte women pass around small glasses of weird-smelling juice that seemed to mock the woman's previous advice. I take one sip and put it down, but Mom drinks hers.

In five minutes, the same woman walks back to the stage; but instead of obese; she's smartly dressed in a sleeveless shift, looks like she doesn't have an ounce of fat. While the audience gasps, she explains her dress had been created to demonstrate how she looked before she lost ninety pounds.

By the time we get home, Mom changes her mind and decides to recommend that Think Thin offers Candy a job. I liked her better fat.

When I awake Wednesday, it feels like the day I took the plea. How had I gotten myself into this mess? I drag myself to work. The morning passes slowly. In the afternoon, I pick up supplies. Nick's behind the counter. "Good to see you, Kristin. Seeing you makes my day. You've probably been thinking about me too, huh?"

"Not really," I answer with a complete lack of wit. It's too hot outside for Samantha so we just wander around the store. On the way to the car, Nick stops to pet Samantha. She seems delighted to see him.

After he loads up, he walks to the driver's seat apparently undaunted with my lack of enthusiasm. "Hey, Kristin, how about meeting me for a drink after work? My treat."

"I can't, Nick, I'm busy; and anyway, I'm seeing someone," (at least until tonight) I add under my breath.

"Well, let me know when you change your mind," he smiles again unfazed by my answer.

Too bad I don't care about Nick. After today, I'll need a new boyfriend.

The day over, I hurry home, change into a new skirt I'd bought for a thin occasion. Between off-and-on dieting and anxiety, I'd lost seven pounds. I put on the skirt and a matching blouse. I look presentable. As I walk out of the house, Mom examines me, "You look nice." I almost believe her. She rarely gives compliments. "Good luck," she adds, as I walk out the door. Mom has convinced herself Kelly's such a great guy he won't mind an ex-con.

I'm meeting Kelly at Le Bistro; the season's new "in" place. My cousin works there. The menu includes unique salads, as well as a large selection of burgers for Kelly, and alcohol. I can't have this talk without a glass or two of wine.

Kelly's waiting. He grins when he sees me and grabs me for a long kiss. He's starved. Wants to order right away. I have a Chinese Chicken Salad and a glass of pinot grigio. Kelly has the burger-of-the-day with caramelized onions, mushrooms and Swiss cheese; fries, and some exotic ale. Why do guys always get to eat what they want?

Kelly talks about the conference and how innovative other courts' IT systems are. I tell him about taking the dogs to Mt. Lemmon as I try to calm the butterflies in my stomach. I finally can't stand it and blurt out, "Kelly, I'm sorry I can't go to the wedding."

"It's not because of work, is it?"

"No, I wish it were."

"What do you mean by that? Why can't you go?"

"It's a long story, and I'm afraid you'll hate me afterwards."

"I can't imagine anything you'd say that would make me hate you. You don't have another boyfriend do you?"

"No, it's worse."

"Worse? You act like you're going to prison or something."

"Close. I'm on parole, and my parole officer won't let me go."

"On parole? You've been in prison?"

"Yeah . . . I got out about six months ago."

"For what?"

"Cocaine. The cops found it in my house. I didn't know it was there. Remember, I told you about my ex-boyfriend, Josh? He put it there——at least I guess he did."

"Calm down and tell me what happened so I can understand it."

"Okay. Josh and I were living together. The night before I got arrested, two guys I didn't know showed up to see Josh. He left with them. Said he'd be back soon. He didn't come back that night. Or the next morning. Angie came over around eleven. I was getting ready to go out for coffee with her when the police showed up. They had a search warrant." Kelly looks at me says nothing. "I was scared, but I didn't think there was anything illegal in the house. The next thing I knew, they found all this cocaine. They took me to jail."

"Did you have a trial?"

"No, I decided to plead guilty to avoid a lot longer prison sentence."

"Why did you plead guilty if you were innocent? Didn't you have a lawyer?"

"Yes, a good one, Becky Bernini."

"I know her. Everyone says she's terrific."

"She is. She said the only chance I had was to rat out Josh. I couldn't do it. If I went to trial and lost, it was a minimum of five years. They offered me a plea of no more than two, so I took it."

"How much cocaine was there?"

"Eighty pounds."

"Eighty pounds?"

"Yeah."

"You loved this Josh so much you went to prison for him?"

"It's not that simple. It was only my word that it was Josh's stuff. If the jury didn't believe me, I was looking at five to fifteen years."

"You didn't answer my question about caring for him."

"I guess I did care about him then. But that's all in the past. It was over before I met you. I'm a different person now."

"So if the wedding hadn't come up, when were you going to tell me all this . . . never?"

"I don't know, Kelly. I wanted to, but it's not easy to explain." I start to cry. "You're such a terrific guy; I love your family; and I knew when I told you, we were going to be over."

"You've explained it fine. You lied to me, used drugs, went to prison for a drug dealer, and tried to keep it all a secret. You think I'm a moron."

"No, no, it's not like that. I was afraid." I can hardly talk.

"Come on, I'll take you home." He throws some money on the table, and we walk silently to the car. Even now, he opens the door for me.

"Can't we talk about this some more? I don't want it to end like this."

Kelly says nothing. He drives to my house and lets me out. He watches me walk to the door. I look at him and mouth, "Please, Kelly."

He drives away.

CHAPTER
THIRTY-TWO

Two weeks and a day since Kelly and I broke up. I'm miserable but without work, I'd be worse. The dogs sense my sadness and rally 'round me. Sara never asks what's the matter, but you don't have to be psychic to know something is. She keeps me busy and repeats often our workplace's family.

Angie and Art left last Sunday for a two-week Hawaiian vacation. They'd invited me, but I had no interest. Sitting on a beautiful beach, watching happy couples? No thanks. Not the way I look in a bathing suit. Amazingly, I'd stayed on my diet.

Mom hadn't said anything, but I feel her disappointment. The wedding's off. My daughter fucked up again. Of course, Mom would never say 'fucked up.' Sometimes, I think I stay on my diet to prove I could do one thing right.

The day of Kelly's last dog class, I take pains to look good. One of my duties is to make graduation certificates, which include a picture of the dog and his people. On Dusty's certificate, I put a picture I took after our first date. As time for the group nears, I become increasingly anxious. Will Kelly talk to me? Can I act professional if he ignores me? I needn't have bothered . . . Kelly doesn't show. "Go ahead and mail Kelly the certificate," was all Sara said.

The same day shortly before we close, I get a call from Parole. "PO Cooper wants to know if you could come in this week instead of your regular appointment."

"Am I in trouble?"

"How would I know? He said he'd like to see you, but if it'll cause problems at your work, just come in your regular time."

My drug tests are clean. I can't think of any rules I'd broken. What if the lab misreads my drug test? The women in prison say it happens all the time. Part of me wants to wait, but I'm too curious. "I can come in early tomorrow morning."

"He has an eight o'clock."

I check with Sara. She says fine. I tell her Kelly and I aren't seeing each other any more. I think she knows.

"I'm sorry," Sara says. "You and he seemed right together. You sure it's over?"

"Pretty sure." I change the subject. I don't want her to know more than she does. I feel pathetic enough.

. . . .

"Did Parole contact you?" Mom asks soon as I walk through the door.

"Yeah, Mr. Cooper wants to see me, so I'm going tomorrow. I wonder what he wants."

"Did you do something wrong?"

"No, Mom, I didn't do anything wrong. You always think the worst."

"Something must be going on for him to want to see you right away."

"The person who called said it was up to me. Mr. Cooper didn't want me to get in trouble at work. He said I could come the regular time if I wanted to. Doesn't seem that big a deal. Maybe the lab messed up my drug test."

"Labs don't make mistakes, Kristin. If the drug test reads positive, it means you used drugs."

"Well, I haven't; but other people said that happened to them."

"You're so gullible. You must have heard that in prison." Wow, she acknowledged I was incarcerated not in summer camp.

Prisoners. The lowest of the low. Some are. Women who make up stuff about cellmates to curry favor with guards or get a deal. Women who steal your last dollar or read your letters. Women who hurt you if you look at them wrong. But that's not the whole story.

Crystal was so small she looked like she could be in high school. She was terrified of being in jail. Spent most of her time in the fetal position on her bunk. Barely said a word to anyone. No one saw her laugh or smile except when she had a visit with her daughter, Brandy.

A letter came from Family Court. Her cellie said she began to shake soon as she saw it. Didn't read it right away. Held it. Stared at it. Took a long time before she opened it. Began to howl like a wounded animal. We all heard her.

Her cellmate tried to quiet her, keep her from a write-up. CO Cornel walked up to her cell, and said loud enough for the floor to hear, "You're not the first to lose your kid, and you won't be the last. They're better off without you. Stop that racquet or you're going to solitary."

The noise continued and two guards dragged her out screaming. Three days later she returned looking even smaller and more scared then before.

The women in our pod put aside their petty feuds and rallied round her; made sure she ate and kept her from getting written up again. Some bought her treats. One read to her. We listened to her talk about her daughter hour after hour. Just when she seemed better, she hung herself. The note she left said only, Brandy, I love you always. Mom would never understand. I wouldn't have before either.

. . . .

I'm pissed at everyone—-Mom, Kelly, Cooper. To avoid time alone with Mom, I take Sparkie for a long walk. Twice on the walk back, I have to stop to give him a rest. All that exercise lets me sleep well.

The drive to parole takes forever. I hit every light. As usual, half of Tucson streets are under construction. My stop at Starbucks puts me back fifteen minutes. I love to have it 'my' way, but the two people in front of me take so long they could've ordered a five-course gourmet dinner. I space out after I hear, "four shots of espresso, extra whipped cream and something about temperature." I'm five minutes late. Mr. Cooper's late too.

"Morning, Kristin," he greets me with a big smile.

"So, am I in trouble?"

"Should you be?"

"No, but why'd you call me in?"

"It's good news. Because of budget cuts, we can't afford to replace two officers who retired. We've been ordered to cut our caseloads and terminate people we think can make it without supervision."

I stare at him. "Aren't you happy? You're off parole. You can live where you want, go where you want."

"Yeah, of course."

"I have some paperwork for you to sign, but once you do, that'll be it. You've done well, Kristin. All your tests have been clean, you're working, and you haven't broken any rules. I talked to your employer, and she has only good things to say about you. Your mom too. It's rare to have people like you. It makes my job a lot more pleasant.

"My supervisor told me he denied you permission to go out of state. Said you requested it too late? Where did you want to go?"

"To a wedding in LA with my . . . uh boyfriend?"

"Too bad I wasn't here. Maybe I could have worked it out."

"The other man said thirty days' notice, no exceptions. I didn't get invited to the wedding in enough time."

"The rule is thirty days; but once in a while, I've worked things out for a parolee if they've been as compliant as you have."

"You're joking, right?"

"Why would I joke about that?"

Oh, my God. If he hadn't been on vacation, I could've gone to the wedding, and Kelly and I'd be together. I can't believe it.

"Something the matter?"

"No, nothing."

He stands up and puts out his hand. "Best of luck. If you think of it, let me know how you're doing. If I can ever help you, don't hesitate to ask. I wish all my cases were this easy."

I'm about to walk out when I think about Ina. "There's something you can do. I want to find out what happened to someone I was in jail with, can you do that?"

"If the person's in prison or on parole and you have their full name, I can. It's public record."

"I have that and their DOC number."

"That's even better. I'll be back shortly."

I wait impatient, hope she won't be in the system. In a few minutes, he comes back. "Ina Jeffries is doing a six-year sentence. She's in the Winslow facility, eligible for parole after eighty percent." Six years, shit. And I'm upset about Kelly.

THIRTY-THREE

"Mom, I'm off parole."

"Off parole, what do you mean?"

"Just what I said." What's wrong with her?

"What happened?"

"That appointment with Mr. Cooper. I wasn't in trouble. They don't have enough officers, so people who are doing fine get off early. Isn't that great?"

"I guess."

"What do you mean 'you guess'?"

"Are you sure it's been long enough for you to be on your own?"

As usual she only sees the bad side. "God, Mom, you still think I'm a criminal. I thought you'd be proud of me."

"I am, but it's partially chance; you know, like being in the right place at the right time."

"Right place at the right time. That's not true. If I were in the right place at the right time, Mr. Cooper wouldn't have been on vacation and I'd be with Kelly. You realize I can move out now."

"Is that what you plan to do?"

"Of course," I answer blithely; but now that I can, I'm not sure I want to.

"At least wait till the start of next month. That'll give you a couple weeks to look for a place."

"Okay, I will."

I put little effort into moving. I'm used to living here; the routine of work, dinner with Mom, walks with Sparkie. Mom does most of the house stuff. Her healthy meals and vigilance help keep me on my diet.

My one splurge is after I leave the parole office. It begins at Starbucks with mocha Frappuccino, a maple scone and several donuts. Ashamed someone would think the food's all for me, I ask for the donuts "to go," mumble they're for my roommates. Like the skinny barista cared. Next, Baskin-Robbins. I have French vanilla and chocolate fudge. My stomach bulges. I berate myself all the way home and for the next several days when I weigh in. (Mom, of course, put scales in both bathrooms.)

Angie and Art make a huge deal about me getting off parole. Angie complains I didn't call them in Hawaii to tell them. They want to have a party—-the two of them will use any excuse—-but I nix it. I'm not ready. I can't tell anyone why I want to celebrate. Martha Stewart doesn't have a menu and decorations for a Get Off Parole Party; and Hallmark, the only institution that celebrates occasions more than Angie and Art, doesn't design Getting Off Parole cards.

"Angie, you think it'd be okay to send Kelly a note, tell him I'm off parole? I won't say I miss him or anything."

"I don't know. You'll feel bad if he doesn't respond."

"I couldn't feel worse. How about if I write it and show you? You can tell me what you think."

I spend the next few days writing versions of "the note."

Dear Kelly,

I'm off parole. I want to get back together. Call me.

Dear Kelly,

Stop being a jerk. Haven't you ever made a mistake? Why are you such a wimp? You know we'd be good together. Call me today.

Dear Kelly,

I got off parole early because I was doing great. I've lost ten pounds. I miss Dusty and would love to take him for a walk, and then we could have dinner. It could work.

I finally compromised on:

Dear Kelly,

I wanted to let you know I got off parole early. I'm glad I had a chance to meet you and wish you the best. Give Dusty a pat for me.

Sincerely, Kristin

I call Angie and read it to her. "What do you think?"

"Same thing I said before. Don't get your hopes up. I know you care about him, but he probably meant what he said."

I hang up, the phone rings immediately. Angie again?

"Hi, Angie?"

"Kristin, is that you?"

"Josh?" Instinctively I look around, glad Mom's not in the room.

"It's so great to hear your voice. I've missed you so much . . . Kristin, say something. You probably hate me and have every right. I'm a different person. I'm clean, have a good job. I've saved some money, and I want to pay you back."

"Pay me back? You think you can put a price on the days I spent in prison?"

"No, no I didn't mean that. I want to make things right."

"Way too late. I spent two years in prison. I was strip-searched. Strip-searched. I'm a felon. I have a record."

"I was an asshole, but it's more complicated than you realize. These guys were after me. Said I owed them half a million dollars. They sent thugs to the apartment. If they found me, they would have tortured me or killed me maybe both. Please, Kristin, I want to see you."

"Where've you been all this time? Why did you stay away?"

"Albuquerque. Thought it was far enough away to be safe. I had no connections there. I got a job in a restaurant and worked my way up to sous chef. I didn't think it was safe to come back here sooner. Can't we talk in person?"

I don't know what to say. My brain says he hasn't changed. He's no good. He left me once, and he'll do it again. But I want to see him . . . My heart's beating faster. I have butterflies in my stomach. To kill time, I ask, "What if Mom answered the phone? She hates you."

"She didn't. I'd have asked to talk to you. What's up with you? Are you with someone?"

I don't know what to say. Don't want him to think I can't get a date. I compromise on, "No one serious."

"Are you working?"

" Yeah. Angie's Aunt Sara has a dog-training place. I've been there a couple months. Let me think about it. Give me your number. I'll call if I want to see you."

"I'll only be here two days. Got to go back to work Thursday. I'm staying at Leslie's. Her number is 435-1560."

"I gotta go." I lie.

"Call me. I'll be at our Starbucks at seven tonight and tomorrow. It can't hurt to talk." He hangs up before I can say anything further.

Leslie's? I don't want to talk to that bitch. Another reason to stay away. What the hell's a sous chef? I never knew he could cook anything except tasteless mac and cheese. Maybe I should talk to Angie. No, she'll just tell me to stay away.

"Kristin, who was on the phone?" Mom calls from the other room.

"Just Sara. She's out of the office tomorrow morning and wanted to give me some information about a research assignment." Josh is in my life two minutes and I lie.

THIRTY-FOUR

I don't care about work. Only Josh. I pick up the phone, put it down.

Today I need to avoid Sara. I'm afraid to make eye contact. I don't want her to know I've talked to Josh. I don't think psychics rely on eye contact but . . .

This morning I start in day-care. We have a new client, a feisty Springer spaniel, Buddy. His person's a short, well-dressed man who announces loudly he's a Judge and expects The Dignified Dog to live up to its name. "When I made arrangement to bring Buddy in, I told the owner my requirements, but to make sure, I'm going to repeat them to you. He doesn't like to do his business in front of other dogs or people. He must have his privacy. When someone takes him outside, have them turn their back."

When it's outside time for large dogs, Buddy goes out willingly. I'm trying to figure out the best way to leave him alone when he lifts his leg and pees in front of the other dogs, any random onlookers, and myself.

As I bring the dogs back in, I hear the intercom, "Kristin, call, line two."

I rarely get calls—-it's Josh. "Hello," I say almost breathless.

"It's me. Having a good day? How 'bout lunch?"

Lunch is too soon. I don't want him to see me in work clothes. "I don't have time for lunch today."

"Oh, come on, Kristin, you work with dogs."

"My work's important whether you think so or not."

"You're right, sorry. Dinner then. What time you get off?"

"I told my Mom I'd eat with her. She'll get suspicious if I can't tell her where I'm going."

"You report to your mother. You're, uh, twenty-four years old."

"Twenty-five. I wouldn't be living with her if I hadn't just gotten off parole."

"I guess I don't realize how much you suffered because of me. Kristin, please come to Starbucks. Meeting me doesn't commit you to anything. You owe it to me to let me explain what happened. Why I did what I did. I had good reasons."

He's right. Its just talk. I don't have to see him again. "All right, I'll meet you at Starbucks."

"Great, see you there." He's gone.

What have I done? I daydream about tonight, when barking tells me the dogs need attention. I quiet them down, when again, the intercom. "Kristin, line one." Line one's in-house. It's Sara. "Sam's on his way to cover; I'd like to talk to you." Could she want to discuss Josh? When Sam arrives, I give him a brief run-down on the dogs. He laughs hysterically when I tell him about Buddy. "I can't wait to tell my friends. Buddy, the bashful dog." He's still chuckling as I leave.

"Morning Kristin. Anything new?" Sara asks. What does she mean?

"Ah, no, nothing," I stammer. "You mean with Buddy?"

"Buddy? Oh, how's he doing? I expect problems when a person makes a ridiculous statement like 'his dog has to pee in private.' It's his person's problem, but could certainly affect Buddy. I thought about telling his person we were full, but decided it would be good for Buddy to be in a sane place."

"He peed like any other dog this morning."

"Big surprise. Maybe we should have a class to teach people about dogs instead of teach dogs to fit in with people. Might make more sense. But it'd be a lot harder."

People's obedience class. "Standing in Your Dog's Paws." Theodore and Samantha stand in front of a group of humans next to a box filled with chocolate candies for use as rewards. We'd have lessons on responsibilities of a dog owner; no stupid tricks; proper response to bathroom accidents; animal charities; and, of course, Theodore would teach, "Show your dog you care with lots of snacks."

Samantha would be head teacher. "Please don't call any of us 'the dog.' We have names and like to be called by them. How would you like to be treated like this: 'Here human, or good human, give it a treat.' "

"I want to talk about the week," Sara says, interrupting my fantasy. "I have two interviews about the consequences of leaving pets in the car in this heat, and one about dogs who are afraid of thunder. If the monsoon ever starts, we'll have lots of freaked-out animals. I'm comfortable with these subjects so I don't need help, but I have an assignment for you. I want you to think about characteristics dogs have that make people want to have them in their lives. I know there're many, but see if you can decide on three."

"I'm not sure what you mean."

"I know it's vague, but I have an idea for a project. You can observe people with their dogs, do research or ask people their opinion, whatever you want. Just narrow it to three. I also want you to pick up supplies on Wednesday with Samantha. She's asked for you lately." At the mention of her name, Samantha wags her tail and looks at us.

The rest of the day passes with agonizing slowness. Every time I look at my watch, it's only a minute or two later. To take my mind off Josh, I think about the assignment. Why do people love dogs? They love you unconditionally, they're loyal, they have beautiful eyes. Josh has beautiful eyes.

Around three, I hear thunder and, miraculously, it rains. Every summer people complain it's been exceptionally hot, wish the monsoons would start. Day after day, the clouds build-up, sky darkens and no rain.

Dogs bark and whimper. I'd better give Sam a hand. Sara and Taylor are both in classes and can't help. Samantha's fearless and loves storms, but Theodore's afraid. Lucky, he's in daycare today. When I get there, Rivet, a large lab mix, is cowered under a table; and Theodore's trembling nearby. I tried to calm them while Sam does the same with some of the others.

Because of Spark, I'd had experience with fearful dogs. At the first thunderclap, he runs under Mom's bed. If someone's home, he's okay. The neighbors say if he's alone, he howls. He was outside once when it stormed unexpectedly, and he got out of the yard. Mom was frantic. I was with

Scott then, and the two of us drove around the neighborhood for hours but couldn't find him. Three hours later a neighbor calls. She found Sparkie under her front porch. Since then, Mom makes sure he isn't alone in a storm.

A few minutes before five, Sara asks me to go with her to meet a woman who trains service dogs. Sara has never suggested we get together after hours. Did she know I was meeting Josh? "I'm sorry, I can't," I explain. "I have plans tonight."

"No problem, another time," she says. "Have a nice evening."

I walk to my car, feeling unsettled. Josh's in my life less than twenty-four hours, and I lied to Mom and let Sara down.

THIRTY-FIVE

At dinner, I pretend everything's normal; but Mom looks at me quizzically. I clean the kitchen without being asked; tell her I'm off to meet friends at Starbucks.

I wonder what she thinks when I leave wearing a sexy new top and tight jeans, my hair and make-up redone. I have lies ready if she comments, but she just says good by. Is it less a lie because it stays in my head? Maybe she thinks one of the friends is a guy.

I pull into Starbucks early. I check for Josh's car but realize I don't know what he drives. I don't want to be first. At ten after seven, I can't stand it any longer.

He's at our corner table drinking coffee. He looks cleaner, more prosperous. He gets up grabs me in a bear hug.

"You look terrific, babe." He takes my hand and pulls me over to the table.

In front of my chair's a latte, a maple scone, and a small wrapped box. "Soy latte and maple scones, your favorites. Open the box."

Josh has never bought me a present. I don't know what to expect. I'm touched but suspicious. I don't want the scone, but I don't want to mention the word "diet." I open the box, worry that whatever it is, is too expensive, too cheap, or I won't like it. A silver and turquoise bracelet. I can't tell if it's real or a flea market trinket. "Josh, it's lovely."

"Put it on." I hold out my hand. "I like it," he says. "Tell me about your job."

"I love it. The people are wonderful. The hard part was finding one. Soon as anyone knew about my record, forget it. I sent out a ton of resumes and went to a lot of interviews. Luckily, Angie's Aunt Sara needed an assistant. Angie said her aunt thinks she psychic, so she'd decide whether to hire me based on her 'vibes' instead of my record."

"You don't believe that shit?"

"Well, she hired me, and I like it there."

"I can see why you'd pretend to believe it, but she's not here now."

"She knows things about me that I never told her. I'm not sure what to believe."

Josh looks at me, shakes his head. "Let me tell you about this gig I lucked into. A few nights after I get to Albuquerque, I walk into this British pub to have a beer. I tell the bartender I'm looking for a job. One of the waitresses walks in and quits. I tell him I'd been a waiter before, and he hires me. Start the next day. A couple weeks later, one of the cooks quits. They're desperate. I tell them I can cook and have experience with British food, and I'm in."

I look at my scone. "I never saw you cook anything restaurant quality, let alone British food."

"I'm sure I told you about my Uncle Sid? He lived in London. When he came back, he taught me how to make some British dishes. Most of them suck. They have no taste over there." I've ignored the scone but now I take a bite.

"I don't remember any Uncle Sid. Too bad you never cooked for me."

Josh ignores my comment. "The owner and I hit it off. He thinks I'm a genius. He wants to open a place in Tucson, and I'll be the manager. It's going to take a while to get that going. I was hoping you'd come to Albuquerque."

"You want me to leave Tucson? That's crazy. I have a job here and friends. I don't want to leave. Why should I go with you after what you did to me?"

"Kristin, I feel terrible about it. I know I did the wrong thing; but at the time, I didn't know what else to do."

"What happened that night? Who were those guys? How'd you get involved with them?"

" One question at a time. You remember Heavy, the guy that sold dope downtown? They hung with him. One night, they asked if I wanted to make a grand by stashing some blow for a night. One night. We were so broke . . ."

"Why couldn't they store it at their place?"

"They said the dude they were selling it to wouldn't buy anything if it was stored at their place. Too high profile. Lots of partying, drugs, the cops had been there a couple times. I said yes, and they brought it over that night. I thought they'd leave it and go, but they invited me to their place to smoke some Turkish hash. Thought I'd be home in an hour or so."

"Why weren't you?"

"Whatever the stuff was, it was stronger than shit. I passed out. When I got up in the morning, they were gone."

"How come you didn't tell me you were going to stash the stuff? It was my place too."

"Why you hassling me about that now?"

"Hassling you? I went to prison. You write a stupid letter to tell me you're gonna leave town. I never hear from you again." I get up to leave, try to hide my tears.

"Kristin, sit down. To tell you the truth, one of the reasons I left was your mom. When I came home that morning and you weren't there, I was frantic. I checked our friends, and then I called your mom's. She told me the best thing I could do for you was to move away."

"You're lying. I know Mom didn't like you, but she'd never tell you to let me take the rap."

"Ask her yourself if you don't believe me. She didn't want you to take the rap, but she made me promise to leave. Look, Kristin, when I found out what happened, I didn't know what to do. I thought about going to the cops, but I didn't know Carlos or JT's last names or anything about them. If the cops asked me where I met them, I'd have to mention Heavy. He'd get pissed if he found out I'd snitched him off. He might make something up about me dealing or try to hurt me."

"You could have tried to help me."

"I did. I talked to a lawyer. He told me that if I copped to anything, it wouldn't save you. I know it was wrong, but give me a chance. I've changed. I'd have kept in touch, but I promised your mom."

"Why'd you contact me now?"

"I can't stop thinking about you. I missed you."

"I don't know what to think." I look down at my plate. The scone's gone. Another big moment in my life, and I'm counting calories. Could Mom have done what Josh said?

Josh moves closer and puts his arm around me. It feels good, really good—-like I'm home after a long vacation. We sit like that a long time.

THIRTY-SIX

Kelly places the note from Kristin on his nightstand. Each time he reads it, he thinks about the conversation with his mom. At first, he makes vague excuses about why Kristin hadn't been around, but a few days before the wedding he has to say something. "Kristin and I aren't going out any more, so she's not coming."

His sisters tried to find out why, but soon tire of asking. His older brother makes remarks about her looking for a "real stud," but Kelly keeps his cool, doesn't respond.

Al's wedding meets his expectations—-he feels lonely. Everyone his age's paired up and having fun. Al's bride, Emily, is perfectly dressed, perfect looking and perfectly boring. Too bad he couldn't bring Kristin. She could liven things up—-tell prison stories or just be with him. He almost calls her, but knows he'd be sorry.

A few days after the wedding, he and his mom are alone at the dinner table. "You seem unhappy; does it have something to do with Kristin?"

"I guess."

"Do you feel like telling me?"

"I don't know. It didn't end because of a silly fight or the usual reasons people break up. I'm not sure how I feel."

"It might help to talk. If you're worried about shocking me, don't. I can handle it." Kelly laughs.

"A few days before I had to make the plane reservations, Kristin told me she had been in prison and was still on parole."

"Prison? Parole? Wow! Is that why she couldn't go?"

"Yeah. She had to get permission from her parole officer to leave the state. He was out of town, or she waited too long to ask or something. I'm not sure of the details other than she couldn't get permission."

"Let me make another pot of coffee." She gets up and walks toward the kitchen. "Don't stop talking. I can hear you. Why was she in prison?"

"She said she was innocent, but doesn't everyone? It's kind of a complicated story, but the cops found lots of cocaine at her house."

"She doesn't look like a drug addict to me."

"When did you become an expert on what drug addicts look like?" Kelly asks with a smile.

"I'm not, of course. But I read the newspapers, watch TV. I don't live in a cave. From everything I've read, drug addicts are skinny and unhealthy looking."

"When she explained it, she said the drugs belonged to her ex-boyfriend. She didn't know the stuff was in the house when the cops showed up with a search warrant."

"I gather you don't believe her."

He got up and poured himself a cup of coffee. He had never asked himself whether he believed her or not. "I'm not sure. It could be true, I guess, but how could she be with a guy who'd deal cocaine? When she got arrested, he split town and left her to take the fall."

"Poor girl, if it's true."

"I asked her why she didn't tell the cops the drugs were her boyfriend's. She said she couldn't turn him in no matter what he did to her."

"Are you upset about the drugs or her loyalty to another man, especially one who seems like such a jackass?"

"Jackass. I've never heard you talk that way."

"Well, the situation seems to call for it. I know we only saw her once, but she impressed me as a decent person." Kelly's surprised. Decent's a high compliment from Mom. First she says jackass, and then calls someone who was in prison decent.

"I got a note from her a few days ago, telling me she got off parole early."

"Did she say anything else?"

"Just wished me luck."

"Seems to me she was trying to leave the door open for you to see her again."

"You'd really want me to go out with someone who was in prison for drug-dealing and has a felony record?"

"Well, honey, people do make mistakes and sometimes change. She got off parole early and has a job, which shows something positive. Life isn't always black and white. The older you get, the more you find that out."

He's expected her to be shocked, no disgusted when she learned about Kristin. She was a stay-at-home mom who spent her life taking care of his dad and the kids. They had a large extended family, but no one had ever been in trouble—-let alone prison—-that he knew of. Uncle Mario was rumored to be involved in illegal gambling, but he'd never been arrested, and it was only rumor. The only criminal behavior they knew about was from TV or movies like The Godfather. Not from a woman he dated.

Maybe he'd been too hasty, too judgmental. On the other hand, he wants to be proud of the woman he's with, not worry someone would find out she's an ex-con, a drug user, maybe a dealer.

He thinks back to the evening he and Kristin ran into her old boyfriend, that lawyer, what's his name. Recalls her unfriendly attitude toward him. Wonders if Kristin had been afraid he'd mention her past. That was the night of their first fight—-their only fight.

He wasn't sure but he had a vague recollection he'd told Kristin how he felt about anyone involved with drugs. Could his attitude be part of the reason she didn't tell him?

After mulling it over, Kelly decides to send Kristin a note. As she had done, he rewrites it several times and finally settles on:

Dear Kristin,

Congratulations on getting off parole early. You must have done well. Thanks for sending the graduation picture of Dusty and me. I'm sorry things didn't work out differently.

Kelly

The letter sits on his dresser for a while, but he finally mails it, not knowing what he wants to happen.

THIRTY-SEVEN

I don't get home till two. Mom's asleep. She must have had to get up early to give up her parental policing duty. Good thing. Confused as I feel, I might blurt out the truth and demand to know what she said to Josh.

In bed, I sleep fitfully, think about Josh, and how to confront Mom. I can't sleep. Maybe it's the wine. Two glasses is a binge for me. Only lack of a place prevented sex with Josh. He'd do it in a car, the park, anyplace, but I didn't want our first time in two years to be that way. Last night, I wished I had my own place. This morning, I'm glad I still live here.

As I dress, I ignore the radio till I hear, "Government officials in Phoenix, Arizona have issued a warning to residents not to go outside, even to the mailbox, without shoes." Well, duh, what kind of idiot would walk outside without shoes? Tucson's high temperature hovered around one hundred seven the last several days, hot enough for second degree burns if you touch metal. Phoenix reached one hundred fourteen. Maybe there's a moron story in here to share with Josh. Could this be a positive omen?

"You got home late." Mom disturbs my vision of hundreds of Phoenicians running from their mailboxes, their feet going up in flames.

"Yeah."

"I thought you were going to Starbucks."

"I did."

"Don't they close around nine?"

"I guess." I'm twenty-five years old, for God sakes. Mom looks at me exasperated, but she says nothing else and neither do I. If I say more, I'd have to admit I'd seen Josh. I wasn't ready to. Maybe tonight.

. . . .

"Morning, Kristin, how are you coming on the assignment?" Sara asks as I enter The Dog.

"Ah, okay, but I'm not done," I stammer.

"That's fine, but I don't want you to forget."

"I won't. I'd never forget an assignment. You want it today?"

"End of the week's fine. Theodore said to tell you, you he doesn't care if you call him 'the dog' as long as you give him snacks. That one sure thinks with his stomach." She laughs. I look at Sara in amazement. I hadn't said those thoughts out loud.

This morning, I'm in obedience class. I have the routine down, look forward to seeing the dogs. I'll do double duty and ask people what they value most in their dogs.

Mattie, a miniature schnauzer, comes with Lisa, a tall attractive woman with long hair. I know she's a lawyer. "Sometimes, I come home really down. I'm a public defender, and the last few years, I've tried a lot of serious cases. There are days when all my clients lie. The judge doesn't listen to anything I say. No more probation, off to jail. Mattie senses how I feel, comes over and cuddles with me. I don't have to explain anything. If I could meet a man like that," she laughs.

Public Defender? She must know Bernini. I'd ask her, but she'd want to know how I knew her, and I don't want to tell another lie.

Evan is big, buff, and looks like he works out a lot. Later, I find out he's teaches weight lifting. He brings a black lab puppy. "Roscoe's happy all the time, wants to play. He's always in a good mood and never gets mad at me."

Heather's a pleasant-looking woman who always has a book with her. She's closer to Mom's age than mine. I know her dog, Rivet, from daycare. Clearly of mixed parentage, the dog's large, clumsy and energetic. Heather recently rescued him. "I knew he was my dog when I heard he was found hanging around the library. He's destroyed a sofa, four chairs and my drapes, but I wouldn't trade him for anything. He's as loving and loyal as he is energetic."

The goal of beginner's class is socialization; get the dogs used to being around each other without fighting, and to learn simple commands like "sit," "come," and "stay." In this session, the dogs work on walking on a leash, longer stays, and building relationships with their people. It looks like Mattie will be the star and, as for Rivet, I wonder if he'll pass.

The other dogs are Sweet Pea, a basset hound; and two rescue dogs, Apple and Tee. Apple, a greyhound, was rescued several years ago after she was no longer able to race. Tee, who's estimated to be at least twelve, is the oldest dog Sara ever trained. She was found about six months ago dirty and scrawny-looking living behind a gas station on the Tohono O'odham reservation. Tee appeared light brown. After a bath or two, her rescuers realized the dog was white. She's small and it's impossible to know her parentage. The vet thinks Tee lived most of life on her own. When she examined her, she saw no evidence of prior medical treatment. Tee's affectionate, not afraid of people, which is unusual for a dog with this history. Her people say she still hides half her food every time she's fed.

After class, I take Samantha to pick up supplies. I tell her about my dilemma with Josh. She looks concerned. I'd be curious to find out her take, but I'd have to admit the relationship to Sara. I realize my reluctance to tell anyone about Josh isn't a good sign. Normally, I'd call Angie if a man smiled at me, but I hadn't told her I'd seen Josh.

We barely enter the store, when Nick walks over. "If it isn't my two favorite ladies." He pets Samantha and turns to face me. "I've missed you the past couple weeks. I thought maybe I'd scared you away."

"It's not up to me whether I pick up the supplies." Stupid answer. Now he's going to think I want to see him, and it's Sara who keeps me away.

"Did you hear about the idiot in Phoenix who went to get his mail barefoot and burned his feet? Had to go to the hospital. The guy's an idiot but I don't know why it's all over the radio," Nick says.

"It's because Phoenix City government issued an advisory about going outside with no shoes."

"So that's the story behind it," Nick says. We both laugh. Maybe Josh isn't the only one with a moron list. "Anyone who goes out without shoes in this heat deserves what they get. I don't know about those Phoenix folks. If something stupid happens in this state, it always starts up there."

"I don't think Phoenix has a monopoly on stupidity." Not while I'm in Tucson.

Nick looks up at a man I think is his boss. "I better get your order ready." He leaves, but not before he gives me the usual once over.

Samantha's works the crowd in the store. I sit in a quiet spot—-think about what I should say to Mom. As he finishes my order, Nick calls out, "My offer's still good." I just smile.

I plan to confront Mom when I get home, but before I know it we're eating dinner. I thought of clever ways to find out what I want to know, but instead I just ask, "Mom, did Josh call here after I was arrested?"

"Why would you ask that now?"

"I wondered that's all."

"He called once, the day after you were arrested, I think."

"Why didn't you tell me?"

"Nothing to tell. Why are you concerned if I talked to him or not? That's not the issue. The issue is you went to prison because of him, and he did nothing about it."

"What do you mean 'nothing to tell'? You knew I was dying to hear from him."

"He called to see if you were here. I told him you were in jail."

"Did you tell him to stay away from me, to leave town?"

For a moment, Mom says nothing; but I know what she's going to say. "Which is it, have you talked to him, or were you with him last night?"

"That's not the point. What did you tell him?"

"I told him if he was any kind of a man, he'd turn himself in and tell the police the drugs were his. When he admitted he wasn't going to do that, I told him the best thing he could do for you was stay out of your life."

"How could you? You knew I loved him. You don't understand the half of it. He talked to a lawyer who told him even if he turned himself in, he couldn't help me. If he came forward, both of us would've gone to prison. What good would that do?"

"How long have you been sneaking around with him?"

"I haven't been sneaking around. The only time I saw him was last night."

"What are you going to do?"

"Why should I tell you?"

"Because I'm your mother, and you live here."

"Not for long."

"Kris, I don't know what to say to you. You're smart, you've got a job you seem to like, and you're off parole. You could put what happened behind you. Why would you start up with Josh again? If it weren't for him, you wouldn't have gone to prison or been on parole or have a record. You'd be with a nice man like Scott or be married to Kelly."

"Geez, Mom, would you stop talking about Scott? We broke up more than three years ago. He dumped me? I told you what happened when I saw him. He turned into a snotty jerk. You never gave Josh a chance. You think no one can measure up to Scott."

"That's not fair. I liked Kelly. Before you met Josh, you had a good job, a decent place. He moves in, you quit a perfectly good job, become a part-time waitress at a pizza place, your place turns into a dump, and you sell your possessions to eat."

"That's not Josh's fault. I hated that job. My boss was mean. There was no future. I was gonna quit anyway. The waitress thing was temporary."

"I'm glad your Dad isn't alive to see what you're doing with your life. We brought you up to have respect for the law, not to hang around with a drug dealer."

"Stop it, Mom. Dad would be on my side. He wouldn't have hated Josh. He taught me people could change. You judge people by the worst moments in their lives or by how much they weigh."

"I told you when you moved in you couldn't stay if you see Josh. If you plan on staying, you better find a new place."

"No problem, I'm out of here." I walk into my room slam the door hard as I can.

THIRTY-EIGHT

I'm waiting for Angie. Another Saturday morning at Starbucks. I've avoided her the last few weeks, but she's busy on her story and didn't seem to notice.

She rushes in, dripping sweat. Temperatures have been over one hundred—-business as usual for July—-but the rise in humidity erases the dry heat that makes Tucson livable. It's monsoon season, but instead of the daily deluge, the city has seen only thunder and lightning. Everyone looks hot and irritable.

"God, I hate this fucking weather. Makes me want to cut my hair."

I smile. She says that every summer. There's no way in hell she'd cut her thick, wavy hair. "Tell me about it. I don't even feel like wearing earrings. I've been living in my bathing suit cover."

"You look great, by the way. Thinner," Angie smiles at me approvingly. "Your mom must be in hog heaven. Bad analogy."

"She's so irritated at me she hasn't noticed, or at least pretended not to."

"What'd you do serious enough to keep her from celebrating a weight loss?"

"Where should I start? First, I'm moving out. I rented a small guest-house close to Elm and Tucson. Near where your friend Beth used to live. It's cute and reasonable."

"Your mom's gonna miss you. She's gotten used to you being around. Look, there's almost no line. I'll be right back."

While she's gone, I screw up my courage. Angie won't be pleased to hear about me and Josh, that there is a me and Josh.

Angie returns several minutes later carrying a large iced drink with whipped cream and chocolate sprinkles, plus a blueberry muffin. "Bitch, I hate you," I said, eyeing my skinny latte and the apple I brought with me.

"I may be a bitch but that woman in front of me was a complete idiot. She kept changing her order, couldn't find her credit card, and all the while she's giggling like a little kid. Finally she's done, I start to order, and back she comes, wants to put it on a different card after the transaction's finished. I thought I'd never get back here. So your mom's upset about your moving?"

"Yeah, but it's a little more complicated."

"Complicated? You're holding out on me?"

I ignore her dig and get to it. "The thing is Josh was in town for a few days, and I saw him."

"In town from where?"

"Albuquerque. He's been living there since he left here. Has what seems like a decent job as some kind of chef in a British pub."

"I had no idea he could cook. So he told you he was really, really sorry for letting you rot in jail and leaving town instead of doing anything to help you?"

"He didn't just abandon me. He went to see a lawyer who told him if he went to the cops, the only thing that would happen is he'd get arrested too."

"Josh told you that?"

"Yeah."

"And you believe him?"

"Why shouldn't I?"

"Where do you want me to start? You think Josh would chance talking to a lawyer when he's on the lam? The lawyer could turn him in."

I smile at Angie. For once I know more than her. "A lawyer can't turn you in if you tell him about a crime you already committed. Everyone in prison knows that."

"I still don't believe him. How would Josh know that?"

"He knows more than you think. The big news is he wants to get back together. He asked me to go to Albuquerque with him."

"Kristin, please tell me you said no. You've got a good job, and things are going well. You can't just up and leave."

"Don't worry; I'm not that much of a moron. I'm not going anywhere. The other thing is Josh's boss wants to open a restaurant here and let Josh manage it."

"I don't know what to say. I don't trust Josh, and I'm afraid you're going to get hurt. I wish I could be happy for you."

I drink the last of my latte and stare hungrily at what's left of Angie's muffin. "Right now, everything's up in the air. I don't know if he's going to move back. He seems to have changed—-grown up."

"Josh, grown up. That's something I'd like to see."

"So tell me about the story you're working on?" I ask.

"You can't get me off Josh so easily. Does your mom know about Josh, is that why you're moving?"

"Partially. We got in a fight about something he told me Mom said."

"What?"

"She told him to leave town. The day I got arrested he called her house looking for me. Can you believe she'd do that?

"Are you sure that's what she said. And even if she did, can't you understand her side? She was furious at him. Her daughter's in jail. Because of him."

"But she never told me they talked. All this time I thought Josh never tried to find me. That he just left. She knew I loved him."

"I hope its 'loved', not love."

"Enough about me. Nothing's happened. I want to know about your story."

Angie looks at me for a long moment. Even thought she doesn't approve, I'm glad I told her. When I keep things from her, I feel dishonest. Finally she spoke, "We caught one of the court administrators lying about his credentials. It's serious enough that his job and some others who were supposed to vet him are on the line."

"I guess you can't tell me who." At first, when Angie wouldn't tell me details of stories, I felt hurt. Why didn't she trust me? Now I understood. Angie's integrity was part of what made her such a special person and terrific reporter.

"Not yet. I still need to do more checking. I shouldn't tell you this, but one of the people I have to interview is Kelly."

"Kelly? I've always known Tucson's a small town. I sure screwed that up."

"Don't be so hard on yourself. If Kelly had been a little less rigid . . . "

"Why are you interviewing him? He's not in trouble?"

"No. We think he has information about the person we're investigating. I don't know if he'll cooperate. Want me to say hi from you?" Angie asks as she turns her napkin into a fan and tries without success to create some cool air.

"No, no. You know that note I sent him a note telling him I was off parole? He didn't respond. You were right. Leave it alone."

"Okay. You mention Josh to Sara?"

"No, but you know Sara. I feel like she knows all about it."

THIRTY-NINE

Moving day. Tension between Mom and me hangs over the house, but in the routine of packing and loading boxes, we begin to talk. By the time I'm ready to take over the last load both of us get kinda weepy. When Mom gives me a hug, I hug back hard. I'll miss her.

Sunday, I empty boxes and put stuff away. When the phone rings, I think it's my landlady. She said she'd call when I'm moved in. It's Mom.

"I forgot to tell you I put a couple letters in your jewelry box. I don't know if they're important, but I wanted to let you know. They looked personal."

Intrigued, I rarely get letters, I plan to look after I hang up, but get distracted as I think of changes I need to make to my place. It's furnished, with decorative art on the walls; but I want it to reflect my taste—-whether that's a change for better or worse.

It's not till Monday morning, when I put on my earrings, that I remember the mail. Two letters. Neither has a return address—-one typed, one handwritten. The typed one's an invitation to a Labor Day barbecue at Taylor's. I open the other one—-it's from Kelly.

I read the few lines over and over, try to decipher hidden meaning in the words "its too bad things didn't work out differently." Does Kelly want to get in touch? Is he sorry we've broken up? By the tenth reading, I'm back to earth. His answer's nothing more than politeness. Kelly's that sort. He doesn't want to see me, but he has to do the right thing.

At work, I check the schedule. Daycare in the morning, and class with Sara in the afternoon. Shortly before lunch, she calls and asks if I can meet her in her office around noon. I've done nothing wrong, but I feel anxious. When your boss is psychic, it might be enough to think bad thoughts.

When I get to her office, Sara sits behind her desk, a pensive look on her face. Samantha lies quietly in her bed. Theodore's asleep on the floor snoring loudly.

"Hi Kristin, come on in, have a seat. How are you?"

"Good, I got here as soon as I could."

"Kristin you need to relax. I'm not the warden, and you're not in prison."

"Thanks." I don't know what else to say.

"The reason I want to talk is I heard from Gail. She's the woman whose job you took. She called to tell me she had her baby. Everything went fine. She has a new healthy daughter."

Oh, no, not the end of my job. Before I panic, Sara gives me a reassuring look. "She decided to be a stay-at-home mom. I'm offering you her job—-permanently. And a five percent raise."

"Wow, great, that's wonderful. I love working here."

"I gather that's an acceptance, but you don't have to decide right now."

"There's nothing to decide—-I'll take it."

"Great. Maybe we can start training therapy dogs soon. I've thought about it since I met Kazu. I'd like to discuss your project tomorrow. Will that work for you?"

"Sure."

I don't believe it. I want to call Angie, Mom, Kelly and Josh. Neither Mom nor Angie answers their phones, but I leave messages. I know I can't call Kelly, but maybe another note? As for Josh, I don't know what I feel. Rather than try to figure it out, I decide to finish the project. Now's not the time to let Sara down.

During lunch, I call clients who use daycare. The client list is alphabetical, so I start with Jasper's people, the Abbott's. Jasper, a staff favorite, is an older brown lab that's always well behaved. His person, Walter Abbot, is a middle-aged man, works in city government. Mr. Abbot treats us like you'd treat your kid's nanny. Treats Jasper like his child. He calls to check on him every couple hours. His behavior would annoy us except he's so sweet.

None of us has met his wife. She stays in the car——even in hot weather——when Mr. Abbot brings Jasper in or picks him up. She answers the phone, laughs when I ask what she likes best about Jasper. "Nothing, unless it's that I'll outlive him."

Is that a bad joke? Jasper's terrific. He's smart, friendly, compassionate. "I hate that dog. My husband cares more about his happiness than mine. That Goddamn animal hates me. Gives me dirty looks when Walter's not looking. Acts like I'm the interloper. I don't suppose I could pay you to have him get lost." I'm shocked and don't know how to respond.

Everyone else loves their animals. One woman's concerned their poodle likes her husband better than her, but she raves about the dog. Except for Mrs. Abbott, the clients consider their dogs' part of the family. For some their only family. When the day's over, I've spoken to forty-one owners——I mean peoples.

Shit. I was going to send Ina junk food and a letter. I promise myself to take care of it tomorrow. I've already waited too long. I can't believe she'll be in almost five more years. I hope she has a decent cellie, a job and some money. Has she seen Dwayne? I don't even need to check the list of what's allowed. Some things you never forget.

Josh calls in the afternoon.

"You won't believe this, but my job became permanent today. I got a raise."

"That's terrific. I've got news of my own. My boss decided to follow up on the restaurant deal, so I'll be back soon. Listen, I gotta go. I wanted you to know. I'll call you."

"Wait, I wanna tell you about a woman I talked to today. You won't believe what she said about her dog . . . but he'd already hung up.

FORTY

Two weeks in my new place. I love it. I worried I'd be lonely, spend my evenings with cookies, ice cream and candy. Hadn't happened. Being in control makes me responsible. If I binge, there's no one else to blame. I lose weight. Begin to feel okay about how I look. My social life's no better than when I was behind bars. But following my own rules, feels exhilarating.

In a class called Responsibility I took in prison, the teacher told a story about basketball. When there are referees, players get away with what they can. When there aren't, players call fouls on themselves. I didn't get it then, but I do now.

Josh calls daily. Once sent flowers. No word from Kelly when Angie interviewed him. She said he acted professionally and never mentioned my name. I expected nothing else.

I'm in bed, when someone knocks. Late for company. Only Mom and Angie have come by. Both would call first. No one else has my address. Rapists don't usually knock. I go to the door, look out the peephole. It's Josh. With a suitcase.

"What are you doing here? You're supposed to be in Albuquerque?

"Aren't you glad to see me?" Josh says, as he grabs me for a long hug my body returns before my mind can question it.

"Of course, but why are you here? What's with the suitcase? I'm shocked. You never mentioned anything when we talked."

"It's a surprise. My boss decided the restaurant's a go and sent me to look for a property. I didn't make plans about where to stay. I just wanted to see you."

Did Josh want to stay here? Was he moving here or just in for a few days? "So, how long you gonna be here?"

"I don't know. Depends how things go. If me being here's a problem, I can go to Leslie's or get a motel or something." He looks at me from head to toe. "Looking good. If you're expecting company, let me know . . . "

"I'm in my pj's. Don't be ridiculous. You're welcome here, you know that."

"Great, I'll get the rest of my shit." At least the place's clean, and I'd done some redecorating. I look for a place where Josh can put his stuff. He comes back in with only another small bag.

"I don't have much room, but I'll empty one side of the closet."

"Don't sweat it. I can put my stuff anywhere. I'm starving. Let's order a pizza and garlic bread."

"I'm not hungry but go ahead."

"I hope you don't mind, but I gave your phone number to my boss, Richard, and a few of the staff at Knickers'. Don't be surprised if I get some calls."

Why aren't I ecstatic? From the day I met Josh, all I want is to be with him. He's here. I don't know how I feel. He must have known I'd let him stay, if he gave people my number. Should he have asked first, or should I be flattered? My body continues to melt whenever he's close. Is that enough?

After Josh orders pizza, he asks about the people I work with. "You'll get to meet all of them if you stay. Taylor's second in command, and Sara's SO. He's having a Labor Day barbecue. Everyone from work's going. You'll love Sara. She has these amazing dogs, Samantha and Theodore. She takes them everywhere."

"Sara's the psychic nut job, right?"

"Josh, she's my boss; she just gave me a permanent job and a raise. Sara's one of the most compassionate people I've ever known. Once you meet her, you'll feel differently."

"Maybe, but this psychic shit is too weird."

"Wait till she tells you something about your life that no one else knows, or something about yourself you want to keep secret."

"Can't wait," Josh says a strange expression on his face. "She can't psych me out—-I don't have secrets. I'm going to buy some beer." I follow him out to the car, but he leaves without a word.

I sit in the living room and wonder what's the matter. Have I done something wrong already?

The pizza comes. I pay. Josh follows with a six-pack of Coors.

"Remember the moron files?" Josh says. "I found them the other day when I was packing. I almost threw them out, but I couldn't. I still laugh when I think of those kids in California who go for a hike and bring back 'abandoned puppies' that turn out to be bear cubs." Josh pauses to take another piece of pizza. He seems fine, I feel better.

"Or the father, visiting Yellowstone, who put his daughter on an elk and tries to take a picture? I kind of let it go when you weren't around. I still collect the stories but only in my head."

"I heard one the other day. Some guy in Phoenix burned his feet getting the mail, and the government issued an advisory not to walk barefoot when it's over one hundred."

"Maybe we need a file for government moron stories."

"Shouldn't be hard in Arizona."

Again, Josh gets quiet, but this time in a good way. "You look better than ever."

Josh eats more pizza, finishes the bread. Like Kelly he can eat whatever. It's not fair. He looks thinner than before I went to prison. One piece of pizza left. I try to put food out of my mind.

"Don't you think you should go to bed, make sure you get enough rest for work?" Josh says with a big grin. My body follows him into the bedroom. I feel beautiful.

I should be happy. Josh's here. He wants me. Likes how I look. Kelly sees only damaged goods. So why do I think of Kelly?

CHAPTER
FORTY-ONE

Leaving Josh isn't as hard as I feared. He feels warm and familiar, but when I wake up I can't wait to get to work. Once I get there my mind drifts. I compare Kelly to Josh, Josh to Kelly. Kelly wouldn't let me take the rap for something he did. Josh loves me. Kelly doesn't.

This morning I meet with Sara to discuss my assignment. I'm leery of being alone with her, afraid she knows Josh is at my house, afraid she knows we had sex.

She begins with a training tip. "I worked with a timid dog yesterday—Lola, a rescue, beagle-basset mix. Don't smile at timid dogs. What they see is your teeth bared. Try to keep your mouth closed till they get to know you."

I smile at her, my mouth closed. She laughs. "Taylor told me you're coming to the barbecue. You can bring someone if you like."

"Okay." Maybe she does know. I change the subject. "Where are Samantha and Teddy? I haven't seen them today?"

"Taylor took them to the vet for vaccinations—-nothing to worry about. So what did you decide are the top three reasons people like dogs?"

"The hardest parts cutting it down. I chose their loyalty, always being glad to see you, and not being judgmental," I look at Sara, hoping she won't be too judgmental. Good traits in people too.

"Sounds like your choices validate my experience. I know that dogs, unlike some humans, want to do the right thing. All of us have had the experience of being let down by someone. I think that's why our relationships with animals, especially dogs, are so gratifying. Dogs don't let you down. If you have a dog, you can get through whatever life throws your way, don't you think?"

"I never thought about it that way but, if I'd had one in prison, it would've been easier to survive."

"Too bad they didn't have dog training. It does great things for prisoners. If I ran prisons, I'd make sure every prisoner who wanted a dog would have one."

"I don't think that would go over with ADOC." Sara looks confused. "Arizona Department of Corrections. They don't care about doing great things for inmates. Aren't you worried some inmates would hurt the dogs?" Oh shit, I've forgotten to mail the stuff to Ina again. Tonight for sure.

"From what I've read, even violent prisoners treat dogs decently when they're inside even if they wouldn't on the outside. Dogs don't rat you off. They're affectionate if you treat them right (and often if you don't). They don't judge you no matter what you did to wind up incarcerated. I'm not surprised you worry about the dogs. I've noticed how much compassion you've shown since you started here."

"It's easy. I love all the dogs, especially Theodore and Samantha."

"Those two are special. You probably know Taylor and I live together. When I met him, I saw the strong bond he had with his dogs and realized he had the same characteristics I love in animals. Its fool proof to imagine your partner as a dog - see if he measures up. Before you get serious with any man you should check out how dogs react to him. I wouldn't be with Taylor if Samantha and Theodore had disapproved."

I think about Josh. He's usually happy to see me, isn't great at not being judgmental, and as for loyalty, he flunks big time. I wonder if it matters he isn't a dog lover? Samantha would disapprove of him, but maybe not Theodore, as both love to eat, especially snacks. I must have been in a daydream as I hear Sara say,

" . . . your own dog class. I have some articles I want you to read, and you need to take a class at the Humane Society." My own class?

"Wow that's terrific. I'll start reading and call the Humane Society right away."

I go back to my desk. Sara never said why she gave me that assignment. I start to read the articles, when the phone rings. "Kristin, could you stop by tonight on your way home?" Mom asks.

"Something wrong? You okay?"

"Nothing to worry about. I just need to talk to you."

"Okay, see you then." I hang up, with an uncomfortable feeling that stays with me. I expect Josh to complain when I tell him I'll be late. To my surprise, he seems fine, offers to pick up dinner.

I walk into Mom's house, not sure what to expect. Can it be about Josh? Soon as she sees me, she gives me a big hug. Probably not about Josh. "I don't want to make a big deal, but I'm going to have a hysterectomy. The date isn't for sure yet, but probably in the next ten days or so."

"Mom, why didn't you tell me you weren't feeling well. It's not like cancer is it?"

"No, not cancer or anything like it. I've had some symptoms but nothing serious, and my doctor thinks I should get it done."

"What do you need me to do? Do you want me to stay with you after the surgery? I'll take you to the hospital."

"Slow down, honey. Your Aunt Lauren's coming in from California. She's planned to visit anyway, and she went through this a few years ago. There are two things you can help with, though: She doesn't drive at night, and she's allergic to dogs."

"So you want me to take Sparkie while she's here? That's great. I'd love to. As to night driving, if you and Aunt Lauren need a ride to go dancing or something, no problem." Mom laughs.

"Probably driving's not an issue, but it's good to know you're available if something comes up."

I'm ambivalent about leaving. I should stay for dinner with her, but I know Josh will be mad if I don't come home. Before I can decide, she announces she has plans for dinner and needs to take off.

Too late to go to the post office. I let Ina down again.

FORTY-TWO

I'm ready to go. No Josh. We should have left fifteen minutes ago. I check the mirror for the fiftieth time. I'm wearing an old denim skirt I couldn't fit into till recently. I've paired it with a purple and blue flowered shirt that emphasizes my curves, but's not tight enough to be slutty.

What if Josh doesn't like Sara or Taylor? What if Samantha or Theodore doesn't like him? Is he late on purpose? I can't imagine he's worry about fitting in. Probably forgot. It's something that means a lot to me. Not him. I try to calm down. Nothing wrong with being fashionably late. I hear his car finally.

"I was afraid you forget."

"How could I? You mention it at least twice a day. Forget a party at the husband of the fortune teller?"

"She's not a fortune teller and Taylor's not her husband. They live together but they're not married."

"Smart move there," he mumbles. "I'm late because I was talking to the ex-owner of Sage, and time got away from me. Sage and Thyme get it?" I nod my head no. "You're so bloody stupid sometimes. Sage is that restaurant on the East Side that went out of business a month or so ago. Sage and Thyme, spices." He shakes his head. "I gotta change my shirt."

Bloody? Now he's English. I can't focus on the other words. Everything has to be okay today. A few minutes later, we're on our way. "I might get some moron stories today," Josh says.

"I like these people. They're not idiots, the opposite in fact."

"Tell me a little about each one. It'll make it easier to remember them."

"Sure. Sara Sanchez is my boss. She's about fiftylate fifties, but looks younger. Fairly tall, slender build. Long brown hair with some gray streaks. She usually wears broom skirts, even to work. Kind of an old-fashioned dresser, but it works for her."

"Broom skirts, like a witch, appropriate for one who thinks she's psychic."

I ignore him and continue. "Taylor Lawrence, he's her SO, not sure of his age, maybe late 50's. He's second in command but he's never seemed like my boss. Taylor's tall, silver hair, and big blue eyes. Helped me out when I first started. The dogs adore him."

"Sounds like you do too. He read tarot cards or anything?"

"Josh stop. You're being ridiculous. Sam's a part-time employee. He's a college student, eighteen or nineteen. Lanky, red hair. Shy. He still hasn't figured out adult conversation, but he's sweet.

"Angie and Art might be there. I told you Angie's Sara's niece? Angie's hot after some story, and it's close to deadline, so they might not make it."

"What about the others? Isn't there someone named Samantha you talk about a lot?"

"Samantha's one of Sara's dogs. She's a black lab, really smart."

"A dog. And she'll be there?"

"Of course. Along with Theodore, who's a brown mutt, really cute. As for other people, I assume there'll be more, but I don't know who."

The rest of the ride passes quickly. Josh makes no further sarcastic remarks.

At least twenty people are milling about when we arrive. I'm embarrassed for a moment when I introduce Josh. I can't decide what to call him; he isn't my fiancé, a word I hate. Lover makes me uncomfortable, but boyfriend's worse—-sounds like high school. I settle for friend, but each time I use it, Josh looks unhappy.

Samantha and Theodore have been cleaned and brushed. Samantha has a big red bow in her fur, and seems to like it. She walks around the crowd, head held high, showing off. Theodore has no decorations—-unless you count food on the corner of his mouth. A third dog I've never seen before, a black and white English bulldog's wearing a blue bandana with the 'I'm the boss of you look,' characteristic of its breed. Taylor sees me eye the dog and walks over. "I see you've met Magic."

"So you guys have three dogs?"

"Four, but Rusty, the fourth one is older and doesn't like crowds. He's a sweet old boy. I'll take you to meet him if you want."

"Okay." I turn to let Josh know where I'm going. He's talking to Sara, so I go off with Taylor, fight an impulse to stay and listen to their conversation—-make sure Josh doesn't say anything stupid about psychics or anything else.

Rusty's a delight, a multicolored boxer mix, whose savvy in the way older dogs are. Taylor and I fuss over him. For a few minutes we sit quietly.

"Sara tells me you're doing great and she wants you to teach your own obedience classes. That's quite a compliment." Rusty moves closer to me and snuggles up as if he understands what Taylor said, wants to congratulate me.

"She's never done that with anyone before. I'm not surprised; you have great instincts with dogs and their people. I love the dogs, but their people make me crazy. They want dogs to be like them. Get mad when dogs do dog things like chase birds. People talk incessantly about nothing, but get irritated when their dog barks to let them know someone or some animal is close by."

I don't know what to say. I adore compliments, but I'm not sure I deserve this one. "I don't know if I ever thanked you for helping me when I started at The Dog. You're wrong about me. I might be good with dogs' people, but not people in general. You heard about me and Kelly and how I messed that up." Why am I telling him?

"I heard you and Kelly were seeing each other. I didn't know it was over till I saw you with someone new today. Whatever happened with Kelly, it's his loss." Again, I'm unsure what to say and settle for giving Taylor a big grin. We sit with Rusty for a few more minutes until I decide I better go find Josh.

"Rusty's great, but I need to go back to the party. Josh doesn't know anyone."

"I better get back too. I'm the host after all." Taylor and I walk back together. I wonder if Josh is still with Sara. In the back yard, Sara's surrounded by a group of people, but not Josh. I spot him in animated conversation with an attractive young woman in a short red dress, which shows off her perfect figure.

I walk toward them with a sense of dread. I look good, but compared to her . . . Why are perfect women always around to remind you of what you aren't? Can Josh want me if he can have her? I stand next to Josh, a fixed smile on my face, and wait for him to introduce me or include me in the conversation. They're talking about how hard it is to run a restaurant.

After what seems forever, Josh turns to me. "Kristin, this is Brie," (of course her name's Brie). "She works at The Blue Sky. Brie, this is Kristin." What happened to Kristin, my friend, or Kristin who works with Sara at The Dignified Dog, or Kristin who went to prison instead of me?

Brie fakes a smile, and I see her straight white teeth in her perfect mouth below her perfect nose. They continue their conversation. Neither includes me. I feel invisible. I try to look unconcerned as I leave them.

I look for anyone but Sara to talk to. She'd know how I feel. One pitying glance would make me cry. Angie and Art aren't here. I'm about to despair when Samantha saves me. She sits down, gives me her paw and looks at me as if to say, "Are you okay, can I help?" Minutes later, Josh comes over like everything's fine.

"Josh this is Samantha. I was telling you about her on the way over." Samantha wags her tail and looks intensely at Josh.

" Why would you introduce me to a dog?" Josh says as he looks at me, not Samantha. Samantha puts out her paw, but Josh ignores it. As we walk to the buffet table, I see Samantha and Theodore standing side-by-side looking at Josh, their tails silent and their faces sad.

The rest of the barbecue's much the same. Brie fills a plate to the brim with ribs, chicken, corn, garlic bread, beans (no salad, of course), followed by seconds and an enormous plate of cake and ice cream. It figures she can eat like a horse. I eat a small piece of chicken and some veggies and hope it will fill me up. Not even close. I try another piece of chicken, then a small bite of cookie, and then it's all over. I ate a dozen or more cookies as I watch Brie and Josh flirt.

Finally, we can leave. As we say goodbye, Sara gives me a big hug and pulls me aside. Is she going to warn me about Josh? "Kristin, so glad you came. I need to remind you not to d take your responsibilities lightly. A dog's life may depend on it," and moves away. What the hell did that mean?

"What did you think of the party?" I ask Josh as we walk to the car.

"Better than I expected. Good food."

"I notice you had a good old time with Brie?" I say before I can stop myself.

"No more than you did with Taylor. We're not there two minutes, when you disappear somewhere with the man all the dogs adore."

"That was nothing. He was showing me their other dog. It doesn't like crowds."

"A new twist on showing your etchings—-dogs who want to be alone with only you and him."

"Look, Taylor's way too old for me, and he's with Sara."

"I was just talking business with Brie. The place she used to work went out of business. When I hear a restaurant fails, I want to know more. Maybe there's a property available, or maybe I'll learn something. I thought you wanted me to be friendly."

"With the people I work with. I don't even know why the hell she was there."

"There's nothing to be jealous about. She's getting married at the end of the month."

I start to argue, but what's the point? What's wrong with me that I get hysterical 'cause my boyfriend talks to another woman at a party in front of twenty people? But how does he know she's getting married. You don't find that out talking about menu planning.

FORTY-THREE

Tuesday, my first lesson on 'separation anxiety.' Not me and Josh, but Gertie, a brown and white Shepherd mix; and Beth, her person. My job's to watch the interaction between the two while Sara talks with them.

After she welcomes dog and human, Sara asks Beth to explain why she's here. "I adopted Gertie about a month ago. She's nine. The second I got her we bonded. She's terrific when I'm with her; when I leave the house, I don't know what she'll do. She shreds furniture, paper—-anything she can find; chews shoes; makes a colossal mess."

"Do you know anything about her life before you adopted her?"

"Oh, yes. I've known her since she was a pup. Alan and Susan, good friends of mine, adopted Gertie from the Humane Society. They had no kids and treated her like their child. Took her everywhere, had her groomed often, and showered her with attention."

"Sounds like dog heaven; what happened?"

"They broke up. Joint custody was the plan, but they were so bitter it couldn't work. They decided to find her a good home. Susan joked if they'd been married and got divorced, a judge would force them to figure it out. It was hard to find someone to adopt him due to her advanced age. I wanted her, but I'm closer to Susan than Alan, so he was against it. When they couldn't find anyone else, he agreed. I'd tell you what a jerk he is, but I don't think it has anything to do with Gertie's problem."

"How did you work the transition from them to you?"

"I took a week off work and spent it with her. It wasn't till I went back she started being destructive."

"Did you know her routine when she lived with Alan and Susan?"

"Not really; I never thought about that."

"Kristin, why don't you tell us what you've observed?"

I answer slowly—-don't want to mess up. "Gertie's totally focused on Beth. She sits on top of her feet. Doesn't seem interested in us or the dog stuff around the room—-even treats. She's friendly, but when you or I pet her, she looks at Beth."

Sara smiles, "You're right on point. It's a classic case of separation anxiety. Not unusual. This behavior's common in older dogs that have been with one family since birth and suddenly everything changes. New environment, new people, different routine. Probably new rules. Maybe at the old place they can beg at the table, but not at their new home. Or vice-versa. People get nervous moving, and they know what's happening. Dogs cling to their new owner, who becomes the pack leader. If that person leaves, they get anxious—-especially if the person lives alone."

"Maybe it's partially my fault. I've encouraged Gertie to be with me all the time. My husband died a few years ago, my daughter's away at college, and I'm kind of lonely."

"It's not a question of fault. You can't love your dog too much, but a healthy dog (like a healthy person) needs some degree of independence. The good news is it's usually fixable."

"Glad to hear that."

"To promote her independence, you need to make sure that sometimes when you're home, you're not always together. Does she sleep in your bed?"

"Yeah she does."

"I suggest you buy her a dog bed and only let her on yours for special treats. You also need to be aware of your routine before leaving the house. If she knows you always dry your hair before you leave, do that some other time of the day also. Try not to have her associate certain behaviors with your leaving. The last fifteen minutes before you leave, don't pay much attention to her. When you leave, say good by once calmly. Since dogs act out more the first hour or so, leave her a Kong or something similar so she'll have something to do."

"I guess I've made too big a deal when I leave. I say stuff like 'Mommy's gonna miss you.' You know, stupid talk like that."

"It's great to talk to your dog. They want us to talk to them. Don't blame yourself. It's a common problem and, with a few changes in your behavior, you'll see changes in Gertie's. I can tell she's a smart girl, aren't you?" she says to Gertie, who wags her tail but keeps her eye on Beth.

Over the next few days, instead of Josh versus Kelly, I compare Josh's behavior to dogs'. I know dogs are loyal to their people, but are they loyal to each other? Male dogs go for any female in heat. Maybe males of all species have that in common. I close my eyes and picture Josh chasing Brie who has turned into a perfectly groomed white standard poodle.

When I'm not imagining Josh humping women who turn into dogs, I worry about what Sara said at the barbecue. Was it a careless remark or more serious? Sara isn't the careless type. Did she mean my dog class? If she's psychic, why can't she explain her warning?

Mom's going into the hospital tomorrow. Aunt Lauren's flying in late tonight. I offer to pick her up, but Mom insists she'll do it. The two of us are going to dinner together. Afterwards, I'll take Sparkie so he won't upset Aunt Lauren's allergies. Josh didn't care that I won't be home for dinner. Said he had other plans. Something to do with the restaurant.

I ask Mom to tell me all about the surgery. I think I'm more anxious than she is. For once, she encourages me to eat whatever I want—-including dessert. "What's the deal with wanting me to eat?"

"I've probably been too hard on you about your weight. You need to enjoy yourself sometimes. You look terrific."

"Thanks, Mom, but I blew it big time last weekend at Taylor's barbecue. I ate at least a dozen cookies, big cookies."

"What do you want me to say, Kristin? Obviously you feel guilty."

"I do, so I've tried to be extra good since."

"Look, everyone slips. It's what you do after that that counts. How are things with you and Josh?" Mom asks, absent her usual sarcasm.

"Good. He hasn't found a spot for his restaurant yet, but I'm sure it's just a matter of time." Wish I could tell her what I really think. Why is it taking so long? When he's out does he meet with people in the business, or is he with other women? He always wants to know where I go, but when I ask him, he just says, "I have plans" unless I act jealous and cry. Then he tells me something, (maybe a lie) or screams at me and takes off. More than anything, I'd like to discuss Kelly.

I have salad and no dessert, probably because Mom's given me permission to eat. I encourage Mom to order dessert, and she does. I want to prolong dinner. Tell her I'm worried, that I love her; but I can't get the words out. "Don't worry, I'll take good care of Sparkie and come to the hospital often."

"Thanks, but I'll only be there two days. I'll be fine."

Josh's out when I get home. I show Sparkie around, put out his dish, water bowl and toys. He slept with Mom at home, but I'd borrowed a small dog bed and set it up in the bedroom. He ignores it and jumps on our bed.

I start to read one of the books Sara gave me when the phone rings. "Hello, I answer."

"Is Josh there?" a feminine voice asks.

"He's not here; can I take a message?"

"Are you Leslie?"

"No, Leslie doesn't live here. Who are you?" I ask.

"Who are you?" she replies.

"Kristen." Good manners trump my concern.

"I'm Crystal. Tell Josh I called."

"Can I give him your number?"

"He has it." And she hangs up.

Crystal? Who the hell's she? Josh never mentioned her? Why does she think I'm Leslie? Did he pretend he's staying with her? Didn't want her to know, he's with me? What's Josh's fascination with girls with slutty names—Brie, and now Crystal? Maybe there's nothing to worry about. She could be his sister or a coworker. Maybe I'll change my name to Brandy. I try to get back to my book. Instead I doze off. Awaken as Josh puts the key in the door.

"Hey, Kristin, did I wake you. It's only ten. Good meeting tonight. Looks like I've found the right property. I'll call Richard tomorrow morning." I say nothing.

"What's up, why so quiet?"

"You got a call earlier. Someone named Crystal wants you to call her."

"And that's what's bothering you? Crystal works at The Red Knicker. I told you some of the staff might call."

"She wasn't very nice. Wanted to know who I was, seemed surprised I wasn't Leslie."

"As to the Leslie part, she's confused. I stayed at Leslie's last time, and I said I might stay with her again. I wasn't sure you'd let me stay."

"I thought you called the restaurant and gave them this number. You didn't tell them you lived with me?"

"I did, but I didn't talk to her. Maybe she didn't get the message. Kristin, you've got to chill. You can't give me grief about every female I talk to. She's just somebody I worked with. Maybe she has a message from the boss."

"Then why was she such a bitch?" And why wouldn't the boss call with his own message.

"You can't blame that on me. Maybe she has PMS."

Asshole. I don't answer. I'm not sure if I'm jealous and insecure, or Josh's a liar. I look at Josh who morphs into a Rottweiler. He's chasing a strange woman I imagine to be Crystal who slowly changes into a basset hound as he begins to hump her.

"Come on, Kristin. Let's not argue."

Josh walks into the bedroom. "Kristin, what the hell's this dog doing in our bed?"

"That's Sparkie, my mom's dog. He's here while she has surgery . . . don't you remember?"

"Oh, yeah. But why's he on the bed?"

"He sleeps with Mom. I got him a dog bed. I'm trying to teach him to sleep in it."

" Try harder. I don't want to sleep with a damn dog. Dog bed? As far as I'm concerned dogs should sleep outside or on the floor. They don't need special beds. You better not expect me to take care of it."

"He's a him not an it. Don't worry. I'll watch him. The only thing is Sparkie's afraid of thunder. When it storms, he needs someone to be with him and reassure him. If he's left alone, he tries to run away. I'm sure I told you about the time he ran away from my mom's house."

"Yeah."

"Don't worry. I'll take Sparkie to work with me. Nights, I'll be here. The way this monsoon has crapped out, there's not much chance of rain anyway."

But I'm wrong.

FORTY-FOUR

"You sure put your mother through hell," Aunt Lauren mumbles, her mouth full of hard candy. Aunt Lauren and I had both arrived at University Hospital by six to see Mom before surgery. Mom's upbeat and laughs off our concerns.

"Sparkie doing okay?" she asks. She seems more worried about him than her operation.

Not long after we arrive, the nurse kicks us out and suggests we go to the surgical waiting room. Aunt Lauren stops at the gift shop and buys a large box of hard candy. I think it's for Mom, but she opens it. I get a latte, but for once, I'm not hungry.

The small waiting room's almost filled. A woman about Mom's age sits alone, her head down. A man and a woman hold hands and share a news-paper. Across the room, a group of people obviously related chat quietly. A TV's on set to the Today Show. No one watches. We take the only empty seats next to the lone woman. Everyone seems somber, and some cry.

"It wasn't an easy time for me either," I answer aloud. Screw you, I say in my head. Mom's on the operating table, and you're giving me shit.

"It's not supposed to be easy for people who deal drugs. That's the point of prison."

"I'm innocent. I wasn't dealing drugs. I'm sure Mom told you the drugs weren't mine."

"Yeah, they belonged to that no-good boyfriend of yours. How could you date a guy that treated you like that? Any self-respecting woman would stay away from him. How can you live with a drug dealer, a criminal?"

"Is that what Mom told you?"

"No, but she's always been naïve. This is my opinion."

"Life's going well for me now. I got off parole early, and I have a good job."

"You have a job. Surely you could find something better to do than babysit dogs. You have a college degree." I drain my coffee and watch Aunt Lauren stuff candy in her mouth. We were never close. I hadn't seen her much over the years, but she'd never attacked me like this.

"I love my job. It's more than babysitting dogs. I'm training to teach obedience classes. I got a promotion and a raise. Just 'cause you don't like dogs doesn't mean what I do doesn't matter." I answer, my voice rising.

"Can't you two stop arguing? My daughter might not live through surgery. Find somewhere else to scream at each other." The room grows silent. Everyone looks at us.

"I'm so sorry. We'll be quiet." I look at Aunt Lauren, and she nods her head almost imperceptibly. "Can I get you something to drink or anything?" I ask the woman.

"No, nothing." I raise my eyes to look at her. She's younger than I thought. Her hair's shiny and brown without a trace of gray. It reaches her shoulders and has the appearance of being well cared for, but today, it hangs in uneven waves. Her eyes are red and swollen. It's a warm September day but she's dressed in jeans and a purple sweater. The hospital's very cold. I'm uncomfortable in my shorts and a t-shirt. Too late to do anything about it now.

"What happened to your daughter?" I ask. I want to make up for my bad behavior.

"She's a freshmen at the U of A. I got a call yesterday afternoon. She'd been in an accident. I flew in last night. My husband's on a business trip. I had to come alone. He's on his way. Beth's majoring in chemistry. She's got broken bones, internal injuries; they're afraid she's bleeding in the brain . . . " the words tumbled out.

"I'm so sorry. I went to the U of A." What a stupid thing to say. Think of something intelligent. "This is an excellent hospital. It's attached to the medical school. She couldn't get better care anywhere. Please let me get you a drink."

She eyed my drink. "I'd love a cup of coffee."

"How about a latte or cappuccino or something?"

"Black coffee would be fine."

I walk out of the room toward the coffee cart. Aunt Lauren follows. I don't want to talk to her.

"Maybe it would be better if you go back in there and talk to that woman," I say. "She seems like she'd like to talk to someone and you're closer to her age." It least it will get her away from me.

"I will, but I came out here to talk to you. I'm sorry I gave you a hard time. I'm worried about Louise, and I guess I'm taking it out on you. I meant what I said about your—-boyfriend and the job, but I know now's not the time or place."

"Fine," I mumble. Just leave me alone. She walks back toward the waiting room.

By the time I get back with the coffee, Aunt Lauren and the woman (who I find out later is Robin Lindstrom) are deep in conversation. The other family's gone. I hand her the coffee and sit down, glad I don't have to talk. I open my book and pretend to read. After what seems like forever—-but is only about two hours—-a petite woman in a white coat comes into the room and calls my name.

"Hi, I'm Doctor Lee. Your mom's surgery went very well. There was no evidence of cancer or other abnormalities, and she came through it fine. She's in recovery, and you can see her shortly. Do you have any questions?"

"No," we both say almost in unison.

We say good by to Mrs. Lindstrom, wish her luck. I want to be happy that Mom's fine, but how can I when this woman's daughter might die, and my aunt thinks I'm stupid and worthless?

FORTY-FIVE

The sky's dark, the wind's picking up, and lightning flashes in the distance. Like everyone else in the city, I want rain instead of the high humidity that makes my clothes cling and sweat run down my face. But not tonight. I promised Mom I'd pick up her prescription and get her some groceries, but I don't want to leave Sparkie if there's a storm.

Sparkie and I come home from The Dog hot and cranky. Josh's car's parked in his usual spot, but the house's quiet. No TV, no music. "Josh, you here?" Nothing. I walk into the bedroom. He's sprawled across the bed. "Josh, wake up."

"I'm asleep, leave me alone."

"Asleep? It's after five—-are you sick?"

"No."

"Aren't you hungry?"

"No, leave me alone."

"Josh, wake up. We gotta eat, and you have to watch Sparkie. I need to get some stuff for Mom."

"Take him with you and shut up."

I sit down on the bed. Sparkie follows me. "I told you my aunt's allergic, and it's too hot to leave him in the car."

"Don't yell. I'll get up in a minute. What's the damn dog doing on the bed," he shouts as Sparkie jumps off?

"I'm not yelling. Don't cuss at Sparkie. He's scared of storms. I've told you about the time he ran away."

"About five hundred times. So what if I cuss at him? He's a dog. He doesn't understand. You're nicer to that fucking, excuse me, disgusting dog than you are to me."

"Dogs know more than you think. Sparkie's not disgusting."

"Shut up, Kristin. I'm half asleep."

I don't want to fight. "I'm sorry. I didn't mean to wake you. I hardly had time for lunch, and I'm starving. If you don't want to eat, I'll just grab something."

"Okay, okay, give me a couple of minutes." Josh walks into the bathroom, combs his fingers through his hair. "I have good news. I'll tell you when I get out."

Why's he asleep this time of day? That's how depressed women in prison behave when they can get away with it. There was that Leticia who never got up except for meals. Missed court. She was transferred to the mental health unit or suicide watch. I never saw her again. What kind of good news? The restaurant? The kitchen's still a mess from this morning. Why would I think he'd clean up?

Josh walks in the kitchen, awake now. I'm doing dishes, but he doesn't say a word, doesn't even notice. "The good news is I have a part-time gig bar tending at the Downtown. I saw a want ad, and they hired me. I'm surprised because I didn't give any notice when I split last time. They're short-handed. I start tonight, which is why I wanted to get some rest."

"Tonight, you can't start tonight. You have to stay with Sparkie. Why do you need a part-time job? What about the restaurant?"

"Don't worry about tonight. I don't have to be there until ten. Won't you be back by then?"

"Of course. But why do you need another job?"

"The restaurant won't open for the next month or so. I need some cash to tide me over. The boss can't pay me much while nothing's happening."

I don't know what to say. Last time he worked there, our life went to hell. A loud clap of thunder and finally, rain. Sparkie whines and crawls under the kitchen table.

"Don't cry, Spark, it'll be all right." I pick him up and cradle him like a baby. He's shaking.

"Maybe we shouldn't go out. Sparkie's already upset."

"I'll make something. There're enough eggs and cheese for omelets; maybe the storm will stop by then," Josh says.

We eat dinner and watch Seinfeld. The lightning and thunder continue, as does the rain. I eat, as Sparkie sits on my lap. A weather bulletin interrupts the show to broadcast flash flood warnings until 10 p.m. As we finish, the rain stops.

"I hate to leave Sparkie, but I promised Mom. I could leave him in the car it's cool enough; but if there's thunder, he'll go crazy."

"Don't be ridiculous, Kristin. I can watch a dog for an hour or so."

"You don't care about him. He's scared and needs someone who's understands. I don't want you to be mean to him."

"I won't. Watch." He sits down next to Sparkie and pats his ears. Sparkie looks at him as if he isn't sure. Josh takes the last piece of cheddar cheese. "Good Sparkie, good boy, eat this." Sparkie takes it and begins to wag his tail. When Josh walks back toward the kitchen, Sparkie follows. "See, go ahead and take care of your mom."

"Promise you won't leave till I get back?"

"I promise, I promise. Get going already. The sooner you go, the sooner you'll get back." He picks up Sparkie and pets him.

I grab my purse and take off.

"Stupid fucking mutt," Josh drops Sparkie on the floor as he hears the door close.

Tucson Boulevard's a mess. In most cities, traffic would be unaffected; but in Tucson when it rains, people act like there's black ice. Out of frustration, I tailgate the driver in front of me. Almost hit him when he stops for no reason. I try to calm down, but I can't.

A two-minute trip to Walgreen's takes ten. Five cars in the drive-through. I go inside. Two people ahead of me. The male clerk flirts with the first one a young blonde. He's in no hurry to help the next in line, a large unkempt woman who's clearly upset and keeps muttering "fucking shit" under her breath. After enough time has passed to arrange a complicated rendezvous, it's the second woman's turn.

Before the clerk gets a word out, two women rush out from the back of the prescription area and whisper to the clerk. I hear "cat," "medicine," and "drive-through." The male clerk in our line goes to the drive-in window. A young woman waits on the strange woman in front of me. "Can I help you ma'am?"

"My prescription's supposed to be ready today. I was here earlier, and you didn't have it. My doctor called it in. Don't tell me you don't have it, I . . . "

"Phone number, please."

"3 2 3 - 4 1 5 4," she says slowly and loudly, "never get any Goddamn help."

"Gruenfeld?" The woman nods. "I have two ready—-$24.50." She pays and leaves with another chorus of "fucking shit."

Finally my turn, but before anyone helps me, I hear "You said it'd be ready at seven. The clock says 7:02. What's wrong with this place? I'm not moving till I get kitty's medicine."

"You can't block the drive, or we'll have to call the police."

"Go ahead. Call them. Call anyone you damn well please. I'm not moving till kitty gets her pills. I can't afford to leave and come back."

"You don't have to leave—-you can come in and sit down and wait. It'll be only a few minutes."

The woman says nothing.

"Code 11, Code 11," blares from the intercom. All the clerks vanish. Thunder claps. Normally, I'd enjoy the drama. Another story for Josh. Why is it when you're in a hurry, shit happens?

After what seems like forever—-but likely less than a minute—a different clerk returns. "I think the rain brings out the crazies," she says quietly. I get Mom's prescriptions without a problem and am about to leave, when a large man in a doctor's coat appears from the back part of the pharmacy and goes to the window.

"We have Bruno's tabs; it'll be $10. I need you to verify your address."

"Why do you need my address? That's my personal business." She holds out a ten-dollar bill. "I've waited too long. Poor Bruno needs his medicine."

"I'm sorry, ma'am, but under federal law, I can't dispense medication unless you provide your address." He looks calmly at her. "You wouldn't want someone else to get kitty's meds, say a dog or someone, would you?"

"No, but . . . "

"Up to you, Mrs. Dover. If you want the medicine, I need the address."

"3130 North Fontana," she hisses. He hands her the bag, and she drives away.

Why didn't the police show? Busy? The rain always caused more than a usual amount of accidents. Mostly fender-benders, but likely a few serious ones. Someone always ignores DO NOT ENTER WHEN FLOODED signs and next thing you know their car floats down the wash with them in it. The legislature had passed the Stupid Motorist Law that required driver's to pay the cost of rescue. But it doesn't stop idiots from trying to save a few minutes.

Shopping's uneventful. I grab eggs, chicken soup for Mom, and the oldest coffee cake and cheapest candy for Aunt Lauren. It rains hard at the store, but when I get to Mom's, it's dry. The monsoon's weird that way. It rains very hard but sometimes only in a small area. Once it rained in my back yard but not my front.

"Mom, Aunt Lauren, hi." I put the food in the fridge and go into the living room. Mom's on the couch with an afghan over her. Aunt Lauren sits in a chair wearing an old-fashioned housecoat, and slippers. Her hairs in rollers covered by a pink scarf decorated with garish flowers. For Mom's sake, I hide my feelings.

"Thanks, Kristen; I'm sorry you had to drive in the rain. I heard the flood warnings. It never started here——only lightning and thunder. How about your place?"

"Heavy rain, roads flooded, the usual. How you feeling?"

"Good, a little pain, mostly tired. I saw the surgeon today, and he was pleased. How's Spark; he'll be okay, won't he?"

"Josh's with him. He adores him, don't worry. He'll sit with him till I get back." Was I convincing her or me?

I stay for another ten minutes, chat, but refuse the stale coffee cake. The drive home's quick. The rain had stopped. Lightning was still visible in the distance.

I pull in our street and up to the drive. Josh's car's gone. Where is he? What about Sparkie? I hurry into the house. "Josh, Sparkie. . ." I run through the house and yard. Call Sparkie's name. The back gate's open. What has Josh done? Sparkie's gone.

CHAPTER
FORTY-SIX

Josh let me down again.

I grab a handful of treats and take off. The wind's died down. The air's crisp and clean. The lovely night makes me feel worse. "Sparkie, Sparkie, come here boy, treats Sparkie, treats." How could I trust Josh? Was this what Sara warned me about?

People are out enjoying the storm's aftermath. I stop anyone who'll listen. "Have you seen a small white poodle-mix, he's lost, afraid of storms." I try not to cry. Everyone wants to help. One old lady babbles on about her cat, Freckles, who went missing during a storm "I finally found him in the closet. I don't know what I would have done if something happened to my baby . . ." In my head, I beg her to shut up. I can't waste time. I need to look for Sparkie. Her voice follows me. I feel guilty leaving her.

One guy asks if I have a picture. Hasn't he ever seen a poodle? Or maybe he saw a poodle alone but can't be sure it's my Sparkie without a photo? Most people say they'll look, but no one's seen him. Finally, I go back—-no Josh, no Sparkie.

I call Angie. She'll know what to do. "Hi, it's me. Sparkie's missing. I don't know what to do . . . Yeah, he's here because of Mom's surgery… I left him with Josh. I'm so stupid. I had to take some meds over to Mom, and when I got home, they were both gone . . . No note . . . See you in a few."

I pace around the house. Shouldn't be long she lives close. The phone rings. I grab it. "Josh?"

"Josh! No, it's Mom. I called to make sure you got home all right and I was worried about Sparkie. Why did you think it was Josh? Wasn't he there?" Oh shit, I can't tell her Sparkie's gone. What if it's all a misunderstanding . . .

"Everything's fine, Mom," I lie try to sound cheerful. "Josh went to the drugstore; and he always forgets what I want and calls, so I just assumed it was him." Angie's at the door. "Listen, Angie's here so I need to let her in. Don't worry, I'll call you tomorrow." Why did I say drugstore, I was just there? Usually I'm a better liar, I've had enough practice.

Maybe Josh's is at the bar. I'm too nervous to look up the number so I call information. "Is Josh there?"

"Josh? No Josh here. Unless you're looking for a customer."

"No." Liar. Thank goodness, I hear Angie at the door.   "Angie, glad you're here." She gives me a hug. "Mom called. Worried about Sparkie because of the storm. I lied. Said he was fine. I couldn't upset her, she's just had surgery and I don't know for sure what's going on."

"Don't worry about that now. We need to call Animal Control and the Humane Society unless you already did. I'm not sure the Humane Society's open this late."

"No, no, I haven't done anything but walk around the neighborhood."

"You don't want Animal Control to call your Mom if they find him. If I know your Mom, Sparkie's licensed."

"Yeah, licensed and has a chip. I'll get the phone book."

"Kristin, let me call. You're too upset. Look up the number."

I fumble through the phonebook and finally find it in the government section. "791-5454." Angie dials. Why don't they answer, come on, come, on?

"Hi, I want to see if my dog's been found. He got out . . . I'll hold." Angie rolls her eyes.

What's taking so long . . .? I pace back and forth.

"My dog got out tonight during the storm. I want to see if he's been picked up... Kristin White but the dog's not mine, he's my mom's. Her name's Louise White. She's ill and I'm taking care of him..." Holding her hand over the phone she whispered, "What's your Mom's address?"

"5468 N. Orange Grove."

Angie repeats it to the person on the phone. "White Poodle, male, Sparkie. What difference does it make whether he's neutered?" She looks at me shrugs. I nod yes. "Yes, he's neutered. It's 326-5868. Oh and he has a chip. You want the chip number?"

"Don't know," I answer.

"No, I don't have the number on the chip. Yes, I'll hold."

Please have him. Please let him be there. I promise I'll break up with Josh, be a better daughter...

"Okay. And please can you make sure you call the number I gave you, not Louise White. She's just had surgery and I don't want her upset. Thanks." She turned to me, "They haven't picked him up. They promised me they would call you, not your mom. Like it matters if he's neutered. Do they think he's out looking for a sex partner?"

"Call the Humane Society, 491-DOGS now." She dials, hangs up.

"Recording, they're not open till 7 a.m. Make some tea and if he isn't back by the time we finish, we'll drive around."

"I need to go now. Tea won't help. We're wasting time."

"You're wrong. Tea always helps. It'll only take a few minutes."

Angie walks into the kitchen and puts on the teapot. "Constant Comment okay?"

"Sure." I watch the water boil and think about Sparkie. I put two sugars in Angie's cup and sweetener in mine. We drink the tea in silence.

"Okay, I drank the tea, let's go."

"Let's take my car unless you think he won't get in." Angie says.

"No, he'd get in anyone's car, go anywhere with anyone. That's part of what worries me. Someone could take him. He's a sweet, trusting dog. Mom will never forgive me if something happens."

As we walk out the door, the phone rings. I run to pick it up. "It's Animal Control, maybe they found him." I whisper to Angie.

"Yes this is Kristin White . . . Sparkie, a white poodle."

"Oh my God, where? Is he all right? How do you know it's him? . . . Oh God Angie. . .. No, I have someone with me . . ." I look at Angie. "I don't know he's my Mom's dog. She'll have to decide. . . Can I call you back? I understand." I hang up the phone and start to cry.

"He's dead. Hit by a car-three blocks from here. They said he died immediately. At least they didn't call her. It'd be horrible if she found out from a stranger. They want to know if I want the ashes so we can bury him. I don't maybe Mom does?"

"You want to call her?"

"We have forty-eight hours to decide. I'm so stupid I forgot to mention he was wearing a blue-jeweled collar with his name on it. I always hated it. It's so poodly. Mom will want it back."

"Don't call her tonight. No reason to, nothing she can do." Angie walks into the kitchen makes a call and comes back with more tea. Like tea would make it better.

"I'll tell her tomorrow. I'm such an ass. How could I trust Josh? If he let me do prison time why'd I think he'd take care of a dog. I'll never forgive myself. He's such a sweet dog. I love him so much."

"You're not an ass. I called Art a few minutes ago and told him to make up the extra bed. You're spending the night at our house, no arguments. I wonder where Josh went that's so fucking important."

"He said he had to work but he wasn't scheduled till later. He didn't need to leave." The doorbell chimes. No one but Angie, Mom and Josh know my address and Josh wouldn't ring the bell. I open the door, "Sara, what are you doing here? How'd do you know where I live?"

She walks in hugs me. "I'm so sorry Kristin. Sparkie was a wonderful dog. Not a mean bone in his body. I know how much you loved him."

"But how did you know. I just found out." Sara looks at me but doesn't say anything. "You even warned me and I didn't get it."

"Don't beat yourself up. I wasn't specific enough. They're many dogs in your life. I knew one was in danger but not which one. Have you told your mom?"

"No, I was going to wait till tomorrow."

"Good. It's better to get this kind of news in the morning. When you talk to you mom, make sure she knows Sparkie didn't suffer. Never knew what hit him. He had a great life with your mom. He knew he was loved." She sticks her hand in her bag and hands me several photos of Sparkie at day care. "Be sure to tell her, Sparkie's spirit will always be with her."

"I will. Mom will love these."

"I'm going to leave unless there's anything I can do for you."

"No, there's nothing. I'm going to spend the night at Angie's. I'll be fine." I grab the clothes and cosmetics I've put together. I start to write a note to Josh but stop myself. Why leave a note? Let him worry.

Sara walks out with us. "Thanks for coming over."

"Don't be silly. Feel free to take whatever time off you want." And she's gone.

FORTY-SEVEN

I walk into the Dog anxious and tired. I have that sick feeling in my stomach when you fear something horrible, really horrible going to happen and you can't do anything to stop it. Like you're going to get fired or have to tell your mom her dog is dead and it's your fault.

I barely open the door when Samantha and Teddy run over to me, almost knock me down. I fall into one of the office beanbag chairs. The dogs fall on top of me. Theodore puts his head on my lap. Samantha gives me kisses, sits down and offers me her paw. They're sorry about Sparkie but want to remind me I have them.

I pet them and my stomach unclenches a bit when Taylor walks in, "Kristin, I'm so sorry. Sparkie was terrific. We all loved him." I look at Taylor but don't reply. What's there to say?

A few minutes later he breaks the silence, "Sara has a dentist's appointment and won't be in till later. She gave me a copy of a talk she's giving next week. She wants you to read it. See if you find any problems." He hands it to me. "You're scheduled in day care later but take off any time you need. I can cover."

"I have to leave at noon but I should be back in time. I'll let you know if anything comes up."

I read the article but can't concentrate. I dread calling Mom. Shit. Get it over with. For the first time I'm thankful to hear Aunt Lauren's voice.

"Hi Aunt Lauren, it's me. I'm bringing lunch over from a sandwich place Mom likes. I know what she wants but how about you? They have all kinds of sandwiches."

She says nothing for what seems like several minutes. It's just a Goddamn sandwich. "Whatever you think I'd like." How the hell would I know? I don't know any kind of sandwich that features candy.

"Okay, see you sometime after twelve." I get off the phone before Mom asks to talk.

Sara's talk "Should You Own a Dog and If So What Kind" begins with a list of factors to consider. Before I start to read, I grab the newspaper and check the obituaries. Hope I won't see the name Lindstrom. Good it's not there. I try to concentrate on Sara's talk when I hear the intercom, "Kristin, line 2." I hope it's not Mom or Aunt Lauren about her stupid sandwich.

"This is Kristin."

"Where the hell were you last night? I get home you're not there, no note. You don't come home at all. What kind of shit's that?"

"My note? Where was your note? You're such a jerk. Think only of yourself as usual. How could you have left Sparkie alone after everything I told you?"

"I'm a jerk. Where'd you spend the night anyway? Or should I say with who? I left because they needed me at the bar. It's a new job. I can't blow them off."

"You knew I'd be home in a few minutes. You could have waited. I didn't spend the night with anyone. I'm not you. That's not important. Sparkie's dead."

"Dead. What happened?"

"You tell me. When I got back you weren't there, Sparkie wasn't there and the gate in the back was open." I unclench my fist try to breathe.

"He was fine when I left. I figured you'd be home in a few minutes. The rain had stopped."

"But you didn't check the back gate?"

"Well neither did you."

"Don't blame me. Sparkie was fine when I left. I didn't leave him alone."

"How'd he die?"

"He was run over."

"Shit. I suppose your mom blamed it on me?"

"I haven't told her yet but I'm the one to blame."

"Oh come on Kristin, it's not your fault. You took great care of him."

"No, I didn't. I left him with you. How could I have done such a stupid thing? I know you. You did a drug deal in our house without telling me. When I got arrested you did nothing to help me. You left town to save your own ass. I'm not only stupid enough to get back with you but I leave a helpless animal with you."

"Not that shit again."

"You don't get it. I want you out of my house and out of my life. Don't be there when I get home or I'll call the cops. Tell them you're harassing me."

"Kristin calm down, don't be hysterical. You don't mean it."

You're wrong. I do. I should never have let you back in my life. Leave me alone." I hang up. I sit there staring into space. "Kristin, line two." I don't answer.

I run into day care to look for Taylor. "Taylor, did you get that call."

"Yes."

"Was it the same person who called a few minutes ago?"

"It sounded like your friend Josh."

"He's not my friend. I don't want to talk to him."

"No problem. I'll take care of it. Don't answer the phone and don't take any calls unless I page you."

"Thanks, Taylor"

"I can't leave day care now but I'll check on you later."

Eleven o'clock. Might as well get it over with. I stop at The Glad Bag, get my Mom a veggie on wheat and Aunt Lauren, turkey on white with nothing else on it. I'm not hungry but I order white meat chicken on multigrain with no cheese or mayo. My diet's second nature now, even in crisis.

The sandwiches are ready in record time and the ride to Mom's takes only a few minutes. Why do you catch every green when you want to kill time and every red when you're late?

I walk in the house try to act normal. "Are you sick?" Mom asks within seconds.

"No, I'm fine," I lie. "Just didn't get much sleep last?" I put the food out and try to eat.

"I can't wait till Spark comes home."

"Sometimes I think you like that dog more than me." Aunt Lauren says.

"Don't be ridiculous. You're my one and only sister." They both laugh like their words mean than is obvious to me.

I put my head down cover my face. "What is it Kristin, Nothing could be that bad?"

"It's that bad Mom, it is.

"Did you and Josh have a fight?"

"We broke up. I kicked him out but that's not it."

"Honey, I don't know what to say. You know I never liked him but I want you to be happy."

"No, you were right," I sob. "If I had listened to you none of this would have happened."

"None of what Kris? You're not in some kind of trouble?"

"No, no, it's not me. Mom, I don't know how to tell you this. It's Sparkie. He got out last night when I was here. Josh was supposed to watch him but like the jerk he is he left him alone. He got out. I looked all over."

"Oh, no Kristin. Where is he?"

"Mom, I'm so very sorry. He got run over by a car and died."

"Sparkie dead? My Sparkie." She begins to weep.

"I'm so sorry Mom. He didn't suffer. The animal control people said he died instantly. Sara said to tell you his spirit will always be here with you."

"What kind of nonsense is that," Aunt Lauren interrupts.

"Lauren, it's not nonsense. Stay out of this. You're not a dog person. Kristin, you poor thing. How horrible coming home, Sparkie not there. You must have been frantic."

"I was. I walked all over the neighborhood. I couldn't find him. I called Animal Control. Angie came to help me look." I grab my purse. "Everyone at The Dog loved Sparkie. Sara took some pictures of him and wants you to have them." I hand her the photographs.

"They're lovely." She kisses one of the pictures. "Thank her for me."

"I will. I could put the pictures in an album."

"Great idea." She smiles at me without a trace of anger.

"I want to have a funeral, no a ceremony for him in a few days, when I feel better. Just the few people who cared about him."

I think for a moment. "I'm going to ask Angie, and I hope you don't mind if I bring Sara and maybe Taylor who works at The Dog and was great with him."

"Of course I don't mind."

"Speaking of funerals, Animal Control wanted to know if you want Sparkie's ashes. They said I had to let them know in forty-eight hours. I didn't think you would but . . ."

She sobs again. "His body, oh my God, he must have broken bones and maybe he's bloody, my poor Sparkie. No, I don't want to see him like that."

"I'm so sorry Mom. It's all my fault. I wouldn't blame you for being angry at me."

"I'm not angry at you. I know you'd never do anything to hurt Sparkie. You loved him as much as I did."

"I did Mom. I loved him so much." Before I can stop her she gets off the couch and gives me a long hug. Neither of us wants to let go.

FORTY-EIGHT

My ordeal's over. By the time I leave Mom, she's calm. Soon as I get back to the Dog, I call Animal Control. The woman that answers is either new or just stupid. "What do you mean you don't want the body, is the dog dead?"

Of course he's dead, moron. "Yes, Sparkie was hit by a car and you have him."

"Oh you mean you don't want his remains."

"Yes, that's what I mean." Remains. A body's still my dog but remains. I picture Sparkie running, frightened, the car swerves unable to avoid him– he shrieks and shrieks–now there's only a mound of blood, fur and bones. I can't bear to see it. I tune it out. One thing prison taught is to shut out what you can't take in.

Taylor and I work together the rest of the day. Sara hasn't returned from the dentist and leaves word not to worry about her talk till tomorrow. I'm calmer but furious with Josh. As soon as we finish afternoon chores, Taylor confronts me. "I don't want to pry but I'm concerned. Josh called a few times after you left and seemed angry."

"Yeah, I broke up with him. It's a long story. I started going with him a couple years ago." I wonder what Sara told him.

"Sara hasn't told you about me and Josh?"

"Sara's the most discreet person that ever lived. After my gossipy ex-wife, it's a blessing."

"He left me in let's just say a bad situation. We didn't have contact for more than two years. A few months ago, he wanted to get back together. I should've been smart enough to say no. It's not that I don't want to tell you about it, but I can't now."

"I just wondered if I could help."

"I don't know if anyone can. I told him to move out. He's been staying at my place. He has some stuff there but not much. I don't know what he'll do."

"Why don't I follow you home, make sure he's gone. I don't like his attitude."

"I think he's a coward but, I'll let you know. Thanks."

The rest of the afternoon passes quickly. Day care gets crazy with fourteen dogs including a four-month-old pit bull mix named Bandit. Normally, we don't take them so young, but Bandit was owned by a friend of Sam's and was only going to be here for two days. Bandit lives in an apartment with no other pets and didn't know how to act around other dogs. He would approach them to play, and, when they came towards him run away.

I can't decide whether to have Taylor follow me. I don't want to involve people in my problems. If Josh is there and sees Taylor, it might be worse. He's already accused me of flirting with Taylor. Why should I care what Josh think? I'm done with him. "Taylor, if you're still willing, I'll take you up on your offer."

The closer I get to home the more stress I feel. I turn on to my street and I'm relieved Josh's car isn't there. I unlock the door, Taylor's behind me. We walk through the house. No Josh. His stuff's gone. Keys on the coffee table next to a piece of paper that reads Fuck You. I turn it over before Taylor sees it.

"Thanks Taylor. His stuff's gone."

"You sure he won't come back?"

"Pretty sure. He doesn't have a key now so if he knocks, I'll call the cops. I'm okay honest. He probably has another girlfriend anyway."

Taylor seems reluctant to leave. "I guess I better go. Remember if you need us or want to stay over call."

"I will."

After he leaves I'm at loose ends. I take off my work clothes, my earrings. Go to put them away. My jewelry box's a mess. Josh has taken the bracelet he gave me. Good riddens. I'm lucky he didn't take everything. Not worth the bother.

The light on the answering machine blinks . . . Josh? I turn it on. "You have five new messages."

"10:35a.m. Hi it's Crystal. Josh call me."

"11:05a.m. Josh, it's Crystal. I've got my tickets for the weekend. Call me so we can make plans."

"12:08p.m. Fuck you."

"12:11p.m. Fucking bitch." Josh isn't very original.

"3:34 p.m. Josh, its Crystal. Call me."

Crystal. Just a friend. I believed him. Again. Arrest, prison, humiliation, felony record, losing Kelly. I give him another chance because he says he loves me. He flirts in front of me. I still believe his lies. I trust him with Sparkie. He doesn't know what love is.

The phone interrupts my self-depreciation. What if it's Josh or that woman? Screw it. If's it's Josh I'll be strong. If it's Crystal I have a few things to tell her.

"This is Kristin."

Silence. "Um, I'm trying to reach Josh, is he there."

"Is this Crystal?"

"Yes."

"Hi Crystal, can I take a message, Josh isn't here now."

"I guess . . . I'm supposed to fly down this weekend. I need to tell him what flight I'm on so he can pick me up."

"I'll tell him. He told me you'd be calling. How long you two been an item?"

"About a year. I met him after I started working at the Knicker. Are you his cousin or something?"

"No, that's Leslie. I'm his girlfriend." (Till today anyway.)

More silence. "I don't believe you. Josh wouldn't lie to me. He loves me. We were going to live together when his restaurant opens. Why should I believe you?"

"He lied to me for year too. I don't care if you believe me. Josh and I started going together three years ago. He did a drug deal. I took the rap, spent two years in prison. He moved to Albuquerque because he owed some drug dealers tons of money for cocaine the cops seized. When he came back here, he begged me to get back together. He's lived her every since."

"Josh dealing? It doesn't make sense that you would go to jail not him. You're lying."

"Ask him not that he'll tell you the truth. Better yet call his cousin Leslie and check it out. Her name's Leslie Berry, B-E-R-R-Y, she's in the book." I hang up and smile for the first time today.

CHAPTER
FORTY-NINE

I push the off button on the alarm. The clock says 7:15. Weird, the alarm's set for 6:45. And it's Saturday. I snuggle back under the covers and drift off. I hear the alarm again. But now I realize it's the phone. I answer- expect the worst.

"Hello."

"Hi, Kristin, its Angie. Sounds like I woke you."

"Not only did you wake me but scared the crap out of me. I thought something happened to Mom."

"Didn't mean to scare you but I just saw some news that might interest you. The Sunday wedding section has an engagement listed you'll want to know about."

Josh? Couldn't be. Too fast and he'd never think of a newspaper announcement. If he ever gets married, he'd do it in a sleazy Las Vegas wedding chapel. "Who is it?"

"Think Kristin."

"Come on Angie, I just woke up. Tell me."

"Scott, who else. Big picture of him and the future wife. Wedding at the Tucson Country Club."

"Who's he marrying? Do we know her?

"Never heard of her. Patricia Amy Miller-Austin, aka Patti. Past President of Kappa Kappa Gamma, majored in Art History. No current employment listed. She's blonde and totally vapid looking."

"Figures. Good thing he dumped me or his folks would be reading, 'Scott Downing is marrying the former Kristin White, no sorority affiliation, employed at The Dignified Dog, and recently released from Arizona Department of Corrections.' Since you woke me, you owe me some coffee. Any chance you can take a break."

"Sure, Starbucks eight-thirty. I'll bring a copy of the fiancé's picture."

I force myself out of bed. No clean clothes. As I put on my most presentable jeans, I flash back to the day I was arrested. My laundry needed doing that day, too. I'd just put on my cleanest jeans to have coffee with Angie, and her Aunt Sara when the police came. I'd never had that coffee, but now I work for Sara.

My habits hadn't changed but I had. I'd miss Josh, but he was history. Forever. I finally understood what he'd done to me, no, what I let him do.

I hurry through my morning routine. Hadn't seen Angie lately. She had been in and out of town on assignment. I'd been busy with work and spent time with Mom. Hadn't had a scone in ages. Sweets remind me of Ina. I'd sent her a note and some money but gotten no response. I hope she's all right.

No traffic so I beat Angie. I get my latte, treat myself to a maple scone and wait. She bursts in exotic looking in a long colorful skirt, bright orange-scooped neck shirt and several bangles. For a moment, I feel ugly and jealous, but I cut off those feelings. I'm doing fine. I wait eagerly while she orders.

"Glad you didn't feel the need to dress up. Here take a look at Scott's future and be glad you're not it. He wants a trophy wife and he's not even thirty. You're way too cool for him." Angie sits down with some kind of Frappuccino and coffee cake.

"Yeah, I'm celebrating my luck." I point to my scone and smile at her. How lucky I am to have her friendship. She never deserted me while I was in prison. For the second time my thoughts turn to Ina. "Remember my roommate in jail? The one who craved sweets?"

"Ana or something. Got a really bad deal."

"Ina, but yeah that's her. I promised myself I'd send her money and food every so often. She has nobody. I did for a while but then I stopped. A week or so ago I sent her some money and a note but haven't heard anything back."

"That's not very long. So you know where she is?"

"She was at Winslow but who knows if she's still there. I haven't gotten my letter back but who knows what DOC does with mail. It always took an awful long for me to get your letters. Mr. Cooper gave me a number you can call to find out where inmates are. She's listed in Winslow but I don't trust it. I could call Bernini."

"You keep in touch with her?"

"I've talked to her once or twice. Ran into her at the mall one day. It's kind of like seeing your boss outside work. She had on jeans and a t-shirt. You'd never guess she was a lawyer. She looks even younger dressed that way." I finish the scone, wish I hadn't eaten it so fast.

"Your mom okay? I was worried the way you answered the phone."

"She's great. She just looked so fragile after the surgery. I still feel responsible about Sparkie."

"I guess it's gonna take you awhile to get over that. She didn't start to blame you?"

"No, she's been wonderful even about Josh. Not one 'I told you so.' We're getting along well. She's changed since the surgery. Compliments me about how I look. Stopped remarks about my weight."

"Maybe you've changed too."

"You're right. I realize she's not going to live forever. She's the only close family I have. I never minded being an only child until now."

Angie laughs. "I wouldn't trade my family for anything but sometimes it's a mixed blessing. Someone's always in crisis and that's the one Mom and Dad focus on. My brother Phil's a complete screw-up. Always tries to borrow money or shows up at the house drunk. Art's family's worse. His sisters fight all the time and there's always one not speaking to another one. I'm glad about you and your mom. Has she found another dog? I heard her mention getting one at lunch."

"She's extra busy at work because of the time she missed. When things calm down she's going to look. Wants me to help her. We're going to the Humane Society unless Sara finds one first"

"Good, she needs a dog."

I debate another scone while Angie brings me up to date on her life. Before I can decide, it's time for her to go. I don't get a chance to tell her what happened with Aunt Lauren. "See you soon," a quick hug and she walks out the door.

No more food. It's time to go home and do laundry.

FIFTY

Almost the same time Saturday morning that Kristin's awakened by Angie's call, Scott leaves for work. This is his third year with Finer, Hegland and Zapata. If he wants to make partner, now's no time to slack off.

As he walks into The Albert Valdez building where the law firm offices, he realizes the building's coffee shop is closed. Shit, I should have stopped on the way. He pauses to decide if it's worth a two blocks walk to The Coffee Mug but decides against it. Maybe someone else's in and made coffee. It won't be cappuccino but any's better than none. Not a good way to start the morning, he muses as he rides up in the empty elevator.

The office lights are on and he hears conversation. Good news for the coffee. As he opens the door, he sees two strange men fiddling with the receptionist's computer. He's about to ask what they're doing here when he remembers Hegland told him the firm hired a computer consultant. As he walks past them to his office, one of them waves, 'Hi Scott, how are you?"

"Fine, How about you," he replies on automatic pilot. Scott knows he'd met the man someplace before but can't place him. Not that it mattered; he isn't anyone important.

His office's a mess. Boxes all over, desk piled high with files. His fiancée, Patti, pouted when he told her he couldn't go wedding shopping but he was delighted to bow out. She'd better get used to me having obligations if she wants to continue to shop as her life's work. Her daddy wouldn't be pleased if Scott didn't make partner. And if he weren't pleased, he wouldn't continue being so generous.

His mood lifts when he opens the large brown file folder that takes up half his desk. Peterson vs. Newton. His first real case. No clerking for one of the other partners. He can make the decisions. It's his to evaluate, hopefully settle for a whooping sum of money or win at trial if it came to that.

The firm's clients, the Peterson's, were driving to Phoenix to visit their grandchildren in their recently purchased top of the line Lincoln. Mr. Peterson had just entered 1-10 when he was hit head-on by Newton driving on the wrong side of the freeway. Newton, unhurt, his Mercedes totaled, had been arrested at the scene, charged with felony DUI. This was not his first arrest for drunk driving. He has plenty of insurance, several homes, a gun collection and would be capable of paying beyond policy limits.

Mr. Peterson had been in the hospital for almost a week but was expected to recover completely. Unfortunately, his wife was still in a coma, and even if she came out of it, doctors believe she suffered severe brain damage. Several depositions had been set for next week and Scott wanted to be prepared.

He'd read through the accident reports when he became aware of a conversation outside his door.

"Kelly, I need to take a smoke break you wanna start the next one without me."

"Sure Keith, go ahead."

When he hears the name Kelly, Scott realizes why the computer guy is familiar. Kelly's the Superior Court main IT guy. They'd been on some stupid court committee together. A few months earlier he's seen him with Kristin somewhere.

Someone, likely Kelly, knocks on the door. "Come in."

"Hi Scott, I need to look at your computer. Hope this isn't too inconvenient."

"No problem. I didn't know you did private work. I thought you just worked at the court."

"I just started consulting recently. Keith Dawdle, the other guy who's with me, and I plan to start our own firm but we're not quite ready to quit our jobs. Soon I hope."

"Give me your card. I'd be happy to pass your name around."

"Thanks, thanks a lot." Kelly stops fiddling with Scott's computer. Digs in his wallet for the card and hands it to Scott. "How are things going with you?"

"Terrific just got engaged. Getting married next April. Maybe you've heard of my fiancée, Patty Austin-Miller. She's from a very prominent Tucson family. Her dad's a big-time developer."

"Sorry don't think I know her."

"I'll introduce you some time. You still see Kristin?"

"No, we're not together any more."

"I'm not surprised. You dodged a bullet with her. I'm sure you know she was in prison. When she first got arrested, I went to see her in jail to see if I could help her out. For old time sake. She tried to convince me she didn't know anything about the drugs. I mean, come on, she's either a lot stupider than I thought or she really was a doper."

"You didn't believe the drugs were her boyfriend's, what's his name?"

"They probably were but how could she not know what he was into. Eighty pounds is a lot of blow. When I saw her, she was still trying to protect that loser. She defended him to me."

"Misplaced loyalty or she really loved him."

"Or she figured it was him or no one. You should have seen her at the jail. Maybe better you didn't. She used to be attractive but she really porked out, let herself go." He looked stealthily at Kelly, realized he might have insulted the guy. "When I saw her with you, she had obviously gotten it together. You're too good for her anyway."

"I guess the important thing is she's doing well now." Scott said feeling uncomfortable.

"Of course you're right. I tried to help her all I could. I wrote a letter to the prosecutor on her behalf."

"That was considerate of you. I must be going. I'm done in here and there's several more we have to check."

"Well thanks, best of luck with your company and as I said I'll recommend you when I can."

"Thanks Scott." He walked out closed the door behind him.

Strange guy. Why bother defending her? It's not like they're together. He ought to be glad she's out of his life. I certainly am. Without further thought, he went back to reading the file. Dropped Kelly's card in the wastebasket.

FIFTY-ONE

Kelly spent most of Saturday at Finer, Hegland and Zapata. He didn't see Scott again but their conversation circled though his mind; "She's a lot stupider than I thought," "She was trying to protect that loser," "She really porked out."

Why did Scott's attitude surprise him? When he and Kristin ran into Scott, he wasn't just a wine snob but arrogant. Kelly knew Scott hadn't recognized when he said hello this morning, even though they'd met several times. Scott always acted like he was better than everyone else. In spite of his hot shit attitude, Kelly expected Scott to speak of Kristin with some level of decency. They almost married for God sakes.

When anyone asks him, why he and Kristin broke up, he says it didn't work out. Other than his mom, he'd never told anyone Kristin had been in prison. He wasn't a gossip; he believed Kristin had made a mistake but it was no one else's business.

'She even defended him to me.' Shouldn't you stand behind people you care about? His family always stood together when one of them had a problem. Of course no one in his family had been in prison or even arrested. There was a huge difference in defending your brother who was accused by a neighbor of damaging his flower garden with his bike or when his sister had been bullied at school.

He often thought about Kristin. Was she still at the Dignified Dog? Did she have a new boyfriend? Think about him? His mom asked about her but otherwise he never heard her name. When Angie requested to interview him, part of him believed her motivation had to do with Kristin. It didn't. Angie acted professional. Didn't mention Kristin at all. They don't hang out with the same crowd so there's little chance he'd run into her unless he made an effort. More of an effort than his wishy-washy note.

On the other hand, could he trust her? Wouldn't she lie to him again if the circumstances were right? He'd seen friends who'd broken up with a girlfriend and gotten back together. The second time never seemed to work. Why would things with Kristin be any different? They were still the same people.

Dusty'd be happy if he contacted her. He never took to another person as he had to her. He sometimes thought Dusty missed her. When a woman who looked like her walked by, he'd run towards her, sniff, get all excited. When he realized it wasn't her, he'd put his tail between his legs and walk away. A dog shouldn't govern your love life even a special dog like Dusty.

He and Keith had plans to go to a party that night. One of the court clerks had gotten engaged. She and her fiancé, a probation officer, had invited half the court staff and probation department to celebrate. Kelly looked forward to going. He was interested in a new sexy PO, Julie Cuomo, who told him she'd be there.

Keith's license was suspended due to a DUI. Kelly planned to pick him up. Why had it never bothered him before that Keith had a DUI? Was that so different from Kristin's situation? Keith was on probation, couldn't drink so he probably wouldn't want to stay long. Kelly was concerned as wanted to make a night of it, but once they got there, he couldn't get in a party mood.

As soon as he walked in, he saw Julie. "Hi Kelly, what's happening?" she called to him from across the room. She grabbed two Bud Lites from a cooler and walked towards him.

"I'm good, spent the day on a private consulting job." He took one of the beers, opened it and took a swig. Julie had moved to Tucson from Boston. She was a tall woman who looked like she worked out with weights, but Kelly was attracted more by her smile and charming Boston accent. They hadn't gone out yet but flirted when they ran into each other at the courthouse. His mom would be happy if he dated an Italian girl.

"I didn't know you wanted to start a business."

"You're almost the only one that doesn't. What'd you do today?" His eyes swept over her body. She looked better than he'd imaged in jeans and a tight white shirt instead of the modest outfits she wore to work. "Sleep mostly; I did a cop ride along last night. Required part of our training. We went to this one call, a guy's daughter ran away. The guy was really belligerent to the cop…"

He became aware she was quiet, looking at him oddly. He'd lost track of what she said as his mind reflected back on the conversation with Scott.

"I'm sorry, I drifted off. Work problem. Please start over." Julie looked reluctant, "Please, it isn't you. I want to hear the rest of the story."

Julie started again and told him how well the young officer had handled the belligerent dad and about an arrest of a suspected armed robber. Kelly listened and made all the appropriate responses. They had talked nonstop for a long time when another PO walked over. "Julie, I'm tired, can't keep my eyes open. I need to go home get some sleep. If you're ready come on, but feel free to get another ride." Julie looked at him.

This was the chance he'd waited for, but he didn't take it, "It's been great talking with you, hope to see you in court soon," he said. She smiled at him and walked away with the other PO.

What's wrong with me? Kelly wondered. He stayed another hour talked to whoever crossed his path but he never became engaged in any conversation. Over and over he replayed his conversation with Scott. He believed Kristin hadn't known about the drugs. Why hadn't he defended her? Time to leave. He found Keith talking to one of the other IT guys. "Hey, Kelly, you strike out. I saw that PO chick leave."

"Not my night I guess. You ready?"

"Sure, not much fun when I can't even have a beer."

CHAPTER

FIFTY-TWO

Kelly sleeps poorly. Tosses and turns. Why he didn't pursue his chance with Julie? Mostly he thinks of Kristin.

He falls into a troubled slumber, dreams Kristin's about to drown. Instead of saving her, he works on an old computer installing a software program. He wakes up sweaty and confused when Dusty jumps onto the bed likely in response to his groans.

The clock radio reads 4:30, but he gets up. He brews a pot of coffee and works on the report for the law firm until he hears the paper land on his front porch. Beginning with the sports page, he carefully reads the paper. When he finishes, it's late enough to call his mom who gets up at six every morning. They arrange to meet for coffee after she goes to church.

By the time his mom arrives, he's eaten his Denver omelet, potatoes, and toast and ordered each of them a fresh cup of coffee. They make small talk until his Mom confronts him, "What's up Kelly? I love your company but I know there's some reason you wanted to see me."

"Aw Mom, can't I just want to see you without the family around?"

"Yes, but I know you well enough that it's something else."

Kelly drinks more coffee and calls to the waitress. "How 'bout one of those cinnamon rolls? Mom you want one?" She shakes her head no.

"I had this disturbing conversation yesterday. I was at a law firm doing a consult and ran into this guy, Scott. He's a lawyer I know casually. He dated Kristin for a couple years before I met her. They almost got married."

"Kristin okay? She's not hurt or in trouble or anything?"

"No, it's nothing like that. He hadn't seen her in years except once with me."

"What did he say that got you so upset?"

Kelly waits till the waitress brings the cinnamon roll and walks away. "He totally trashed her. Couldn't believe she didn't know about the drugs. Couldn't believe how stupid she was to be loyal to a guy who landed her in prison. Said she was fat. Stuff like that."

"He knew you dated her?"

"Yeah."

"Sounds like a jerk with no compassion for anyone. How did the subject of Kristin come up?"

"I didn't bring up her. I think he asked if we were still going out. I said no. He said something like I figured you were smart enough to dump her. Then he just went on and on."

"In my day a decent man didn't talk about an ex like that. So he's a gossipmonger besides everything else."

"Yeah. When he sensed I didn't agree with him, he told me he wrote a letter to the judge on her behalf like that made things right."

Kelley's mom grabs a piece of his roll. "He sensed you didn't agree? You didn't stand up for Kristin?"

"I didn't really say much of anything. I can't stop thinking about what he said."

"What bothers you most?"

"I'm not sure. I can't believe he has such a bad opinion about her."

"Are you sure it's his attitude that's concerns you?"

Kelly doesn't answer. He concentrates on his sweet roll. After a few minutes, she tells him the family news. Cousin Al's wife's expecting their first child. His brother Tony's soccer team won their last two soccer games, and Tony scored his first goal. Dad might buy a new car.

They chat inconsequentially till Kelly stops talking and looks at her. "You're right, of course. I was feeling bad I didn't treat Kristin well either. She shouldn't have lied to me, but I can see why she did it. Thanks, Mom."

Kelly pays and they leave. As soon as Kelly gets back home, he picks up the phone, dials Kristin's number. "Hi, this is Kristin."

"Kristin, it's Kelly."

ABOUT THE AUTHOR

Barbara lives with her husband Kenney and her two dogs Toby and Teddy. Now retired, she spent the last 30 years as a criminal defense attorney and later a Superior Court Judge.

In 2001, she was diagnosed with transverse myelitis.

Barbara considers herself lucky to have a large family including Ben, Rob, Alex, Caleb and Nini and grandkids Margot, Kate and Charles.

She is at work on her next novel about a public defender who commits a serious ethical violation during a murder trial.

Made in the USA
San Bernardino, CA
15 January 2013